THE TANGIER TAJINE

THE TANGIER TAJINE

THE SEVETH KIT ASTON MYSTERY

JACK MURRAY

Books by Jack Murray

Copyright © 2023 by Jack Murray

ISBN: 9798356430961
Imprint: Independently published

Cover by Jack Murray after J.C. Leyendecker and Mead Schaeffer

For Monica, Lavinia, Anne, and our angel, Baby Edward

Stew

noun
1. a dish of meat and vegetables cooked slowly in liquid in a closed dish or pan.
   "lamb stew"

2. a state of great anxiety or agitation.
   "she's **in a** right old **stew**"

verb
3. (with reference to meat, fruit, or other food) cook or be cooked slowly in liquid in a closed dish or pan.

4. remain in a heated or stifling atmosphere.
   "sweaty clothes left to stew in a plastic bag"

Tajine

noun
1. a large, heavy North African cooking pot with a conical lid
2. a North African stew with vegetables, olives, lemon, garlic and spices, cooked in a tajine

Part 1: Source and mix ingredients

Morocco 1905

The shadow of war looms large over Europe. There are potential flashpoints everywhere: the Far East, the Balkans, Alsace & Lorraine and Morocco.

In Morocco, Sultan Abdul Aziz's power is waning. His misrule means the country is in debt to the European powers causing unrest among the people. Britain has made concessions on the control of Morocco to France and Spain in return for a free hand in Egypt and the Suez Canal. Tangier is, effectively, under joint control of the European powers which suits Britain as it ensures the security of Gibraltar at the mouth of the Mediterranean.

Germany has been outflanked by the entente cordiale between Britain and France in 1904. They have no clear idea whether to support the independence of the Sultan in Morocco or merely pay lip service to the status quo. Meanwhile, lawlessness and rebellion are building in the country, stirred partly by Germany supplying weapons to Rif rebels in the mountains.

In order to settle the Moroccan question finally, the Germans propose a conference which is scheduled to take place in Algeciras, a town in southern Spain, in early 1906.

They want to assert the independence of Morocco and drive a wedge between France and Britain...

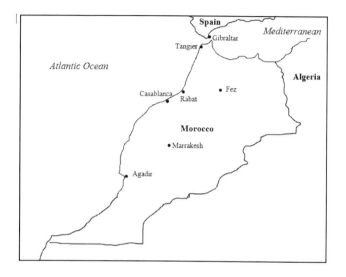

Morocco

Prologue

Tangier, Morocco: December 1905

'Have you ever murdered anyone?'

Eustace Frost addressed this unusual question to his wife, Agatha one evening in Tangier. Even by his own lofty standards it was rather uncommon. She met the question with a sideways glance. What she saw was her husband of thirty years. A curious lop-sided grin broke out across a face lit by the soft translucence of the moon which made his eyes twinkle.

'It has crossed my mind once or twice,' said Agatha cryptically. The smile on her husband's face widened. He rose from his seat into a curious crouch and ducked through the doorway of the carriage. Agatha followed him, taking his extended hand to climb down onto the street. It was still crowded with food sellers, clothes sellers and people carrying carpets.

Air was in short supply. It felt as if the heat had evaporated leaving just enough to sustain life but little more. Agatha felt hot and she was rarely anything less than bothered. Perhaps it was her time of life. She was nearing sixty. Her frame was sturdier than it once had been.

Eustace, meanwhile, was still as slim as ever. She did not resent this so much as the fact that his diet over the last thirty years had consisted of a remarkable amount of champagne mixed with a gargantuan amount of brandy. How did he do it? It never seemed to affect him either physically or in his behaviour. He was always the same. She smiled in acceptance. This was the man she'd married.

Eustace turned to the carriage driver. He nodded briefly and a moment later, the landau departed. Eustace led Agatha along a path lit by candles towards a large white building. All around were men dressed in white djellabas with a red fez on their heads patrolling the front garden like the security guards they were. The guards ignored the couple as they walked towards the arched doorway. A sign by the door proclaimed: *Deutsche Gesandtschaft.* The German Legation.

Standing outside the door, smoking, was an overweight man of around forty years of age with thick grey hair and even thicker whiskers. He was dressed in a white suit but had a distinctly military bearing. He smiled briefly at the approaching couple then threw away his cigarette, turned towards the doorway and walked inside without saying anything. This was Doctor Thierry Arnaud.

'I'm fairly certain these things are doing him more harm than good,' observed Eustace, under his breath.

Agatha did not look at her husband as she replied, 'and I'm fairly certain the amount you drink is not doing you much good either.'

'He's a doctor,' pointed out Eustace by way of riposte.

They entered through the door, smiling to the doorman or slave or both. This was Morocco after all. Agatha wondered if he was a slave. Such practices had not yet been eradicated despite the enlightenment of thought and purity of intention brought by the Europeans, mused Agatha sourly. Imagine. Anyone would think that the Europeans were more interested in exploiting the country rather than sharing its ideas on things like human rights.

They entered a wide hallway crowded with officials, servants and tradesmen. A loud murmur of conversation and music greeted them as they walked through the high-ceilinged reception into a large room crowded with European men wearing uniforms or dinner suits. Mingling with them were a small number of women and an even smaller number of the local population. This was a distinctly European affair. The uniforms were French, Spanish, British and German; the wine was French and the music, if Eustace guessed correctly, was Bavarian *volksmusic*.

'Oh Lord,' said Eustace, as he heard the accordions and brass. 'Please don't yodel.'

Just at that moment the male singer, a German officer by the name of Willy Krapp, began to sing in various pitches, 'yodelleheeyodelyodelyodeleheehee'

'Perhaps we should postpone this,' said Eustace cringing at the aural onslaught being inflicted by the smiling lederhosen-clad male singer. He seemed particularly pleased by the flexibility of his vocal chords. A quick glance at some of the French and Spanish officers by Agatha suggested they were less enamoured. However, their reaction was nothing as compared to the Moroccan visitors who looked on askance at the yodeller. They glared in anger at the man in the black shorts with braces and white shirt. It was as if they thought the performer was somehow making fun of the *Adhan*, the Muslim call to prayer.

This thought made Eustace stifle his laughter, but his mood of merriment changed suddenly as he became uncomfortably aware that the singer was staring right at him and smiling.

'I think that's Wilhelm. He seems to have taken a fancy to you,' commented Agatha, a hint of triumph in her voice.

'If he were to wink at me, Agatha, I swear we are leaving.'

'Not until we've done what we came here to do,' replied Agatha.

Yes, there was business to be conducted. Someone to be shot. Eustace and Agatha's eyes swept the room as they made their way towards their host who was standing as far away from the cacophony as he could decently manage without insulting his junior officer who was providing what passed for vocal entertainment this evening.

Oberleutnant Uwe Kessel was a man of around thirty who radiated all the bonhomie one has come to expect from a Teutonic military man. His face was proudly decorated with a few tiny scars; badges of honour from *Mensur*, the sword-fighting art peculiar to Germany. Peculiar barely covered Eustace's view of such a barbaric ritual. Standing beside the captain was a young, bearded man who seemed no more smitten by the music and appeared to wince at every oom-pah.

'That's Albert Bartels,' whispered Eustace.

'He's awfully young,' replied Agatha. 'Are you sure?'

'Young and dangerous. He's been running guns to the Berbers for a while now. The French would love to have proof of this. Young Toussaint, for example, over there. He'd love to catch Bartels in the act.' Eustace indicated a rather rotund young man with a highly waxed moustache dressed in a French policeman's uniform; he was a captain also but looked an altogether less formidable one than the German. He stood near Bartels who, every so often, would turn to the captain and offer a toast. This was greeted by a scowl from Toussaint. 'Can you see Gabrielle anywhere? I want this to be over with.'

Agatha could not have agreed more and said so. She reached into the small clutch purse and felt the steel of the revolver. All at once, despite the heat, she felt a chill descend on her. She trusted Eustace with her life and Lord only knows she'd had to over the years, but she was older now. Wisdom and experience counted for something, yet neither of those friends could provide the comfort she needed at that moment.

She was afraid.

A loud voice from the other side of the room momentarily distracted the couple from the acoustic horrorfest being delivered by Herr Krapp. They turned to see a man of middling height and middling age approach them with a broad smile, arm outstretched. He was dressed impeccably in perfectly cut dinner suit.

'I thought you two would be here,' said the man shaking Eustace's hand.

9

'Hello Walter,' said Eustace, a little too loudly. Although one might have interpreted this as a riposte to the caterwauling of the singer and Agatha certainly suspected this to be the case, it served another purpose, which the new arrival knew very well.

The 'Walter' in question was Walter Burton Harris, The Times correspondent. He had based himself in Tangier a few decades previously at the age of nineteen and was now a well-known figure in the social milieu of the town, a friend to everyone except, perhaps, his wife who had recently left him.

'Wonderful singing, what?' said Harris just as Herr Krapp overextended himself on the upper register of one note which resulted in a coughing fit. The band mercifully stopped playing to allow the ailing yodeller a moment to regain his voice.

Eustace listened to Krapp whose face was red and seemed in imminent danger of exploding. The two Englishmen braced themselves.

'Best bit of his performance so far,' murmured Eustace. 'Have you seen Gabrielle or Emily?'

'The Sharifa arrived an hour ago. No, I haven't seen Gabrielle. Did you see the guards outside by the way?'

'Yes, they looked like Raisuli's men.'

'They are Raisuli's men,' confirmed Harris grimly. Oddly, he noted, Eustace seemed quite chuffed by this. As ever, you could never quite predict what Eustace was thinking. He liked this about him and was glad he was on their side. He dreaded to think what he might have been like had he been born a Junker. Germany would have an empire by now. They still might, the way things were going.

Agatha and Eustace exchanged glances. The news about Raisuli's men only confirmed what both had thought when they arrived. Despite this being the German Legation, the security outside was distinctly Berber.

'I suppose we should have expected it,' said Agatha, trying to keep her voice steady. Sometimes being English and its requirements around the tautness of the upper regions of ones chops was decidedly annoying. Sometimes shouting out in frustration in the manner of a southern European was just the ticket. She noticed that Eustace was more relaxed about this, however. He was smiling once more as in remembering a funny off joke.

The three of them scanned the room in search of Gabrielle Fish and the Sharifa of Wazan, Emily Keene. Agatha spotted the Sharifa first. The two ladies' eyes met and soon she began to move her way through the crowd of diplomats and officers towards Agatha and Eustace.

The Sharifa was one of those English ladies who was sturdy of build, decided of opinion and hardier than a mountain goat. She could have been Agatha's sister such was the resemblance between the two ladies in age, attitude and acumen. Perhaps one significant difference was that Agatha, despite being noted in her youth for possessing a stubborn streak, one which only grew with age, had not run off and married a Moroccan nobleman as Emily Keene had done, some thirty years earlier. This level of obstinacy to family wishes was, perhaps, too much even for Agatha.

'Agatha, thank goodness you're here,' said the Sharifa.

11

'Where's Gabrielle?' asked Agatha.

'She has the document, but she fears the Germans are suspicious. Which means they will be keeping an eye on her too. She doesn't think they will let her leave. Agatha, I'm sure of it. I can see the way they are looking at Walter and me. They're just looking for an excuse to arrest her. What are we going to do?'

'Eustace has a plan,' replied Agatha, not without a trace of nerves. This must have been evident for Emily as she glanced from Agatha to Eustace who had taken the opportunity to avail himself of a glass of champagne. Agatha had been too nervous to accept hers. Eustace had a glass of champagne in each hand. So too did Walter Harris, noted Agatha grimly. It was all just a game to them. Did they ever grow up? They were men. This was an answer of sorts to the question posed.

'There's no chance Eustace's plan is simple and easy to accomplish?' asked the Sharifa hopefully.

Agatha's roll of the eyes caused the Sharifa's shoulders to slump perceptibly.

'Just once...'

'I know,' agreed Agatha shaking her head. Her husband had an aversion to simplicity bordering on outright hostility. For him, the simplest route between two points usually involved a detour via Vladivostok. Frustratingly for Agatha, Eustace's Byzantine thinking was peculiarly adapted to the murky world in which they ploughed a furrow: the world of diplomacy where a misplaced syllable could cause a chill between countries, a harsh tone of voice, an incident and the wrong word, conflict. Europe was on the brink of a war.

The only thing that had not been decided was when this war would take place, who would be in each team and what would be the spark. There were any number of potential conflagration points.

Morocco was one of the biggest pieces of tinder waiting to catch fire.

'Be careful,' warned the Sharifa. Agatha looked at her old friend with affection. Emily Keene had followed her heart for good or for ill, just as she had. She doubted her friend regretted her life away from England for one second. Nor did she. Then a thought struck her.

'Is Raisuli here?'

'No. I think that would have been just too provocative even for our German friends, but Berrada is here in his place.'

'I think I'd have preferred to take my chances with Raisuli.'

'I agree. Berrada is just a thug with responsibility. Sometimes Raisuli surprises you.'

The two ladies parted to look for Gabrielle Fish. Eustace and Walter Harris, meanwhile, had been joined by a third man they had passed earlier with whiskers that would have been considered flamboyant during the Regency. The three men were speaking rapidly in French.

'Dr Arnaud, I presume,' said Eustace.

This was met with a raised eyebrow and half a smile.

'Eustace, what are you going to do? Berrada is here and if he's here, Raisuli is skulking somewhere in the shadows.'

'Don't worry about them,' replied Eustace calmly. For once, the smile on his face had disappeared. Arnaud

13

wondered if he was nervous. This would be a first. 'You know what you have to do.'

'I do, Eustace, but his men are everywhere.'

'That's the point, Thierry. That's the point,' replied Eustace, as obtuse as ever. He really was quite infuriating. Arnaud wondered how Agatha ever put up with him. Perhaps she liked him as much as he did. Moments later Arnaud felt a glass of champagne being put into his hand. 'Drink, Thierry. It'll help.'

Arnaud gulped the champagne down in a single move before placing it on a tray and grabbing another. This piece of bravado was singularly ill-advised as the bubbles raced straight to his head almost causing him to pass out. He didn't and immediately felt better.

Eustace felt a hand grip his arm. He turned to Walter Harris and then followed the direction of the journalist's gaze. Berrada had entered the room. With him came a charge, an electric current and an angry buzzing murmur that filled the night air with a nervous tension. Eustace decided to take his own advice and gulped down the rest of his champagne before reaching for another glass.

*

Agatha moved slowly through the room throwing out smiles and the occasional "hello" to the guests. She avoided the German military as much as possible. Her eyes scanned around the room looking for Gabrielle Fish who was dressed as a servant. This was her usual mode of dress, but only on occasion did she have to don a German servant's livery. While she was surveying the room, Agatha bumped into a rather large man. She turned to apologise before realising it was Berrada.

The large man looked at Agatha with dark eyes full of loathing. He said nothing, hoping that his mere presence would be enough to intimidate the woman. It usually worked with others.

'Ahh Berrada,' said Agatha before continuing in Arabic, 'I thought I smelled goat. Shouldn't you be off torturing some innocent soul?'

It was all Berrada could do to stop himself lashing out at the woman in front of him. Something in her eyes suggested she would have hit back, but what would have been the point? His face twisted into a snarl and then he spun away, stalking off into the crowd. He too was surveying the room. Agatha had no doubt he was looking for Gabrielle Fish. She had to find her first. The thought of what she had to do then chilled her.

On the makeshift stage, Willy Krapp was yodelling like the goat herder Agatha had accused Berrada of being. She glanced around and saw Eustace talking to the German officer they'd spied when they entered. The two men were wincing at the performance on the stage.

*

'Interesting,' said Eustace, indicating with his newly refilled glass, the singer on the stage. 'That is Willy isn't it? I never knew he had such a talent.'

Obertleutnant Uwe Kessel's mouth flickered into a smile. He made no attempt to hide his horror at the extraordinary undulating shrieks emanating from somewhere around his subordinate's feet.

15

'Who says Germans do not have a sense of humour?' said Kessel archly.

Eustace exploded into laughter. He glanced at the German. Kessel was around thirty years of age, tall, regal of bearing and good-looking, despite the occasional scar around his face from his days as a student practicing *Mensur*. The folly of youth. Such diversions had seemed so attractive then. The pain he felt came not from the Stoßmensur inflicting the scar so much as the realisation of his own stupidity. The senselessness of it all. The violence. His weakness in needing to be accepted by people he despised. Those scars ran deep; the shame would last a lifetime, but they were as nothing to the scars that would rent bodies if war broke out. It was in the air here tonight. He could feel it, touch it even.

Kessel watched Eustace shake his head and saunter off into the crowd, drink in hand. No, make that two hands. He smiled briefly at the sight of the Englishman.

The smile would last less than a few seconds.

*

Agatha was near the stage. The sound of the brass was deafening, but she needed to stand on a step to see better. When you are around five feet tall, such exigencies exist. She could see nothing from her position. The throng in front of her was thick with army men and diplomats drinking and trying to chat over the noise of the *volksmusic*.

Events moved quickly.

Agatha caught sight of Eustace. He had just left Kessel and was wandering nonchalantly amongst the throng when he stopped suddenly. His eyes were directed towards the side of the room. He swung around and seemed to grab a

16

man that Agatha recognised as Dr Thierry Arnaud, an old friend from the French legation. Then he was looking around once more. Agatha realised he was looking for her. She glanced in the direction that Eustace had originally been looking.

She saw Gabrielle Fish standing near a table with food. To her right she could see Albert Bartels moving through the crowd towards her from one side and Captain Toussaint from the other. It was like they were in a race to find her. They weren't the only ones. Berrada had also woken up to her presence. His large body was finding it difficult to navigate its way through the swarm of people.

Agatha could have kicked herself. Of course! As a servant she would be expected to bring the food in from the kitchen. She leapt down from the step. To be fair, it wasn't a high step and virtually scattered a group of Spanish diplomats as she ploughed towards Gabrielle.

On stage, the band and Willy were performing the end of the song and the music rose to a volume that was making ears bleed for peace and quiet.

Like a medieval battering ram, Agatha ripped through the crowd. She reached her quarry moments ahead of Eustace. Further back, encountering rather robust reactions from the guests was Berrada. Agatha did not hesitate. Just as the band reached its crescendo, she pulled out her revolver and shouted, 'Traitor!'

Then she shot Gabrielle Fish in the chest.

1

16 YEARS LATER

Grosvenor Square, London: 3rd July 1921

Kit Aston stood back from the window and gazed out onto Grosvenor Square. It was a summer's day in England which is to say there was a black belly of cloud threatening rain and plenty of it. Neither the clouds nor the weather were occupying Kit's mind at that point. It was the unfamiliar car sitting further up the road.

'Still there?' asked a female voice. This was Mary Aston. She was reading the morning newspaper and sipping a cup of tea with Simpkins, their adopted cat, sitting on her knee.

'Yes,' replied Kit. 'I don't think it's the same two men though. Neither of these have a moustache.'

'Why not call the police or send Harry along to find out what they want?'

'No fun in that, darling.'

Mary grinned and looked up at her husband. She liked to look at him when he was not aware. She suspected the feeling was mutual. They had been married less than five months. She hoped it would always be like this that secret thrill. They heard some voices outside the room. This broke the moment well and truly. The couple looked at one another and rolled their eyes at the same moment.

'It sounds as if our guests have surfaced,' observed Mary.

The guests in question were Hugo and Gloria Fowles and her brother George. Followers of these chronicles will perhaps recall how their romance was sealed over the putting green at Troon Golf Club the previous year. On this occasion, Kit had managed to save his good, if rather impetuous and accident-prone friend, Reggie Pilbream from an unwise union with the then Gloria Mansfield. Now this is not to decry the young woman in question nor her ability to grip a wood and play a round. Far from it, the problem lay in the personality of her young brother.

A year on from when we last met George, time had done nothing to narrow the gap between his excess of energy and his maturity. In short, his unfortunate predisposition towards malevolent mischief had grown rather than lessened: he was a horrible child.

The first person to appear in the room, much to the surprise of Kit and Mary, was their old friend Aldric 'Spunky' Stevens. The earliness of the hour was noted by Kit. It was just after eleven in the morning.

'Difficulty sleeping old boy?'

Spunky's face suggested that this was not something he had undertaken voluntarily.

'That little excrescence woke me up. There I was, mid dream with Bessie Love when all of a sudden I was jolted awake by that little so and so jumping on the bed full of cheer.'

19

'I trust you gave him a gentle kick in his rear end,' asked Kit, ignoring the disapproving look on Mary's face.

'It wouldn't have been gentle, let me tell you. I was hoping I could have slept a little longer. It was rather a late one last night. Thanks again for putting me up.'

'You'll stay for the lunch party, won't you?' asked Mary. 'The Lord President of the Council is coming.'

'Balfour? I might do. I wish you'd told me earlier.'

'I did last night,' pointed out Kit. 'You were somewhat the worse for wear, admittedly.'

The door opened at this point and in walked a rather disgruntled Hugo Fowles. He was greeted with muted enthusiasm by the others. Hugo Fowles had been in the war and frequently mentioned the fact. He was not a nice man, but nor was he a cad. A dashing moustache and a solid golf game had helped him bag a rich young woman. Fowles was a good cricketer and could play to a handicap of eight which is to say he actually played off a comfortable 13; unlucky for those players who played against him. In fact his life would've been perfect where it not for...

'George is going to be the death of me,' said Fowles, visibly shaking. 'I don't suppose there's any gin?'

'Is it not a little early?' asked Mary, glancing at the clock. Spunky, however, was already by the drinks cabinet mixing a couple of gins. Exposure to George had that effect on people.

'Do you know what the little blister just told me?'

'No, what did he say?' asked Kit and immediately regretted it.

*

Half an hour earlier:

'Uncle Hugo,' said George excitedly. He always called Hugo, 'Uncle,' much to the former army captain's immense irritation. Unfortunately, the devil-child was the apple of his wife's eye. Therefore giving full vent to his feelings towards the evil sprite was, sadly, not possible. However, it did feed many a fantasy that, if enacted, would certainly have earned Fowles a guarded respect in the Spanish Inquisition as well as thirty years at His Majesty's pleasure.

The boy in question was red-haired, freckled and almost a teenager. Quite what the arrival of puberty and its accompanying hormones would do to the ghastly imp was anyone's guess, but Fowles was not taking an optimistic view of future developments.

'Uncle Hugo,' said the imp in question. 'I've just had the most tremendous wheeze. Do you want to hear about it?'

'Would 'no' deter you?' asked Fowles.

George ignored him and ploughed on regardless.

'Do you know that maid of Kit and Mary's?'

The maid in question was an attractive young Italian named Bella. She was well-named in Fowles' view and had he not been married... However, he was happily married aside from the one blot on the beautiful landscape. George. Still, the mention of the maid, Bella, was enough to pique the interest of Fowles. He picked up a cup of water and turned to face his nemesis. This was mistake.

'I've just seen her in the altogether,' announced George proudly. The smile was wiped off his face as Fowles spat out the water he'd just imbibed drenching George in the process. George was too excited to care, though.

21

'What on earth?' exclaimed Fowles, staring in a demented fashion at the abominable result of too little discipline and too much over-indulging.

'I mean it. I hid in the wardrobe as she was changing,' explained George matter-of-factly.

Perhaps it was the very shamelessness rather than the act itself that sent Fowles' temperature gauge skyward, but before he had time to explode the foul child continued relating his story.

'I saw everything. Do you want to know?'

Hugo certainly did not but was unable to stop the horrid child forging on. George proceeded to describe with a surprising clinical accuracy what he'd seen. Then, before Fowles could dispense some uncle-like wisdom through the agency of a clip round the ear, the boy was off, leaving him close to a state of catatonic shock.

*

'He's a peeping Tom,' concluded Fowles to the shocked and, by now, highly sympathetic, audience.

'I can see why you need a drink,' said Mary, clearly displeased by what she'd heard. She looked at Kit. Her husband was staring at the bust of Canova which had a hat perched over it belonging to Betty. He and Mary had asked that she leave one behind as a memento.

Mary's hopes rose. Kit was planning something. While she had no doubt that her husband was as good a man as had ever walked God's earth, or England as it was better known, she had the feeling that his highly developed intellect, if applied in the cause of mischief, would be a lethal weapon.

'I say chaps,' said Fowles. 'You won't say anything to Gloria. For reasons that surpass all understanding, she dotes on the little blighter.'

A chorus of 'nooo's' greeted this request which seemed to calm the situation and then Kit spoke up.

'Hugo, how would you feel about a little justice heading young George's way. A little life lesson, shall we say?'

Shoulders that had slumped so despondently, straightened, the shaking hand steadied and a pilot light flickered in his eyes. Once more he was Captain Hugo Fowles of the Royal Artillery, a hero of countless encounters in Flanders.

'I say Kit, would you?'

The un-Kit-like evil gleam in his eye suggested that he would and that it would be a good one. The group gathered round to hear what he had in mind. Kit spoke in a hushed voice.

'Our guests are due here in an hour or so but I'm right in thinking Esther and Richard will be here sooner, Mary?'

'Yes, any minute in fact.'

'Good. Here's what I want you to do.'

*

The arrival of Esther Bright was always an event, especially for any man lucky enough to gaze upon her serene beauty. Yet this placid, ethereal exterior hid the beating heart of a rebel, a mischief maker with a sense of humour every bit as wicked as her sister's.

'Esther,' proclaimed Mary, as she entered the house with her husband, Dr Richard Bright, himself no slouch in the Adonis stakes.

'What a perfectly ghastly dress.'

Esther looked ravishing. Richard Bright certainly thought as much. So too did everyone else. Esther stood and looked at her sister in shock. Only then did she detect the merest hint of a shake of the head.

'Is it?' she asked, eyebrow raised.

'I say,' said Richard. 'A bit harsh.'

'No,' replied Kit, looking meaningfully at his great friend, 'Not Esther's colour at all.'

At this point the penny dropped on the beautiful couple that something was afoot. Quite what this was and why it needed such a public airing was unfathomable at this point. Introductions were made to the Fowles' including a young boy whose jaw appeared to be glued to the floor when he shook the hand of Esther. Seconds later he disappeared up the stairs. Kit and Mary exchanged glances. Mary waited a few moments until she heard the distinct sound of a door closing and then she took Esther's hand.

'Come with me.'

On the way up the stairs, Mary explained the situation to a relieved and then delighted Esther. Kit, meanwhile, filled Richard Bright in on the unfolding plan out of earshot of Gloria Fowles who was somewhat taken aback by Mary's condemnation of her sister's attire. She glanced at her own dress and immediately decided that she needed a new wardrobe. Standards were high in this part of the world.

*

George Mansfield arrived in Kit and Mary's room and at once felt immense joy as he realised that not only was there a wardrobe to hide in, but it afforded a wonderful view of

24

the room through the keyhole. He settled into the wardrobe for the show and what a show it would be. Best of all, the wardrobe was full of men's clothes so there was little chance of his being discovered.

The door opened and he heard the voices of the stunning sisters enter the room. Mary was chatting about a dress that would be perfect for her.

'You'll need to take off everything Esther.' George's heart began to race. His eye was glued to the keyhole and his view was perfect. 'I have some undergarments that go with the dress.'

'Very well, Mary. I will take off everything. You better lock the door in case anyone comes in.'

George could barely breathe now and then disaster struck. Mary moved in front of the keyhole blocking his view. He felt like crying but he was young and what is youth if not a boundless belief in the possibilities of the future.

'That's it, take everything off,' said Mary.

'The door is locked?'

'Yes. Just as well. Wouldn't want anyone seeing you like this. I must say Richard is an incredibly lucky man. Not an inch out of place.'

'You don't think my chest is too small?'

'No, Esther. I'm perfectly envious of you.'

'Let me see your chest, Mary.'

George couldn't stop himself groaning from inside the wardrobe.

'Did you hear that?' asked Esther.

'Probably the wind,' said Mary. 'What do you think?'

'I think Kit is a very lucky man too.'

George wasn't feeling lucky. This was turning into the worst moment of his life, but, just as youth will always have a belief in a positive future, adulthood is nothing if not the realisation that life doesn't always turn out the way you want it to. George was about to get an early and valuable lesson in this regard.

'Quickly, Esther. I think we should go now.'

Mary moved away from her key position of blocking the room and George, heart racing in renewed hope saw Esther at last. Alas, she was wearing a new dress, but worse was to come.

'I say, isn't that the key to the wardrobe,' said Mary. She picked it up and went over and placed it in the keyhole.

George's eyes widened in horror. He wanted to shout out, 'No,' but realised this was impossible. The light was now mostly blocked out and then a dire situation deteriorated even further. Mary turned the ley and locked the imp in the wardrobe. George bit back several new and particularly useful words he'd learned from 'Uncle' Hugo. It was only when he heard the bedroom door shut that he was able to give full vent to the fountain of frustration that built up inside him.

Esther and Mary, meanwhile, descended the stairs to join the others. Esther's new dress was met with acclaim by all, although no one, least of all Gloria Fowles, thought the other had been a problem in the slightest. A thought struck Gloria and she aired it immediately.

'Has anyone seen George?'

'I'm sure he's exploring the house, somewhere,' said Kit looking at Mary for confirmation.

'He'll be locked away somewhere, happy as Larry. Don't worry about him, Gloria' replied Mary.

2

Mary was standing by the window and nodded in reply to Kit's unspoken question. The car was still there with the two men. Kit joined her. Behind them the noise was growing louder as the lunch party guests arrived.

'You don't think they're after Arthur, do you?'' asked Mary. She was thinking of the former Prime Minister, Arthur Balfour, who was current Lord President of the Council.

'I can't imagine why,' admitted Kit, stepping back. 'The Lord President is a senior government position, I suppose, but it's not one with policy influence.'

A car pulled up outside the house. A woman dressed in black exited and made her way up the steps of Kit and Mary's Grosvenor Square residence. Aunt Agatha's old house was now in the possession of Kit and Mary. A minute later she entered the room to be greeted by Mary.

'Isabelle,' said Mary greeting an attractive woman who was perhaps closer to fifty than forty. 'Thank you for joining us. I was worried you might be detained because of upcoming Independence Day celebrations.'

'Mary, good to see you again. Yes a busy few days ahead.'

The accent was American. Isabelle Rosling looked around the room in approval. It was difficult to decide whether or not the approval was based on the tasteful décor or the bringing together of such evident wealth. Mary decided it was the former. Isabelle, like Mary, was involved in charity work related to supporting women who had escaped from abusive domestic situations and offered support and protection.

'Arthur Balfour is coming soon.'

'I know,' said Isabelle Rosling, 'I was speaking with Nancy Astor yesterday. She's his date for the afternoon.'

Nancy Astor was the first woman to sit in the House of Parliament as a Member, although she was not the first to be elected. That honour went to Countess Markiewicz who was currently serving time in Holloway prison for activities in support of Irish independence.

'How exciting,' exclaimed Mary. 'I haven't met her before. How do you know her?'

'Oh you know how it is, we Americans stick together.'

In the background, Mary heard Gloria Fowles ask her maid, Bella, if she'd seen George. There was just a hint of concern in her voice. Mary suspected this concern was less to do with George being lost than him indulging in some mischief that might bring shame upon her and her prospective Member of Parliament husband. Mary moved Mrs Rosling away from Gloria towards the Canova bust. As she was doing so, she saw Kit looked surprised by something he'd seen out of the window. As he did not seem unduly concerned she relaxed, but he seemed amused by something.

A minute or two later the source of his surprise became apparent.

Arthur Balfour entered the room with the first female sitting Member of Parliament, Nancy Astor who looked radiant in a teal-coloured dress. Under any circumstances all eyes would have turned to look at them. On this occasion they were upstaged.

'Good Lord,' said Mrs Rosling, her mouth falling open in surprise. 'Isn't that...?'

'Charlie Chaplin,' said Mary, half in shock.

Of course, this being England, the arrival of possibly the most famous man on the planet was greeted with marginally less excitement than an outsider winning the Derby: a mixture of shock, delight and jealousy.

Kit immediately went over to greet the new arrivals.

'Kit, you've met Nancy I take it,' said Arthur Balfour in a tired voice. He perennially seemed fatigued which was when he was probably at his most alert. He was even taller than Kit who stood over six feet himself and, thanks to his moustache, seemed a little sad with life. His clear eyes suggested something altogether different and richer.

Kit shook hands with the Member of Parliament for Plymouth Sutton and then turned his attention to their surprise companion.

'Kit, may I introduce Charlie Chaplin,' said Nancy Astor in a southern American accent.

'This is a delightful surprise Mr Chaplin. Mary and I have watched many of your films. In fact, Mary cried all the way through your last one. I laughed.'

'I'm relieved to hear it,' said Chaplin. This was the first time that Kit had heard the great man speak. It was almost a shock to hear the voice of someone so famous, but whose fame rested in the fact that he had never spoken on screen and communicated only through expression, gesture and action.

Chaplin was diminutive in stature, clean shaven with hair that was hinting it would turn grey imminently. His eyes sparkled with good humour and Kit liked him immediately. The eyes seemed to take in the room and, to Kit's amusement, widened momentarily.

'I suspect that you have either just seen my wife or her sister.'

'Or both,' grinned Chaplin. Kit turned around and saw the Cavendish girls were together, chatting, pretending not to have noticed their guest.

'They do that,' said Kit, thinking out loud. 'Would you like to meet them.'

'I'm not sure my heart could take it.'

'Courage Mr Chaplin. Courage,' said Kit drily and was rewarded by a chuckle. Kit had made the great man laugh. This would be a story to bore people with forever.

Much to the credit of the Cavendish sisters as were, they managed to maintain an air of studied indifference up until the point that Kit introduced Chaplin to them. As ever, the initial impact of the sisters was immediate and devastating, but Chaplin's charisma also worked its own spell and soon they were both grinning like schoolgirls at their great crush. Kit and Richard hovered nearby lest this evident mutual attraction become more concerning.

31

'I gather from Nancy that you are detectives,' said Chaplin.

'That would be Mary,' said Esther.

Chaplin turned to Mary with his eyebrows raised.

'Well,' admitted Mary, Kit and I have been involved with the police from time to time.'

'Anything you can tell me?' inquired the star. His eyes were bright with curiosity. Mary took a deep breath, suddenly feeling a little nervous to be alongside someone so well-known. He was only a little taller than she and so slight, but his movements were those of a dancer.

'Our most recent case was in Monte Carlo. We were involved with a Bluebeard case.'

Chaplin looked mystified. Seeing this, Mary expanded a little on this rather lurid opening.

'Have you heard of Henri Landru? He's the Frenchman accused of murdering a number of ladies who were married to him. We were involved with a connected case.'

'Why on earth did he kill his wives?' asked Chaplin, stupefied. Hugo Fowles, listening nearby, was fascinated. The thought of doing away with his beloved Gloria was inconceivable. George on the other hand...

'For money,' replied Mary. This gave Chaplin pause for thought.

'How interesting.'

'Perhaps you could make a film about it,' suggested Esther, half joking, but Chaplin was already thinking along similar lines given the pensive look on his face. Then he broke into a grin.

'I'm not sure audiences would accept the little fellow as a murderer, do you? Perhaps in the future though, who knows?'

*

Much to Kit and Mary's surprise, Chaplin stayed throughout the lunch and entertained the guest royally with stories of his life in Hollywood alongside screen idols such as Douglas Fairbanks, a particular favourite of Kit's and Mary Pickford.

Towards late afternoon, Harry Miller made an appearance in the room. He did a double take when he almost ran into Chaplin who was built along similar lines to his fellow Londoner, Miller. He went straight over to Kit.

'Sir, the car is still out there. Two different men. They are definitely watching the place. There's a telegram for you too.' He handed Kit an envelope and waited for his instructions.

Something in Kit's face as he read the telegram sent Mary over to him accompanied by Chaplin.

'Is everything all right?'

'No,' said Kit grimly. 'Read this.'

Chaplin could not but help read the communication also. It said:

COME TO TANGIER IMMEDIATELY. IN A STEW. LOOK FOR WALTER OR EMILY.

'Good Lord,' said Mary, 'what can it mean?'

Kit glanced out of the window and then back to Mary and the confused Chaplin.

'I don't know, but I suspect it's connected with our friends watching outside.'

Chaplin hovered close to the window and saw the car with the two men. He looked with concern at Kit and Mary.

'Another case?'

'I hope not,' said Kit just at the same time as Mary said, 'I hope so.'

Kit looked wryly at his wife and then said, 'My Aunt Agatha is in Morocco at the moment with her friends. She can be murder.'

This brought a raised eyebrow and a half-smile from Chaplin.

'Family trade?'

'Yes,' answered Mary on Kit's behalf. 'Very much so.'

'Who are the gentlemen outside?' inquired Chaplin.

'We should very much like to know that ourselves,' responded Kit, glancing out of the window. 'Whoever they are, they'll have seen the telegram arrive. They'll know we will be on our way soon because I suspect they'll already know what caused Aunt Agatha to send the telegram. The question is, how do we leave without them seeing us do so?'

'I have an idea I've been working on that might help you evade their attention,' said Chaplin with a grin. Kit and Mary's eyes both widened which Chaplin took as permission to carry on and explain more.

*

An hour later in which Kit had made various phone calls and Mary had changed into a dark one-piece outfit from Chanel. Chaplin, who had elected to stay on and watch how his suggestion worked out in real life, looked on appreciatively as Mary swept past him ready for her performance.

Miller was the first to leave. He walked past the two men and round the corner to a garage where Kit's Rolls Royce was parked. A few minutes later he drove past and parked a little further away from the curb than road etiquette dictated was acceptable.

Kit shook Chaplin's hand and thanked him for the idea. Mary was a little warmer in her gratitude which brought a happy smile to the star's face.

'I must say, this detective business is immensely satisfying,' commented Chaplin after receiving a hug and a peck on the cheek from Mary. Somewhere upstairs they heard Gloria Fowles calling for George to stop mucking around and come out. Chaplin, who had heard about the episode, burst out into a fit of giggles.

'You should leave before all hell breaks loose.'

Mary and Kit agreed it was time to part company. They moved out to the hallway, through the front door, descending the steps hand in hand just in time to see a taxi pull up close to Miller in the Rolls Royce. The taxi driver and Miller began to exchange words, mostly of one syllable, in a tones of voice that suggested neither would be receiving a Christmas card from the other.

The couple climbed into the Rolls and shut the door. Unseen by the car parked further down the Square, Kit and Mary ducked down and crawled out the door facing the road into the taxi that Miller was having the words with. Their arrival heralded the end of the argument. The taxi headed in one direction, while Miller set off in the other.

Sure enough the parked car was soon in pursuit of Miller and the Rolls that no longer contained Kit and Mary.

*

'Where exactly is Harry leading them?' asked Mary, glancing back to see the two cars embarking on their journey.

'I suggested Harry head down towards the Elephant and Castle. I phoned the MacDonald brothers. They will no doubt provide a warm welcome for our friends.'

Mary was shocked. Worse, she was worried.

'Kit, how could you? What if the two men are hurt?'

'I asked Wag not to use violence. I suspect one look at Haymaker and the two men will happily tell all that they know.'

Mary, reassured, sat back in her chair. She folded her arms and fixed her eyes on Kit. This was always designed to beguile him. It never failed. Ever.

'So where exactly are we going and don't say Morocco. I know that part. Who are Walter and Emily?'

Kit rolled his eyes at this and said, 'Walter Harris is The Times correspondent in Tangier. He's been there for years. Emily Keene, or as she is known, the Sharifa, was married to the Sharif, but he died long ago. She's been there even longer; a little bit like Agatha and Betty if you take my meaning.'

Mary did. Then another thought struck her.

'So how are we travelling?'

Kit's reply was infuriatingly enigmatic.

'You'll soon find out.'

*

It was Sam, Kit's Jack Russell who found young George, an hour later. He stood outside the wardrobe and made such a racket barking that it attracted the attention of Bella, the maid. She opened the wardrobe to find a rather chastened George lying in a crumpled heap on the floor. He'd fallen asleep inside the wardrobe and only just woken, thanks to Sam. By this time, Gloria Fowles was beside herself with worry, Hugo Fowles was enjoying one of the best days of his life.

'What on earth were you doing in there?' demanded the four-handicap love of Hugo Fowles' life. She was not clearly very displeased by the events of the day although George was feeling none too chipper about life at that moment, either. Then he glanced in the direction of Hugo Fowles and realised that destiny was at hand. Exactly what that destiny would be was in the hands of a man he did not particularly like and who he knew detested being called 'uncle.' He looked hopefully at Hugo Fowles, barely able to breathe.

'Well?' demanded Gloria.

'Leave the child alone, Gloria darling. Perhaps he was sleepwalking again.'

'Sleepwalking?' exclaimed Gloria.

Again, asked George in his head. It was an olive branch. Of sorts. In for a penny...

*

'I sometimes feel, Kit, that you deliberately keep things back from me,' said Mary a couple of hours later. It was early evening, and the sky was a glorious mauve. It might have been romantic in any other circumstances.

'Oh? Why do you say that?' asked Kit ingenuously.

Mary rolled her eyes and glanced to her left. Below them was the English channel. Quite a bit below them in fact. A thousand feet or more, apparently. Kit had said this to reassure her. Strangely it had not worked as well as he might have hoped. She was sitting behind Kit who was flying the biplane. The engine chattered, as did Mary's teeth through cold and perhaps a tinge of fear too. The wires whistled all around. Mary was not a bellyacher, so she bit back any complaints about the lurking cramp in her legs and the freezing cold that was invading every pore of her body.

The engine coughed and they proceeded on. Just up ahead, France loomed large and welcoming. Kit assured her that they would be travelling first class from this point on. They would catch a train to Paris and then take the Blue train down to Marseilles before boarding a night boat to Tangier.

That was the plan. They would be in Tangier in three days. Harry Miller would follow separately.

The engine of the aeroplane coughed again. No, it was now more of a bronchial splutter and certainly did not sound like something an aeroplane should do.

Then the engine cut out.

Silence.

The silence persisted. A few thousand feet in the air the silence sounded deafening to Mary's ears. In the seat in front of her, Kit was frantically trying to work the controls. His language had become a little frantic too. Mary decided not to comment on this, focusing her not inconsiderable intellect on the one question that was screaming inside her head. Finally, after another series of oaths she spoke.

'Is it supposed to do this?'

3

48 HOURS EARLIER

Agadir, Morocco: 1st July 1921

'I say, it's rather hot, isn't it?' said Jocelyn 'Sausage' Gossage.

Betty stared down at her friend unsympathetically and pointed out, 'You should try pushing the wheelchair.' A wave of guilt immediately engulfed her. Sausage laughed however which made her feel better. She hated to be unkind, but it was rather hot, and she was becoming fatigued by the effort. Agatha was walking a few steps ahead of them.

'It's somewhere around here,' said Agatha pointing her umbrella in the direction of the sea. Between the umbrella and the sea lay several hundred, if not thousand, graves. 'I don't remember having such trouble last time.'

They marched on and then Agatha spotted a landmark that she recognised. She waved her hand like a general at a battle and her 'men' followed her forward. They reached a white marble stone. It was small and simple, in stark contrast to the extraordinary constructions all around.

40

The top of the headstone read: '*I'm sleeping. Please be quiet.*'

Beneath it read: 'Lord Eustace Leonard Frost – Born 23rd April 1844 – Died 1st July 1911'.

Agatha stared at the headstone barely able to breathe. A part of her life had ended on that dreadful day ten years previously when the German gunboat had entered the port at Agadir, witnessed by Eustace. His last words were, 'There's going to be a war.'

It had taken three years, but his prophesy had come terrifyingly true. The war had almost claimed the life of her favourite nephew. It had claimed the life of Betty's only son. Agatha stared at the headstone through her tears and willed Eustace to appear one last time to her. She'd still have told him off, but he would have laughed and shrugged as he always did.

The trip to Agadir had taken almost twenty hours by boat. They stayed at the grave less than twenty minutes. The heat was just too much for all of them.

'We should return to the car,' said Agatha at last.

They turned and began to walk away slowly. Two cars appeared fifty yards away. One of the cars was a police car. The cars stopped and several men appeared. Two of the men were in uniform. One older man lit a cigarette. A younger man stood near him. He was tall and erect, wearing a straw Panama.

'I say,' said Sausage.

'I wonder what's going on,' asked Betty. The men seemed to be looking and pointing in their direction.

'The young man looks familiar,' said Sausage. 'Where have I seen him before?'

But Agatha's attention was not on the young man. It was on the older man. He was without a hat. His bald head shone in the sunlight. His bushy handlebar moustache crossed his face like weeds in a garden. He sat on the bonnet of his car like a hunter waiting for his prey.

'That's Inspector Berrada,' said Agatha as they drew closer. Betty gasped as she, too, recognised the old man sitting on the car smoking.

'Who's he?' asked Sausage.

'My nemesis,' replied Agatha.

The young man turned away and climbed into the second car before Agatha could see his face, but her attention was, as always, taken by the smile on Berrada's face and the malevolent triumph in his eyes.

'What does he want?' asked Sausage.

'I think he wants to arrest me,' replied Agatha, quickly. 'Perhaps we should go.'

Betty was already on the move.

'I say, chaps,' asked Sausage in that familiar plaintive voice. 'Do tell me what's going on.'

One hand on her hat and the other on her umbrella, Agatha led the way back to the waiting car. The sight of the ladies rushing in his direction had emboldened the driver, Ahmed, to step out of the car and come towards them. Without a word he took over from Betty to help Sausage into the back of the car. Shouts in the distance suggested that Inspector Berrada and the other policemen were somewhat dismayed by the turn of events.

'What is happening your ladyship? asked Ahmed.

'No time,' gasped Agatha. 'Drive.'

In a matter of seconds, Agatha and Betty had joined Sausage in the back. Ahmed rushed around to the driver's seat. Agatha turned and looked through the back window at Berrada. The detective had stopped, turned and was running back to his car.

'He'll have a stroke if he's not careful,' said Agatha unkindly.

'But why is he after you?' exclaimed Sausage. Their car was now moving quickly towards the gates of the cemetery.

'For some reason he thinks I killed Gabrielle Fish. Complete nonsense of course. Anyway, this is a bit of a problem. Ahmed, you'll need to take us somewhere safe.'

'Of course, your ladyship,' grinned the old driver.

'And we'll need to send a telegram as soon as possible.'

Agatha turned to Betty and Sausage. She nodded to them that everything would be all right. Whether she was feeling this particularly herself was not for discussion. She sat back in her seat and took in a few deep breaths.

'Who must I send the telegram to?' asked Ahmed.

'Kit and Mary Aston. They live in Grosvenor Square in London. I need their help.'

'No time for that Agatha,' said Betty turning around. 'Their car is coming.'

Agatha looked out the back window and saw Betty's warning was accurate but did not convey exactly how quickly they were coming. They would be overtaken in a matter of minutes. Just at that moment something licked Agatha's face.

'Oh for goodness sake,' said Agatha. 'Mimi, this is not the time.'

The Mimi in question was a large, female Doberman that Agatha had adopted following her recent involvement with the Bluebeard Club in Monte Carlo.

'I still don't know what possessed you to adopt her,' said Betty coldly. Mimi, sensing Betty's displeasure as only animals can, switched her affections to Betty momentarily before returning to Agatha. The car, meanwhile, reached the gates of the cemetery and then they were through.

'Stop the car,' ordered Agatha suddenly. She pushed Mimi down and opened the car door. For someone over seventy years of age, she was still surprisingly nimble when the mood caught her. Or panic.

Ahmed stopped the car before he had time to consider the wisdom of his actions.

'What are you doing?' shouted Betty.

'What's going on?' appealed Sausage.

The two ladies turned in horror as they saw Agatha close the gates to the cemetery. Quite what the point of this was, escaped them. Their pursuers were almost upon them. The prospect of being arrested and thrown into a Moroccan jail as accomplices loomed large upon their minds and, as prospects went, it was far from inviting.

Agatha's actions had the desired effect. The police car slowed down as it approached the gate. At this point, Agatha did something that, even by her own exacting standards, astonished Betty. From out of her pocket, she extracted a revolver.

'Good Lord,' said Betty.

'She's not going to...' said Sausage.

Agatha fired twice at the car.

Betty spun around and saw what she'd done.

'Well done old girl.'

'What did she do?'

'She just shot the two front tyres of the police car.'

Agatha hastened back into the car, and they set off before the shocked policemen had time to process what had just happened.

'Just a respite,' warned Agatha. They'll be searching for us now. Rail station, harbours. We'll need to find a way of reaching Tangier. That's our only hope.'

Silence.

Agatha was surprised at the lack of reaction and looked at her travelling companions. They were staring at her. So was Mimi. It seemed like everyone felt a more detailed explanation was required for why the police were hunting Agatha and why she had just made matters worse by shooting at them. It was not an unreasonable question even though it had not actually been asked.

'When I said I hadn't killed Gabrielle Fish, I was perhaps guilty of being a little disingenuous.'

'Did you kill her?' exclaimed Sausage, half in shock.

'It rather depends on what you mean by killed, my dear.'

*

'The surest way of getting out of a country unseen is a busy harbour in the early hours. There's always space on a fishing boat,' explained Agatha. She had said similar over the previous few hours as the three women had hidden at Ahmed's house. Her two companions were also her oldest and staunchest friends. They had seen Agatha pull veritable rabbits out of a hat in the past, but they were as one on this idea.

'Does it have to be by boat?'

The speaker might have been either Betty or Sausage. It was hard to tell as they, like Agatha, were dressed in the traditional dress of Muslim women, the Niqab. Only their eyes were visible, and speech was muffled by the veil across their faces.

'You'll have your sea legs in no time,' said Agatha, upbeat as ever.

'Ocean,' said Betty. 'It's a ruddy ocean. Anyway, why can't we just walk into a police station and clear this matter up?'

'Police station?' expostulated Agatha. 'We're not in Paddington Green my dear. Police is more of an idea than a reality outside of Tangier. Berrada's word is law, and he is judge, jury and, trust me on this one, executioner.

'I remember,' said Betty. Her one trip to Morocco had taken place just after Kaiser Wilhelm II had made an unscheduled stop in Tangier in 1905, setting off a chain of events that had led them to this point. 'I saw the face of evil when I met that man.'

'Exactly,' said Agatha. 'We need to make it to Tangier and then over to Spain. It's a pity Ahmed's cousin won't take us any further than Rabat.'

Ahmed appeared at this point and bowed to the ladies. He looked genuinely distraught that he could not be of more help.

'Darid is not my favourite cousin. Not even his family like him very much.'

'Can we trust him?' asked Agatha, instantly alert for treachery.

Ahmed shrugged and replied, 'You have money, and you have a gun. Darid is not a brave man. He respects both.'

It was midnight now. Despite the time of year, it was much cooler in the evening. A sea breeze might have caressed their faces, but Ahmed had insisted they retain their veils at every point until they reached Tangier.

To transport the three ladies, Ahmed borrowed a cart and a donkey from another cousin. The trip down to the port was made through the narrow streets of Agadir. As expected, there was a lot of activity at the port despite the hour.

'We are fortunate with the breeze,' said Ahmed. His English was exceptionally good although he and Agatha often conversed in Arabic.

Near the port, Ahmed diverted the cart away onto a street that ran parallel to the sea. This prompted a question from Sausage.

'I say, aren't we going the wrong way?'

'We're not catching our boat at the port, Sausage. Berrada will have men there.'

Whatever reassurance may have been provided by this point was swiftly lost as they travelled slowly out of the town on a dirt track that hugged the coastline. The journey seemed interminable, and it needed all of the stoicism of three English ladies to bear it without complaint.

After an hour or so they finally reached an inlet. Ahmed brought the cart to a halt and helped the three ladies down. He pointed towards a small beach in a cove ringed by high rocks that seemed to rise vertically into the sky

'Are you strong enough to walk Lady Jocelyn?' asked Ahmed.

'I think so, assuming my back hasn't been broken by the bumps on the road.'

Ahmed laughed and shrugged once more. What can you do? This wasn't England. He shook hands with Betty and Sausage, wishing them a safe journey in the hands of God. Then he turned to Agatha. For a moment they were silent, regarding each other in the moonlight.

'We have had many adventures Lady Agatha.'

'We have Ahmed. I thought those days were behind me when I lost Useless.'

'I miss Lord Frost. He was...'

Ahmed could not think of a word to describe Agatha's husband. He shrugged once more and smiled.

'He was...' agreed Agatha. It seemed about the only way to describe the love of her life.

'Go, Lady Agatha. Darid will be waiting.' He patted Mimi on the head and watched them depart.

The three ladies picked their way down to the rocky beach while Mimi ran on ahead towards a rather alarmed man sitting in a small boat floating beside a makeshift jetty. The fishing boat hardly seemed fit for a pond never mind braving the Atlantic ocean. It was a small wooden craft with a battered off-white sail that appeared to have been repaired many times with cloth of dubious provenance. Agatha and Betty helped their friend across the beach onto the jetty. Sitting in the boat was a man of around fifty. He stayed seated as the three ladies carefully climbed down into the boat.

'Thanks for the help,' said Agatha archly in English. She looked at the man who was to guide them to Rabat. His face suggested, not unreasonably, that he would rather be anywhere than here at that moment. His thick moustache did not move as he watched his three travel companions warily and the dog even more warily. For a moment, the only sound was the lapping of the water against the side of the boat. Then Darid spoke. His accent was thick, his voice harsh.

'Money.'

He said this in English and then repeated it in Arabic.

'No. When we arrive in Rabat,' replied Agatha firmly.

'No. Money.'

Betty felt Sausage grip her hands fearfully. This was not the start to their trip they wanted. Mimi growled. Darid seemed unmoved.

'Don't worry. It's always like this,' said Betty.

For the next minute, which seemed like a lifetime to Sausage, Agatha and Darid volleyed and smashed their way through a verbal rally that concluded with Agatha providing Darid with half the money for the trip and a promise of the rest upon arrival.

'Couldn't we have just agreed this at the start. It's the first thing I thought of when he started on about wanting money,' said Betty.

'Where's the fun in that?' asked Agatha oblivious to her friend's consternation.

'Can I remind you that we are sitting on a small boat in the Atlantic on the run from what passes for Moroccan law and order. Fun is the very last thing that I'm having right now, dear.'

' I do hope Mr Darid knows his way around at night. He looks capable,' said Sausage trying as ever, to see the positive. He looked like a killer to the other two ladies, but they wisely kept their counsel.

'If Mr Darid is what I think he is then most of his work is conducted at night,' said Agatha enigmatically. The smuggler pushed off from the jetty and they were off on a journey by sea that would take them two nights to accomplish.

Darid's first attempt to kill his passengers occurred during Sausage's watch.

Naturally, she had fallen asleep, Mimi snoozing at her feet. The big Doberman, unlike the three ladies, was not keen on sailing at the best of times and was happy to keep her head well and truly down. The attempt was aborted when Darid stubbed his big toe on the wooden floor of the boat and yelped thereby waking Mimi and, by extension, half the coast as she barked frenziedly.

Darid realised there were two challenges to overcome. How to get rid of the guard dog and then how to overpower three, admittedly elderly, ladies to obtain the rich pickings that lay in wait. This would require some thought. Darid was not a thinker.

The rest of the first night's travel passed without incident. They spent daylight hours which would have been too hot to travel midway between Safi and El Jadidi on the western coast of the country, south of Rabat.

As darkness fell and, more importantly, the temperature, Darid set off with his unusual set of passengers. They were close to finishing their already meagre rations. A sullen silence settled over the boat as it skipped along the coastline driven by a very welcome, if rather warm, wind coming from the south.

Sensing that his best opportunity for gains would come when Sausage was on watch, Darid bided his time until he was certain that both Betty and Agatha were asleep. He smiled towards Sausage who, minus veil, responded in kind. She was that sort of Englishwoman who believed the best in everybody even when evidence and experience had proven that their characters were manifestly unworthy of her affection.

Around four in the morning, hunger and fatigue finally saw Sausage give herself up to slumber. Her eyes began to shut, opening occasionally until finally the locks and bolts of deep sleep had been applied. Even then, Darid waited until he was certain that the three ladies were, in boxing parlance, out for the count. He removed the oar from the water that he had been using on occasion to steer the boat and raised it over his head. His method of dealing with Mimi had a certain barbaric simplicity to it. A bash on the head was as good as anything in his view. Even better was the fact that he did not have to move too far. His big toe was still sore from last night's failed attempt.

Oar in hand, he raised it over his head and picked his spot on the comatose canine's black and brown head.

'I wouldn't do that if I were you,' said Agatha in English. Now Darid's grasp of the subjunctive, never mind English, was at best, non-existent, but he understood all too well what a revolver looked like. Agatha cocked it to add an additional level of comprehension.

Darid, wisely, decided to forgo any further attempt at enriching himself through robbery and murder. He was a fisherman, a sometime smuggler. This was his life. It wasn't a bad life all told. He would stick to this.

By the time they reached Rabat, as dawn was breaking on the 3rd of July, relations between the three ladies were somewhere between cordial and testy. All were hungry, all needed a long bath and, most of all, the restorative powers of a large gin, but another day of travel lay in wait. Thankfully, it would be across land, partly by train and partly by car, thanks, once more, to the astonishingly wide-reaching nature of Ahmed's family.

*

A day later, even more fatigued, but, at least, washed, fed and in Tangier, Agatha and her two friends considered their options. A drive past in a taxi had confirmed their suspicion that the British Legation on Rue d'Angleterre was being watched by Berrada's men although whether the man himself had reached Tangier was open to question.

The three ladies were sitting in a café near the Grand Hotel. They could see a couple of men near the entrance to

52

the hotel which suggested that this establishment was being watched also.

'Lucky you sent Kit a telegram in Rabat, Agatha,' said Betty. This was the nearest she had come to praising her friend's perspicacity since their original flight. 'I suspect they have men at every office.'

Agatha merely nodded confirmation of this. Their niqabs were showing all the signs of their extraordinary trip by sea and by land that saw them a few hundred yards away from relative safety. Agatha had been too long in the game to know that this was the most crucial part of the journey and the most difficult.

They could not just walk into the Legation. Berrada's men would intercept them long before they reached the door. Messages were out of the question, as they would be intercepted too. Agatha had no doubt that Walter Harris and the Sharifa, Emily Keene, were under similar observation.

This left them with the prospect of waiting for a random person of an English disposition to pass by so that they could arrive at the Legation under escort. An hour in the café had rendered such a hope forlorn. The longer they stayed, the more suspicious they appeared. Although the Press in Morocco at this point was not pervasive, the news would undoubtedly be out. Agatha shot a glance at the café owner. There was something about the way he was looking at them.

Yes, overall, reflected Agatha, it was a bit of a stew.

She looked at the man behind the bar. He was fidgeting with a cup, standing up and sitting down as if he had piles.

Agatha's spider senses were on alert now. Had he sent someone to inform on them? It would be no surprise if he had. Berrada's tentacles stretched everywhere. He would have every business on the lookout for three independent women in any form of dress.

'We should leave,' said Agatha.

'Why?' asked Sausage who had just been on the point of ordering another coffee.

Betty had been with Agatha in too many precarious situations to question the order. She was on her feet immediately. This had the desired impact on Sausage. She rose a little unsteadily and headed for the door in a manner that belied her seventy plus years and recent recovery from a broken leg. A horse-riding accident.

Outside in the café, Agatha considered their limited options.

'I have a plan,' said Agatha.

'You have a plan?' exclaimed Betty in surprise.

It wasn't much of a plan, but it was superior to anything else they had going on for them at that moment.

'We will hire a marketplace trader to take his wares to the British Legation. We'll hide in the back of his cart and when he reaches the door, we'll jump out and force our way in. The door should be open until eleven at the least. They ducked down a side street and headed in the direction of a small market square that Agatha knew would have the traders that they needed. No one saw the small man who appeared from a doorway and began to follow them.

Betty and Sausage struggled to keep up with Agatha as she weaved her way down the narrow street with high

54

whitewashed walls either side. They could hear a tremendous bustle in the distance; this could only be their destination. Soon they were in the square.

What hit them first was the smell. It was the fragrance of the Mediterranean: dead fish and spices. Brightly dressed Rif women were selling fruit and vegetables. The bray of donkeys echoed all around. Mounds of brilliantly coloured spices baskets overflowing with peppercorns dazzled the eyes. Behind them was a small pinkish mosque.

'I say,' said Sausage. 'How lovely.'

'Let's go,' said Agatha who was in no mood to stand and enjoy the view like a tourist.

A voice from behind spoke.

'Please stay where you are Lady Agatha. It is Lady Agatha isn't it?'

Agatha felt something metal and pointed press gently against her ribs. She stopped immediately as instructed. Betty and Sausage pushed on until they heard the urgent note in Agatha's voice.

'Girls. Stop.'

The two ladies stopped and turned around. Betty's face suggested that she was about to give out to her friend until she saw the small man standing next to her. The face was a mask but there was no mistaking the dangerous intent in the eyes. Her heart sank. It was difficult to know what Agatha was thinking. Then her friend tore off her veil and threw it to the ground. Frustration and anger were etched on her face. They had come so far and now...

Agatha turned around slowly to face the man who had found her.

'Good Lord!' she exclaimed, none too happily it must be said. 'What in blue blazes are you doing here?'

4

A farmhouse near Calais: 3rd July 1921

'So with the engine cutting out, we'd no choice but to glide down onto your farm, Monsieur Filbert.'

The Monsieur Filbert in question was a man of around sixty with a huge moustache that made him look like a walrus who had decided, late in life, to take up beetroot farming. He studied the face of the fair-haired Englishman who spoke French flawlessly with a degree of bemusement. He had promised to make good any damage to the field in which they had landed. Filbert was already calculating a rather large profit from the serendipitous accident. Beetroot prices had fallen recently.

The two men were sitting in the kitchen of Filbert's large farmhouse a few miles west of Calais eating toast. In another room, the Englishman's beautiful companion, he claimed wife, was with Madame Filbert borrowing a dress. Like most Frenchmen, he was romantic to the very core of his being. Not for one second did he believe they were husband and wife. Non! They had eloped by plane to France. Everyone knew that France was the home of romance. Madame Filbert was of a like mind and had instantly forgiven them the damage they had caused when she saw just how beautiful the young woman was. At fifty-five, she wasn't so old as not to appreciate the obvious attractions of the tall, blue-eyed gentleman either. Perhaps thirty years ago she might have given the young English woman a run for her money.

The two women emerged from the bedroom. Madame Filbert looked on proudly at the young woman. She had donated an old dress of her daughter's. It was a little old-fashioned, but the young Englishwoman had that certain *je ne sais quoi* that meant a sack cloth would have looked beautiful on her.

Kit certainly thought so too if his smile was any guide. The French couple exchanged knowing looks. Unquestionably they had eloped.

A few minutes later Monsieur Filbert was leading them out to his prized possession. A motor car. Rather like Mary's dress, the car was not the latest model. In fact, it dated back to just before the beginning of the war. Matters over the next few years had meant that it was rarely used. Monsieur Filbert had hidden it away lest it be commandeered by one side or the other.

Beetroot farming's gain was clearly racing's loss. Thanks to Monsieur Filbert's enjoyment of speed, Kit and Mary reached Calais in suitable time to catch the train to Paris. They parted at the station with an assurances of renumeration from Kit and best wishes for their future from the farmer. Right at that moment, Kit and Mary's future involved a few days travel by train and by boat.

'I'll just pop to the telegraph office and let the Majestic know we are coming,' said Kit.

'Can they find us some luggage and clothing too?' said Mary with a grin. She held her arms out and gazed, not without fondness, at her dress. 'We did take off in a bit of a rush.'

'I mentioned that in my original telegram, but yes, now we know what time we'll arrive they can have all of that ready.'

*

Three hours later, rather fatigued and ready for a bath and bed, Kit and Mary strolled into the Hotel Majestic. The Majestic, near the Arc de Triomphe was not, as the name suggested, the pick of the Parisian crop of hotels, but it held a special place in Kit's heart. It had been two years since his last visit. Then he had attended the Paris Peace Conference and investigated a murder that the press called '*The French Diplomat Affair.*' The success of the Peace Conference was a matter of debate for Kit. The reparations levied on a nation that did not believe it had been defeated struck Kit as harsh and likely to store up resentment. This was not the lasting peace that the dead and the maimed from the Great War had earned through their sacrifice.

Mary strolled through the enormous lobby and looked around her. Its opulence marked by the shiny floor, the beautifully manicured plants with hues that harmonised with the colours of the walls and the floor. For Kit it also seemed enormous, but only because it was so empty. Two years previously it had been humming with diplomats, soldiers, politicians and potential terrorists. Now it was

59

nearing eleven at night and sensible folk were either in bed or still out dancing at one of the many jazz clubs. This was for another trip.

They were greeted by the night manager, Eric Dumas. He led the couple up to their room. On the bed, artfully arranged was a selection of clothes provided by Coco Chanel for Mary. Kit picked up outfit, a Breton top and held it up in the air.

'This does not seem long enough. Won't your midriff be on display?' pointed out Kit. It wasn't exactly a complaint.

Mary smiled and shrugged. The shape of her mouth and mischief in her eyes suggested adventurous possibilities.

'Is there anything wrong with my midriff?'

'Not at all. I can say positively that I adore your midriff; I would challenge anyone to say otherwise. I'm just wondering what effect it may have on our French friends and when we reach Tangier.'

He set the top down and picked up a couple of long white dresses that were more modest in their ambition. There were a number of ready-to-wear suits in the wardrobe that Kit had ordered from his usual tailor in Paris. Except for his dinner suit, they were all light coloured and suitable for the hot weather they were likely to encounter in Tangier. Near the window was the luggage provided by Louis Vuitton. There were two large trunks and two smaller suitcases.

'I always believe in travelling light,' said Kit drily.

'Such an adventurer,' agreed Mary, putting one arm on his shoulder.

Kit turned to look at her. This took a few seconds longer than such things normally take as Mary had discarded the borrowed dress.

'So, what happened to the dress Madame Filbert gave you?'

*

Around the same time that Kit was happily wondering then ceasing to care about what had happened to Mary's dress, Harry Miller was boarding a boat at Dover. He too was bound for Tangier but would travel separately. Something in Aunt Agatha's telegram had suggested to Kit that her problems may benefit from the presence of Miller. The reason for this was less to do with the need for a servant than the fact that, once upon a time, Miller had been a burglar. His life had been changed, like so many other men and women, by the War. He was one of the lucky ones. Hundreds of thousands had perished or been maimed for life. Now, he was living in a large townhouse on Grosvenor Square, a burglar, the son of a burglar. Yes, he was one of the lucky ones.

Life is never so straightforward, though. When Lord Kit Aston had invited him to be his valet, Miller had never envisaged he would want to do anything else. The last few years had brought him travel and adventure.

Yet, he wanted if not more, then something that he could call his own. He lived at the behest of another man and now, woman. He lived in circumstances that were akin to grace and favour luxury. What was to dislike? Nothing. He adored Kit Aston and Mary too. He loved the adventure, the chance to put his old skills to effective use in

61

causes that were truly noble. Perhaps this was the source of his lingering sense of discontent.

Although he had not spoken to Kit about his feelings, he sensed that the couple were aware he was questioning himself, his life. It was unspoken of course. This was England. One did not speak of feelings when one could make a joke or talk about sport instead. Yet the air was filled with something that Miller could not define. It was not tension; it could never be resentment or indeed disappointment. He and Kit had been through too much together for that ever to sully their relationship. Miller did not know what it was, nor how to define it, never mind put words to it. He was, fundamentally, a man of action.

Perhaps this was the nub of the problem, he realised. Too much of his life was a succession of days in which nothing very much happened, but then all that could change without warning. In those glorious moments when the couple had a case, Miller could be involved in something that genuinely challenged him, scared him senseless, yet invigorated him too. He felt alive, alive in the way he had felt during the War, even amongst, particularly amongst, the dead. He owed it to them, to the mates that hadn't made it to live a life.

His life.

*

As Miller began the journey to Tangier with the ferry crossing over to Calais, another man's journey was ending there. Inspector Berrada was standing in a queue at his usual hotel in Tangier overcome with a combination of fatigue and a mood of discontent. He was never happy at the best of times, although the torture and murder of people did provide more than a modicum of sunshine in a life that was truly dark. Unlike Miller, Berrada accepted that his life was not his to define and shape like potter's clay. This was not to say that he would not have liked to have choices. In all but name he was a slave: a willing slave. His owner, if he could so be described, was Mulai Ahmed al-Raisuli.

The two men had been born a few weeks apart in the village of Zinat, albeit in quite different circumstances. Raisuli was a Sharif, a descendant of the Prophet Mohammad. Yet, despite the difference in rank, they had been friends as children. Their youth had been a wild series of adventures or, as the authorities viewed it, crime.

Raisuli, as ever, pushed the authorities too far and was imprisoned. Berrada visited his friend at the dungeon where he was chained to a wall over those four years. He brought him food, kept him alive. When Raisuli was released as part of the new Sultan's clemency, he had chosen Berrada to follow him. Someone he could trust in his great project: the expulsion, no less, of foreigners from his country and Berrada had followed him willingly, as he had always done.

Yet sometimes, on days such as these, Berrada wished he could go away and retire to a village, take a young wife, enjoy a life that had thus far been devoted to one man. He was in his early fifties now. It was not too late. The great Raisuli would understand. Perhaps this one last case and then he could lie prostrate before the great man and ask him to be released. Perhaps if he could catch Agatha Frost then Raisuli would listen.

He would never listen, of course. Raisuli would not stop until foreign governments ceased to control Morocco. Until every last foreigner had been expelled. Only then, perhaps, would he see that his old friend's work was done. His old village, a wife and some land. Berrada had never been a dreamer, but sometimes these thoughts would cross his mind. They did so now as he stood in the lobby of the hotel. He hated this place, but the Sûreté paid for him to stay here and Raisuli insisted he do so to remind him, every night, of his true job.

All around Berrada a babble of voices assaulted his ears. Under any circumstances he was used to chaos and noise. He was Moroccan. What else was Morocco if not this? Yet these were not *his* voices. These were not *his* people. These were foreign voices. Americans, French, German. He detested them, just like Raisuli. Yet, like Raisuli, he had learned to work with and for the hated foreigner. Raisuli had told him to join the Sûreté. He'd learned to speak French and for fifteen years he'd become part of them.

'Monsieur Berrada,' said a voice, waking Berrada from his brief reverie. It was Lucien Moreau, the owner of the hotel. He smiled mirthlessly at the policeman, perhaps even fearfully. Berrada had that effect on people. Despite his white, European suit and his Panama hat, he would never pass for one of them. Nor would he want to. He was a Berber and would be all his life, whatever he chose to wear. The looks he received from his fellow countrymen he ignored. They did not understand. One day they would. Then they would celebrate his name not just Raisuli's.

'We have your usual room,' said the Frenchman, handing Berrada a large Mortice key from a hook on the wall at the reception.

Berrada sensed a few of the guests were looking at him, but he ignored them. He nodded to the owner of the hotel and grabbed the key. The noise in the lobby seemed to die as he walked through. It was as if the foreigners were protesting at the presence of someone who was not like them. He was the one who should protest. They were the unwelcome ones. This was his country.

He walked slowly towards the stairs. On his way he passed a mirror. He saw an old man looking back at him. The years had not been kind. His weight had spiralled, not unlike his master, his wispy beard was greying and the lines around his eyes ran like cracks on a mud road in summer, the jowls around his mouth hung like cured meat in a market stall. On a good day he resembled an incontinent yak. This was not a good day.

Berrada lumbered up the stairs, desperate to rid himself of the uncomfortable suit and put on his djellaba. He carried two bags, neither heavy, yet they felt like the weight of the world to him. Two days of hard travelling had not helped either. The sooner he caught the Frost woman the better. She was here. She had to be. Where else was there for her to go? He had the evidence now, not that he normally cared about such niceties.

Gabrielle Fish had died that night sixteen years ago. The British had lied. Agatha Frost was a murderer. The man, a

65

Frenchman of all things, had said her capture, her trial and her execution would splinter the unnatural alliance between France and Britain while, elsewhere, the weapons he was smuggling into the country would arm Berrada's brothers in the Rif mountains, just like the German, Bartels, had tried years before. This time they would succeed. The French and the British no longer had the stomach for war and the Spanish were too weak. The tribes would unite and kick the foreigners out of Morocco.

Within a year, maybe two, Raisuli would have his wish. So might Berrada.

5

Tangier: 5th July 1921

'Yes indeed, Lady Agatha, it must seem very strange to see us here. Very strange indeed,' said a rather stout man dressed in a white suit.

Strange barely covered Agatha's view on the matter. She stood in front of two men, one of them holding a gun, neither of whom should have been there. Names from the past, yet no more welcome for that. To have come so far and, at the last minute, be captured. Or something. The look on the large man's face was enigmatic. Sidney Gutmann or Goodman as he now fashioned himself had been her brother's former partner in their San Francisco advertising firm before his innate predisposition to crime, in this case, cooking the books, had led to the dissolution of their partnership. Goodman had taken to a new business, importing goods from Europe, North Africa and the Middle East for his antiques business. The shop in San Francisco, inevitably, was a front for the genuine business of the day, smuggling and fencing stolen antiques.

His sometimes willing, often resentful, partner in the exercise was the diminutive Egyptian, Joel. Thanks to Kit,

Mary and Agatha along with a private investigator named Dashiell Hammett, their business had crumbled following their imprisonment in Turkey for the murder of a sailor. Unfortunately, just as Goodman had finally taken possession of the thing he desired most, the Caravaggio painting of a falcon, created when he was incarcerated at the pleasure of the Knights of St John in Malta, he was relieved of it by a Frenchman named Comte Jean-Valois du Bourbon. By then he was already standing on the wrong side of a revolver and soon to be in the hands of the police.

'Well, Sidney, if this were a book, I would scarcely credit the coincidence,' said Agatha.

Goodman chuckled good-naturedly. He was a large man, tall and wide. He smelled like his perspiration was in a fight to the death with his cheap eau de cologne. The Cologne was losing.

He replied, 'But this is real life not the words of an exceptionally talented writer, Agatha. You are most certainly going to be my guest.'

'Agatha, what's going on?' asked Sausage. Even her steadfastly optimistic view of life had been dented by the sight of the revolver.

The group threaded their way along a narrow street which offered some shade from the relentless sun before reaching a wide flight of stairs with tailor shops and carpenters either side. Goodman was leading them into the deepest, darkest part of Tangier, but only metaphorically. The sun reflecting off the white walls half-blinded the three ladies. Their two male escorts were more practically equipped for the bright conditions with sunglasses.

68

The ladies were in a determinedly uncommunicative mood as they struggled up the gentle slope. None would admit to the discomfort they felt in the heat and the breathless air. As they neared their destination, Goodman sensed that Sausage was finding the gentle climb an uncomfortable one. He offered his arm to Sausage who, much against her will, had to accept. After so long out with a broken leg she was close to the limit of her endurance. Of course, she complained more about Goodman, a kidnapper, helping her than about her own discomfort which had been borne in silence. Goodman merely smiled at this rebellion but helped her anyway. Such is the perversity of the island race.

They finally came to a stop at a small square with a broken fountain. On the other side of the fountain was a large, dilapidated villa in the European style. It certainly gave no reassurance that its interior was in any better state of repair. The white paint on the walls was chipped and there was unmistakable evidence of cracks.

'Be it ever so humble,' said Goodman, smiling benignly to the three ladies.

'It's about the only thing humble about you, Sidney,' retorted Agatha. She glanced at Joel. The Egyptian seemed no more enamoured of the building than they were. In fact, he had been a sullen contrast to the malevolent benevolence of Goodman. Agatha doubted the two men were any fonder of one another than they had seemed previously. This was a marriage of inconvenience.

Joel motioned with the gun that Goodman had given him. It was time to stop admiring their new accommodation and, instead, sample its delights. Goodman bowed to Joel and then with a slight tug, helped Sausage across the square to the villa. Soon the party was ascending a staircase that had once been rickety but had graduated to being a genuine health hazard.

'You should have this fixed,' said Betty sternly. 'Someone could hurt themselves.'

'This is but a temporary accommodation,' said Goodman.

'Is your castle being fixed up at present?' asked Agatha drily.

Goodman ignored the sarcasm with a practiced ease. He had known Agatha, on and off, for thirty years. She'd never liked him and to give the lady her due, he had never given her much reason to do so. While he, Goodman, could not help himself. He held Agatha in a genuinely warm regard that transcended mere respect for her obvious intellectual gifts. She entertained him. He found her brusqueness a delight, her intelligence an endless source of edification when compared with the slyly smart, Joel and her very English sense of privilege, a right that he believed his country had earned on the battlefield and on the playing field, to be the very embodiment of everything that made him proud of his country.

Also, on a number of levels, she could be especially useful to him.

They entered a large room with a dining table and a number of large cushions and wooden chairs. Agatha turned to Goodman with one eyebrow cocked to full derision.

'Make yourselves comfortable ladies,' said Goodman clapping his hands and then opening them expansively. 'Now, what do you say I organise for us some coffees and things to eat?'

There was little to be sarcastic about in this and, as ever, Agatha found Goodman to be a challenge to needle and to get under his skin. That said, there was a lot of skin to get through. Despite being close to six feet in height, their kidnapper weighed in at a more-than-sturdy two hundred and thirty pounds.

'Yes, coffee and something to eat would be welcome,' conceded Agatha.

'Of course,' said Goodman, 'but first if you would give me your gun Agatha. I know you have one. The newspaper claimed you fired upon poor Inspector Berrada. I wish you'd finished him off and saved us all a job.'

Agatha, reluctantly, handed over the weapon. The room was ridiculously hot, and Sausage was beginning to look a little pale. Betty helped her to a chair while Joel, who had said little until this point said, 'I'll open the shutter. Perhaps some air.'

He walked over to the window and tried the shutter, but it resolutely refused to budge. Betty noted the size of the Egyptian and walked over to see if her rather more robust frame might provide the necessary strength. Joel was having none of it though. He was engaged in a life and death struggle with the recalcitrant shutter.

Joel handed Betty his gun and gave it another shake. It gave way, much to his evident delight if his yelp of joy was any indication. Without looking, he put his hand out and Betty instinctively handed the gun back to him.

This little episode was too much for Agatha. She slammed her hand on the table and glared stupefied at Betty.

'Ah,' said Betty, somewhat embarrassed. 'I probably shouldn't have done that.'

'What were you thinking?' demanded Agatha, half turning away and then back again in evident frustration.

Goodman was certainly wondering the same but seemed a little more relaxed about both Joel's usual stupidity and Betty's sense of fair play.

'Don't be hard on her Agatha, my gun wasn't loaded anyway, but your gun, I note, is,' said Goodman holding Agatha's revolver up and assessing the chambers. He emptied the bullets onto the table. 'Dangerous things these. Especially in the wrong hands.' He put the bullets in his pocket and handed the gun back to Agatha. This was met with a look of suspicion.

'Let's face it Agatha. Your options are rather limited at the moment, oh yes. You are wanted by the police. You need a place to stay.' He left the rest unsaid.

This was frustratingly true. Agatha looked around at their surroundings. In truth, things could have been much worse. She fixed her eyes on Goodman.

'What do you want?'

'A coffee right now, I think and then, perhaps an explanation of why you are in such demand with the authorities. Perhaps then I can tell you about a little scheme that Joel and myself are interested in pursuing.'

'Go on,' said Agatha, straightening her back.

'No, you go first, but only after I bring us up some coffee.'

Around twenty minutes later, the group had feasted on strong coffee and several Krachel, sweet buns made with aniseed and sesame seeds.

'These are rather good,' said Betty, reaching for the final bun, her fourth.

'Yes they are rather,' agreed Goodman, who had consumed three of them and had had his eyes on making it four until Betty beat him to the punch. 'So, now that we are all fed and feeling a little better, perhaps Agatha you can tell us a little bit more about why you are on the run. Did you kill Gabrielle Fish?'

'It depends on what you mean by kill,' interjected Betty.

Agatha ignored the explicit sarcasm, dabbed the side of her mouth and began to relate what had happened on the night of December 1905.

*

'You have to remember, 1905 was a vastly different world to the one we live in now. Then we, particularly Eustace, feared a war was imminent. When Kaiser Wilhelm arrived at Tangier and began to speak to the Moroccans on their right to be independent, he was deliberately stirring up trouble. I'm not going to pretend to you that empire and the scramble for Africa was in anyone's interest except Europeans, but try being a slave, or young girl for that matter. Try and see a doctor or be educated. Of course it was exploitation, but some of us tried to push for a fairer way of dealing with those we ruled.'

73

'For good or for ill we threw our lot in with France. They were worried about Morocco. On one side they had a country that was all but ungovernable, they gave that to the Spanish I might add, and kept the parts that might be of some use. On the other, you had our friends in Berlin sending out signals that they would support the right of the Moroccan people to have their own government. The French were certainly feeling a bit windy about the situation and with the Algeciras Conference coming up, they were keen to line everyone up against Germany. They succeeded.'

'Sultan Aziz, the young fool, was never going to survive. We knew this, so did the French and so did the Germans. They were clearly in league with Raisuli to overthrow Aziz, but we had no proof of this. Of course, Raisuli played both sides. He was only interested in his own power base, but we knew he was working with the Germans to destabilise the country while all the time acting as the Pasha of Tangier, it's policeman. So even if we did find proof of German complicity with Raisuli in rebellion, what then? War? The situation was delicate, I can tell you.'

'Unlike the French, who had tried to use local people as their informers, we had one asset that they did not. We had a woman who was actually German. Well, Austrian, but it's the same difference. Gabrielle Heinze, or Fish as we know her through her married name, agreed to act as a contact for one of our spies in the German Legation. She found a job in the German Legation as a maid. She was our maid and a good one so we were doubly fortunate that she could speak the language fluently and knew how to bring silver up beautifully. You don't find many spies like that I can tell you.'

'We also had a young Moroccan woman at the Legation, one of the cooks, who claimed to have important papers, but she had no way of leaving the Legation. She claimed that one of the Germans had passed them to her. He no more wanted war than we did. She was a slave, I might add. Oh yes, the twentieth century and slaves were still being employed. I never met her, but Gabrielle said she was a beautiful young girl. Eustace developed a plan to free her along with the papers. She refused. Perhaps she did not fully trust Gabrielle. They killed her in the end. Berrada killed her, but that's in the future.'

'On the night in question, the young woman left the papers in a place then passed the location on to Gabrielle. There was a party that night at the Legation. They happened frequently, by the way. Not much else to do there in Tangier. Many of the key British and French noteworthy people were there. The French Ambassador, Gerard Lowther, who was ours, various military and diplomatic officials, Walter Harris and Emily Keene too. I can still hear that German *volkmusic* band and Wilhelm singing in my worst nightmares. Awful music. No matter, they were actually quite useful to us in the end.'

'As Eustace had expected and I had hoped, would not be the case, Berrada and his men were acting as security. Useless had a nose for these things. He predicted Raisuli would not be there, and he was mostly right. So we had Gabrielle to find and extract from the Legation, Berrada and his henchmen on security and the German army all

75

around us. I don't mind telling you, I had a few snifters before I walked into the legation that night.'

'I still remember the way Useless froze when he saw Berrada's face. It was if he read his mind. Eustace knew that he knew. I don't know how. He knew Berrada was looking for us to make a move. We didn't know if he knew it was Gabrielle, but Eustace's first instinct was not to trust anyone and assume the worst. You could learn from him Sausage. It's never too late.'

'So we were in a race to find Gabrielle before Berrada and take her out of the Legation, but how? As soon as we located her or tried to move her, Berrada would claim she was a spy and arrest her. As this was technically German soil, as Gabrielle was from Austria and as Berrada was being employed by them, the Germans would be bound to support his judgement. I had no idea what we would do. Useless was in his element, however. He was an escape artist, and this was a locked room.'

'The plan was outrageous of course. I nearly refused when he told me, but then I knew that...well, it's difficult to explain, really. You had to be married to him.'

'By the time we did find Gabrielle that night I was wound up tighter than an old clock. I can't remember ever being so fearful. Well, I can, but still. Gabrielle appeared and we all descended on her like a fog. I was there first, waited for the band to reach their crescendo and shot her. I don't think anyone realised what had happened.'

'I barely recall what we did next. It was all a blur. I saw Doctor Arnaud beside her pronouncing her near death unless she reached a hospital. There was a large halo of blood on her white blouse. Thierry took the papers from her as he examined the wound. He shouted for help to move her and for someone to bring a carriage round. A few security men arrived and helped carry her away past Berrada. He was incandescent I heard. By then, Useless and Walter had dragged me away from the scene and out of the Legation before anyone had woken up to the situation. We were in the waiting carriage. Ahmed was driving.'

'Gabrielle, meanwhile, was in another carriage, driven by our old friend Freddie de Courcey. Fish was inside the carriage waiting for his wife who, it must be said, made a miraculous recovery as soon as they departed. Blank bullets don't really do much damage. Although the pig's blood made a mess of the blouse.'

'Our night wasn't over yet though. About fifty yards away from the Legation, Ahmed was forced to stop. Useless said some things which I certainly won't repeat, it showed he'd been a little more nervous than he'd appeared. Then we heard shouting outside. I thought we had been caught.'

'The carriage door opened, and a man stood looking at us. He was tall, wearing a brown cloak over a white tunic that fell to his knees. His skin was quite light, I remember. Of course, I recognised him immediately although I'd never actually met him. This was Raisuli. An utter brigand. The kidnapper of Pedicaris, Walter Harris and many others. A man who had killed dozens of people in his life without pity. I have never felt such fear, before or since, as I did at that moment staring into those merciless black eyes.'

6

Paris, France: 5 July 1921

He didn't know what had made him do it.

Something inside impelled him. He just had to know. So, against his better judgement and his heart's screams, he went to the hospital. She wouldn't be there of course. She would have moved on. With her husband.

Ida.

Harry Miller trudged through the streets of a city he had last visited two years previously. He passed the shop he'd robbed, the hotel where he'd stayed, the spot where the artist, Marcel Duchamp, had saved Ida's life and helped catch their man. He would like to have stayed longer and relive the moments, but he had a train to catch later in the early afternoon.

The final stop was the former military hospital. The outside had not changed much, but inside it was another world. The last time he'd been here it had been a vast throng of human misery. The lucky survivors of the Great War facing a life of pain, of exclusion, of heart-rending misery due to their injuries.

Miller made his way to the reception of the hospital. During the War he had picked up a decent smattering of French. He searched his memory for the correct words and then addressed the young woman behind the counter.

'Mademoiselle, please can you tell me if either Ida Jennings or Ethel Rance still work at this hospital.' He paused for a moment and realised he was blushing. He added quickly, 'I met them two years ago.'

The young woman seemed to understand, and her smile was sympathetic. She asked Miller to write the names down and then she went into a back office to make inquiries. A minute or two later she returned. Using a pen, she pointed to the second name.

'Ethel Rance works here.'

The young woman wrote down which ward to visit. Miller thanked her and walked through the hospital. The interior was much as he'd remembered it, but the corridors echoed to footsteps not the screams of the dying. The smell was still of disinfectant but, at least, the misery had been cleansed.

The he saw her. She turned and saw him. It took a few seconds for her to register who it was and then an enormous smile split her face.

'Harry!'

Ethel ran towards him and embraced him tightly.

'I knew you'd come. I knew it Harry Miller. I told Ida, I did. You would not be able to stop yourself. Those were my words to her.'

Miller had not seen Ethel in two years since the Paris Peace Conference. She hadn't changed much except for

79

one rather obvious difference. She stood back and laughed in embarrassment.

'Gosh, someone in my condition acting like this. Well, I never. Oh Harry, I can't tell you what this means to see you.'

'And you Ethel. Congratulations by the way. When is the baby due?'

'Oh not for another two months. Gosh, another few weeks you'd have missed me.'

She took both his hands in his and then studied Miller with a well of affection that seemed to grow rather than diminish. Tears welled up in her eyes, but she did nothing to wipe them away.

'What happened Ethel? One minute I'm proposing to her then she...'

Miller couldn't bring himself to say it. Then she married another man. He felt his hands being squeezed a little harder.

'Don't be hard on her Harry. You don't know the story.'

Miller shook his head and tried to control his emotions.

'I don't have long. I have a train to catch.'

Ethel nodded and took a deep breath. She was now fighting to control her own emotions.

'She married a man called Jonathan McKenzie, Harry. She didn't want to, but he insisted. You see he was dying. He died a few hours after the ceremony. He wanted her to have his money, see? He was rich, but he had no heir. He wanted Ida to have it, but you know what she's like. She didn't want anything, but in the end we all persuaded her. She didn't stop working. Gave a lot of it away and then a year ago she decided to leave. Travel. Remember how she wanted to see the world?'

'Don't remind me.' said Miller half-laughing, yet all of a sudden he felt such a surge of happiness he barely knew what to say. 'Where is she now?'

Ethel's smile was sad, yet Miller saw hope in it too.

'I told her you'd come Harry. I really did. Thing is, she made me promise not to say where she was. She said you'd understand if you did come.'

Miller nodded. He understood. They had an agreement, and he would adhere to it. The Eiffel Tower: 21st of February 1924.

He would be there.

*

Agatha watched a rather surly looking Sidney Goodman bring breakfast into their room. It consisted of tea and more of the rather delicious Krachel. Gone was his normally serenely benign manner. Replacing it was something close to sulking.

'What is the matter with you?' asked Agatha, although she was fully aware.

'Nothing.'

'Are you still sore at me over the Raisuli story?'

Goodman glared at Agatha but did not rise to the bait. Instead, he lumbered towards the door.

'It's hardly my fault,' exclaimed Agatha, 'that Raisuli did nothing and just closed the door of the carriage again. Would you have preferred that he arrested then tortured us?'

81

'Well it would have made for a more interesting story if he had,' retorted Goodman.

Agatha was beginning to steam up herself now.

'Hardly for us.'

'Just once,' proclaimed Goodman, raising a finger in the air to emphasise the number, 'I would greatly appreciate it if a woman telling a story could give us a beginning, a middle *and* an end. Why must the poor listener, pardon me, madam, I will be more precise, male listener, always have to endure these interminable stories that go nowhere and have no point?'

'What about the faked murder of Gabrielle Fish? That was interesting,' pointed out Agatha through teeth that were slowly gritting.

'Yes and would that it had been the end of the story. This was a most excellent place to conclude on. Instead, we had to endure a coda that, that...'

He did not know how to finish the sentence without resorting to coarse language which he eschewed normally. To avoid hearing anything else from Agatha, Goodman flounced out of the room .

'Well, I say,' said Sausage. 'He seems rather rude, and he was so polite yesterday.'

Agatha shrugged and walked over to the door. In his anger, Goodman had not locked it. Although escape was not really an option, Goodman's point about where they would go was well made. She opened the door which led out onto a landing and then the staircase. The stairs seemed no more welcoming than before, so she returned to the room and sat down. Her mood was a little more downcast than she let on. Goodman and Joel had not yet revealed what they were planning. They had confirmed what Agatha and the others suspected, there was now a price on their heads. This would make going out in public even more difficult.

Much depended on the arrival of Kit, and she hoped Harry Miller would be with them, but even with a fair wind, it would take days before they all landed in Morocco. Feelings of guilt swept through her as she thought about her friends. Not for one moment would they abandon her, not one thought of recrimination would be in their minds or in their hearts. This made the situation all the more unbearable for her.

'Buck up old girl,' said Betty, sensing her friend's mood. 'We haven't heard what they want us to do yet.' Mimi stirred briefly before returning to sleep.

'Thanks,' said Agatha. 'For all we know they want a ransom. Did you see how Joel's eyes lit up when I told him Kit was coming.'

'You don't think he plans anything untoward do you?'

'They want revenge, but I can't help thinking that they have something else on their mind otherwise why not just claim the reward? No, it's something bigger.'

They did not have long to wait. Ten minutes later, Joel appeared. He was carrying three niqabs.

'If you would please put these on,' said Joel, trying to ignore Mimi who was quickly was on her feet at the arrival of the Egyptian, ears pricked upward to full Satanic effect.

Despite the apparent politeness, there was no mistaking that it was an order. The ladies quickly dressed before the

83

Egyptian led them out of the room to negotiate the stairs. Mimi followed along meekly behind Agatha.

Soon they were on the street being led through a quiet alley that wound up a gentle slope. Somewhere in the distance they could hear the whisper and slap of the Mediterranean against the cliffs.

As tempted as Agatha was to ask Goodman, who met them outside, about their destination, she decided that it might provide a level of infuriation if she, instead, chose to converse on more banal topics.

'Rather muggy today,' said Agatha.

Sausage invariably had no idea about Agatha's mind games and would, as a matter of politeness, engage her without artifice.

'It is rather. I suppose wearing so many layers isn't helping.'

Agatha could see Goodman bristling nicely.

'What material is this, do you think?'

'Cotton, I imagine.'

'I wonder where they manufacture the garments? I suppose they're handmade.'

Goodman stopped in the middle of the street causing a minor pile up behind him. He was rather large.

'Madam, I am no fool. I think you know this,' he snarled. 'Therefore I implore you to cease these commonplaces. I will tell you all in good time.'

Betty noted the smile of satisfaction on her friend's face through the crinkling eyes and grinned back at her. She had seen this so often. It never failed to send pressure gauges rising. Always entertaining in Betty's book. After around ten minutes walking which, from Agatha's memory was actually taking them away from the centre rather than towards it, they reached a large villa on the edge of the town. It was secluded behind a high wall and a number of cypress trees.

'Is this what you wanted to show me, Sidney?'

'It is, oh yes, indeed. Quite a beautiful house, don't you think?'

'Well appointed,' agreed Agatha. 'I imagine it catches the sun in the afternoon.'

'I'm sure you could care less,' replied Goodman.

'Correct, I could care less. Now why are we here?'

'I want you to help me rob this house.'

It took a few seconds for the meaning of the request to be assimilated by the astounded Agatha. Then she erupted into laughter. Neither Betty nor Sausage or, for that matter, Joel, found the idea remotely funny, but to give Goodman his due, he smiled benignly at his guests. Mimi, unsure of what to do, began to bark which quickly wiped the beatific expression from Goodman.

'Madam, I really must insist that you control this beast.'

Agatha patted Mimi which appeared to have the desired effect. Then she fixed Goodman with a look that would have drilled a hole through reinforced concrete.

'Care to expand on this ridiculous idea. I mean, Sidney, unless you are becoming a little confused in your old age, you may have noticed that we are none of us going to see sixty again, except Joel of course.

'It is true that only Joel still enjoys the vigour of youth, but that is of no matter. It is your mind Agatha that I seek to use, not your gymnastic skills for scaling walls.'

85

'I see,' said Agatha doubtfully. 'What do you wish to steal and why?'

'I wish to steal what I believe is mine by right,' explained Goodman reasonably. 'This villa belongs to Comte Jean-Valois du Bourbon.* If you remember, he unlawfully dispossessed me of the painting of the Falcon by Caravaggio. I merely wish to take possession of it again.'

Agatha could not hide her shock at this piece of news. Bourbon had befriended her, Kit and Mary on their passage to the United States before robbing them in San Francisco of the painting that Caravaggio had done while incarcerated by the Knights of St John in Malta.

'The painting is not yours. You stole it.'

'I bought it.'

'You murdered a sailor.'

'To be fair Agatha, he was trying to kill me at the time. Will you help me?'

'Will you help us escape to Spain?'

'Of course,' said Goodman, with an agreeably dangerous smile. 'I will make it my life's mission if you help me in return.'

*See *The Frisco Falcon*

7

Mediterranean Sea, somewhere between Marseilles and Tangier: 6ᵗʰ July 1921

Mary Aston strolled arm in arm with Kit along the deck, gazing at the cloudless sky with the sense of its sublime beauty only comprehensible to those who are in love to the point of rapture. Was it her imagination, but were the colours that bit brighter, the sea that bit calmer and the sea birds singing just for her?

In truth, none of these. While she was woman enough to enjoy romance, she could not abide soppiness in any novel she read or was ever likely to appear in. The sea breeze caressed her face like the kiss of a lover. Stop, she thought. Then she started to giggle. Kit noticed this and asked the question that any man would ask in such a moment when watching the love of his life laughing for no apparent reason.

'Are you planning to kill me?'

'Not yet.'

'That's a relief. I worry when you laugh, and I haven't made a hilarious remark just moments before.'

'I can see the problem,' said Mary, glancing up at Kit. 'If I were going to do away with you, I would really need a replacement in mind.'

'Have you found one?'

'Not yet,' said Mary. The repeated use of the adverb was potentially unsettling for a less confident man, but Kit merely grinned. He was the luckiest man in the world and his wife knew it. So did all of the other passengers who stared at the couple whenever they passed by.

While he was dressed in a light suit, white shirt and light blue tie, Mary was wearing her favoured Breton top without slacks. As it only reached midway down her thigh, Kit was genuinely concerned that the generous expanse of leg on display might cause a few of the Frenchmen on the boat to spontaneously combust.

They found a couple of spare deckchairs, in the shade and sat down. Mary ordered some coffee while Kit went back to The Times crossword. He studied it for a moment and then handed it over to Mary who had been working on it that morning.

'Thanks, I never seem to have time to work on it.'

There was just a hint of accusation in her tone although the smile that accompanied it had just enough mischief in it to make Kit want to distract her one more time. The waiter brought them a large silver pot from which he poured two coffees.

'Four letter word beginning in "C" and ending in "T." The clue reads, "a fathead",' said Mary out loud almost causing Kit to spit out his coffee.

'Gosh. The Times isn't beating about the bush these days.'

'Clot,' replied Mary not looking at Kit, but slapping his leg in recrimination.

'Easy mistake to make,' pointed out Kit. This was never going to wash, but he was laughing now and so was Mary, more importantly.

An older man joined them at the next deckchair along. He had a copy of *L'Equippe*. The headline made for salutary reading.

BRITISH WOMAN SUSPECTED OF MOROCCO MURDER

This cast a pall over an otherwise delightful day. They needed a plan, and they needed one soon. The ferry would arrive in Tangier the next morning and the situation looked fairly bleak. Kit, however, had called upon the services of his old friend Aldric 'Spunky' Stevens, to investigate a little bit more about the alleged murder. The accusation was clearly ludicrous. Gabrielle Fish had been murdered, but not in Tangier. It had happened a few months later in London. Then, it had been nothing more than the act of a madman. A random senseless act that, as so often is the case, ends the life of one for whom had so much more to live. How could the Moroccans and, more critically, the French, believe that this was a lie? How could they accuse the British authorities of covering up such a crime in Tangier by saying she had been murdered some months later. It made no sense. While Spunky was unravelling the knot in London, Kit and Mary would endeavour to return the ladies to the safety of their new home in the south of France.

That was the plan.

But plans, as von Moltke once observed so insightfully, rarely survive contact with the enemy.

*

Kit Aston and Inspector Berrada probably had little in common at the best of times, yet that morning both had chosen remarkably similar attire. Berrada may have viewed his white linen suit with some repugnance, but he had developed a soft spot for the Panama hat and perhaps best of all, his sunglasses. The shade provided to Berrada's eyes was of such benefit to him that he was almost prepared to forgive the relentless march of progress in his country. Almost.

The lobby of the hotel seemed to quieten as he gazed over the balustrade at the top of the stairs. Then he descended slowly like an aging chanteuse in a French nightclub while all eyes were on him. This gave him a quiet satisfaction. A couple of Europeans, or were they the Americans, seemed to confer about who he was. There were a few other people at reception. One was apologising for a ruined carpet. Behind him was a Frenchman who might once have been in the army. You could always tell with the French; always so stiff.

Berrada was in no mood to rush out into the sunshine wearing the hateful suit, so he stayed in the cool of the lobby and waited his turn to hand back his keys. After an age, he was able to give up his keys to Moreau and go for breakfast. So began his day. The first stop was the Palace of Justice. The building made a mockery of its name, it was neither a palace nor did it dispense much justice to people unless they had light skin or deep pockets. The street smelled of mule which, oddly, Berrada did not mind. A few men reached the steps leading up to the palace with the high horseshoe arch just as Berrada arrived. They stepped back to let him up first.

Inside, the palace was every bit as life affirming as the exterior. He wanted to stay only long enough to round up a dozen men to continue the search for Agatha and her friends. By now he'd worked out that they must have found a place to stay. As he had already staked out the houses belonging to Walter Harris and the Sharifa, as well as the port, this meant that they may be at a low rent hotel. The men would be required to visit every hotel and establish if the three women were staying there. He would detail a couple of men to search the markets and establish ad hoc watches among the traders who lived in fear of arrest.

There was a large supply of men to choose from. The French had money and were prepared to spend it on law and order. They increased the size of the Sûreté due to fears that the population, emboldened by the recent activity of Raisuli and the Rif tribes east of the city against the Spanish, might begin to agitate here in Tangier. Nothing would have pleased Berrada more, but Raisuli had insisted he maintain his position.

Another reason for wanting to make this a quick visit was that a telegram had warned him that two French officers were coming down from Paris to review the Agatha Frost case. This was unlikely to bring good news. His orders, from Raisuli, were explicit. Find the old woman and bring her to him.

Just as he had accomplished the task of choosing his search party, he saw the Chief of Police, Colonel Emile Toussaint, motioning for him to come to his office. Berrada cursed silently but obeyed. He trooped over to the office and saw that there were two men already there. Two Frenchmen. These, he realised, were the two from Paris he'd been warned about. Although he was under orders from Raisuli to comply with the French, he was not obligated either to like this or, indeed, to show respect. He suspected the petty tyrant Toussaint was of a like mind. Toussaint treated Tangier like his own fiefdom. He was in his fifties with close cropped hair and a waxed moustache. He and Berrada cordially loathed one another, but neither could do much about the situation.

Toussaint looked from Berrada to the new arrivals with a barely concealed lack of enthusiasm. His heavy eyelids drooped, and he spoke as if the heat had drawn every last ounce of his reserves. Or perhaps he was bored.

Introductions were made. Berrada made a point of treating the arrogant invaders with an undisguised surliness. Normally, this was guaranteed to needle the average French police officer, which was always a moment of joy for him. This time, however, the captain seemed unperturbed by his attitude although the younger man looked like fertile territory to anger. He was a Moroccan dressed up like a European. Just like him. There was a difference tough. He could see the arrogance, the contempt in the young man's eyes. He was one of them now.

'Do you know where Lady Frost is?'

'Would I be here if I did?' said Berrada with a smile that twisted easily into a sneer. He picked at his teeth. Some bread was stuck there, and this seemed as good a time as any to remove it. He would make a point of shaking hands on the way out. That was always guaranteed to disgust his chosen victim as well as show them in a bad light. Europeans put much store in handshakes, which he found personally unhygienic. That being so, he made his hands doubly so with his teeth-picking display.

The French captain's eyes bored into Berrada's. He was not being rude as far as Berrada could tell. His manner was calm, conversational even. Unlike the overfed camel who passed for a Chief of Police, this man was clearly dangerous. Berrada guessed that he was around forty years of age and did not look like someone who would be intimidated easily. The War had done that to people. Berrada was on his guard but saw no reason to stop being his usual self as the questions rained down on him.

'What happened in Agadir?'

'She had a gun. We weren't expecting this. She shot at us.'

'Was she trying to kill you?'

'She was shooting at us.'

'She mustn't be a good shot. I heard she could only hit your tyres,' said the Frenchman. There was just a hint of mockery in his voice. Berrada could feel his own anger rising. All at once he realised what was happening. The

Frenchman was playing him at his own game. He calmed down immediately and resumed his truculent manner.

'What became of her? I mean, you must have been able to find the car, at least?'

Berrada shook his head.

'So she disappeared into thin air.' The Frenchman waved his hand around to emphasize the point. This brought a smile to the face of his young partner. How Berrada would have liked a few minutes with the boy at that moment to dispense a lesson in life about respecting ones elders.

'But you are in Tangier, not Agadir,' continued the captain. 'This suggests that you think she is somewhere in the town.'

'We will find her if she is in Tangier. I won't find her if I stay here talking to you.'

'How did you come by the information that she had murdered the Austrian woman Gabrielle Fish?'

This question was unexpected.

'My sources will be sources no longer if I reveal how.'

The captain nodded without removing his remorseless gaze from Berrada.

'Have you met Lady Frost before?'

'I have never spoken to her,' replied Berrada carefully, affecting a bored tone of voice. The captain nodded as if this confirmed something he already suspected. Berrada ignored the captain and fixed his eyes on Colonel Toussaint. A rivulet of sweat was rolling down his forehead. With any luck it would sting his eye. At the last moment

Berrada's hopes were dashed as a fleshy paw swiped it away.

'Very well, Berrada,' said the Toussaint. 'You may go.

The captain seemed irritated by Toussaint's intervention. He clearly had not finished with the Moroccan yet.

The Frenchman fixed his eyes on Berrada once more, 'I don't doubt you will catch this woman, but when you do, I want you to bring her to me. I expect her and her friends to be unharmed. Is this clear?'

Berrada was already on his feet and heading for the door. Then he stopped himself and attempted to smile. The bread had been successfully excavated. He held out his hand to the young man. The young man could not hide the look of distaste on his and he turned away thereby confirming a small victory in Berrada's mind.

As he left the office, Berrada gave voice to his thoughts by loudly expelling the wind that had been building up that morning. The corridor echoed to the sound of his laughter. Yet a part of him was worried. The arrival of the foreigners showing an interest in the old woman had not been foreseen and how did they know about the man who had first informed him of her arrival?

He would have to tell Raisuli.

Despite these concerns, Berrada left the Palace of Justice confident that he would soon find success. The net was closing in on the resourceful Englishwoman. By the end of the day, none of the ladies would be able to buy a coffee without him knowing about it.

By the end of the day, however, Berrada would be dead.

Early evening found Agatha, Betty and Sausage back in their *de facto* prison cell. A mood of melancholic reflection had descended on the room as they stared out the window. It had probably been brought on by a combination of the heat and a bottle or three of wine procured by their captors. As prison cells went, Agatha had certainly endured more penurious accommodation. Not so Betty and Sausage who had led a much more sedentary life if one excludes golf and horse riding. It was life that formed the subject of the conversation in their room. Discussion around how they could possibly rob the villa had wisely been left in abeyance while Agatha cogitated.

Joel sat in a rather sullen silence as Goodman engaged the ladies in conversation, glass in hand.

'You were married Lady Elizabeth, I remember.'

'Yes. I lost him a few years ago,' the words were barely out of her mouth when the tears welled up in her eyes. She had lost more than just James though. He had passed away just before the world had gone mad. Not so her son. He had perished during the Great War that had laid waste to the young men of Europe. Sausage and Agatha each took hold of a hand.

'We are all widows Sidney,' explained Agatha in an unusually quiet voice.

'I'm so sorry, how thoughtless of me,' said Sidney, genuinely aggrieved.

Sausage shook her head, 'Don't be. Can't be helped. It's life isn't it? We have our time and then we must go.'

'You lost your husband recently?'

96

Sausage nodded, unable to speak. Tears stung her eyes as she thought of the man with whom she had spent forty years of her life. Tommy Pilbream had been a husband, a father and a stalwart of the British Museum. He never liked horses and had never played hockey, so he was not without some flaws, but he had loved Sausage from the first moment he'd met her. The feeling had been mutual. Like Betty, like Agatha, she had married for love and never regretted a day of her life. Fate had given her only one great love, but that was enough. If only Fate had allowed them more time. More time...

'Who'd have thought it would be the flu,' she whispered. 'It seemed nothing at first and then...then it was everything. So many people. That bloody flu.'

It was unusual to hear Sausage so animated, but the Spanish Flu brought out the anger. She had survived. Rather like many of the men that returned home from Flanders, the guilt was sometimes unbearable.

'Were you ever married, Mr Goodman?' asked Betty.

'I never had that good fortune no, Lady Elizabeth, indeed not. I suppose I regret some of the mistakes in my past that led to my being a bachelor.' Betty and Sausage nodded sympathetically. In their minds they saw a woman whom he had loved and lost. In Agatha's mind was the stretch he'd done at San Quentin for fraud.

At this point a polite comment might have been – it's never too late. The truth, in reality, was different. It was too late. That game was over. Indeed, yes.

Goodman topped up their glasses and opened up another bottle of wine as they gazed out over the rooftops of Tangier towards the purple-coloured sea. It's roll and crash followed by silence. Each was lost in a world that no longer existed for them. The tears in their eyes only told half the story of what they lost. Their hearts knew the rest and it would remain a secret; a connection to a time and person they hoped they would one day see again.

8

The port of Tangier: 7ᵗʰ July 1921

It was mid-morning when the ship docked at the port of
Tangier, and it was already hot enough for camels to be
seeking shade and a cold beer. Mary had changed into a
linen dress that was a little more modest than her leg-baring
effort the day before. Paradoxically, this was both a
disappointment and a relief for Kit. It was one thing to be
seen with the most beautiful girl on the ship in an eye-
catching outfit, it was another to cause offence to a culture
unused to such display.

They strolled down the gang plank, each keeping an eye
open for someone who might look either like Aunt Agatha
in disguise or someone who was a messenger. Their eyes
alighted on the same two people. Neither looked like Aunt
Agatha and almost certainly were unlikely to be her
messengers. Their presence, rather like Mary's modest
dress, represented a worrying conflict in his emotions. On
the one hand, Captain Briant was as reassuring presence as
one was likely to find among officers of the law. On the
other, it meant that Kit's presence had been anticipated and

he would be unlikely to enjoy anything resembling autonomy in his efforts to clear his aunt's name.

'Captain Briant,' said Kit shaking the Frenchman's hand, 'we must stop meeting like this.'

Briant laughed as they shook hands. Then he turned to introduce the young man standing beside him. He was in his twenties, dressed in a straw-coloured suit.

'This is Sergeant Raif. He came with me from Paris, but he is originally from Rabat,' said Briant.

Raif smiled but did not offer his hand. Kit guessed that Raif would not just have been chosen for his local knowledge or to act as a translator.

'Will you come with us?' said Raif. He spoke in a lightly accented English.

'Under arrest already?' asked Mary, with a wicked grin. 'This must be some kind of record for you darling.'

The two policemen grinned before Briant replied, 'Your luggage will be sent to the hotel.'

'Is that what they call prison in Tangier?' asked Mary. Briant laughed at this while, at the same time, motioning to a uniformed policeman to take the luggage from the porter who had followed Kit and Mary down the gangplank.

Just then a man approached them, dressed in a djellaba, but was clearly not Moroccan despite his tanned skin. He was tall, in his late fifties and just building up to have it out with the two French policemen before Kit smiled and shook his head.

'Relax Walter, Captain Briant and Sergeant Raif are old friends. Gentlemen, may I introduce Walter Harris, The Times correspondent in Tangier.'

The two policemen shook hands with Harris before Briant, with a wry smile on his face asked him, 'Monsieur Harris, may I ask why it is that the paper of record in England has made no mention of the fact that a noblewoman and former diplomat in Morocco are on the run for a murder?' His English was faultless and a reminder to Kit not to speak out of turn when around him.

'It's arrant nonsense, that's why and as you well know, captain,' said Harris, reasonably.

Kit, Mary and Harris climbed into the back of the car.

'It's good to see you again Walter, pity it has to be in these circs. Did you have any inkling this would happen?'

'Of course not. Gabrielle was murdered in London, poor thing. We all know this. Well, all who are not the French of the species. I say, Briant, what exactly is going on with your lot? They know damn well the murder in the German Legation was faked. You lot were in on it. Benefitted from it too. Had it not been for Gabrielle, you might have a lot of Junkers running Morocco, then where would we be?'

Despite himself, Briant smiled at the unusual Englishman. He was a complication given where they were heading. This became even more apparent a moment later when they passed a road that led to the Grand Hotel where Kit and Mary were staying.

'Haven't you missed the turn?' asked Harris pointing to a road that led away towards the Kasbah.

'No Monsieur, we are not going to this hotel. We are going to another one first.'

Kit and Mary turned to one another. This could mean that they had located Aunt Agatha and the others. Yet, something in Briant's manner suggested that this was not the case. He was not a man who played games. He would have informed them at the start.

'What's happened?' asked Kit warily. Briant remained tight-lipped. Kit suspected it did not augur well for Agatha.

The police car pulled up in a small square. They saw a beautiful if rather dilapidated building with another police car outside. At the entrance were two policemen acting as guards to prevent onlookers entering. The hotel was on three floors. All of the windows, noted Kit, had iron bars. Clearly the management were taking no chances with burglars. The name on the sign read Moreau Hotel.

Across from the hotel were some market stalls, one selling fruit, another had ceramic plates and jugs, another had a twenty-foot square high pile of carpets. The square seemed to have a pulse all of its own: people were dancing, clapping, and singing. Mary listened fascinated by the sound of the ululation sung by the women.

'Please come with us,' said Briant to the three passengers. He ignored the slightly disapproving stare from Raif. The young sergeant glanced towards Mary to make his point. It still failed to land so he did the sensible thing and gave up.

Briant led them through the entrance of the hotel. It was very Moorish in its interior, all except for the one or two guests floating around who were distinctly European. European and truly angry. Kit heard a few voices raised at Briant as he took two stairs at a time.

102

By now Kit was growing increasingly alarmed as to what they would find. If something had happened to Agatha, Betty or Sausage then surely Briant would have said something before now. In fact, just thinking this relaxed him. Briant *would* have handled this differently had it been someone close to Kit.

At the top of the stairs they saw an open corridor with a white balustrade. The first room on the corridor landing was guarded by a policeman. The three English visitors exchanged glances. The group walked up the stairs towards the room guarded by the policeman. When they reached the room, the policeman stood aside and the entered.

It was empty.

The only thing of note was the stain of blood on the carpet floor. It was a rather large stain.

*

Sidney Goodman burst into the room holding his 'captives' or guests as he liked to think of them. They expected coffee and Krachel was absent. Instead, Sidney was looking even more flushed of face than normal.

'I don't much like the stairs either,' said Betty, misreading his anxiety.

'Ladies, I regret to inform you that your situation may have deteriorated overnight.'

Given that they were on the run from the police with Agatha suspected of murder, it was difficult to see how the bar could be set any lower. It was Agatha who gave voice to their thoughts.

'How exactly, Sidney, could our situation be any worse than this? No disrespect to you or Joel or the stairs.'

103

'Is there something wrong with the stairs?' asked Betty with innocent mischief.

'They are rather treacherous,' pointed out Sausage who, true to form, took every statement at face value. Sausage had no enemies.

'No offence taken,' said Goodman. 'There is good news and bad news contained within what I have to tell you.'

The ladies glanced at one another and then back to Goodman. This was taken by Goodman as permission to proceed.

'Inspector Berrada has been found shot dead in his room.'

'Good Lord,' exclaimed Betty and Sausage in unison. 'What happened?'

Rather than point out that Berrada had been shot dead in his room once more, Goodman, related all he knew.

'Yesterday in the early evening a gunshot was heard coming from the inspector's room. The hotel manager and a few of the guests ran to the room of Berrada and when they opened the door the inspector was found dead on the floor, a gunshot wound to his chest. It looks like it may have been suicide as he was found with the gun in his hand.'

Communication delivered, Goodman sat down and wiped his brow.

'No offence to Berrada, but he was a bad lot. I don't think the world will miss him,' said Betty. 'If it's possible for a death to be considered good news then I imagine his would qualify.'

All eyes turned to Agatha who had remained silent while the news was communicated.

'You said bad news, Sidney. Am I to take it that the police are unsure if it was a suicide and that I might be in the frame for his murder?'

'How ever perspicacious of you Agatha,' replied Goodman. 'You really have lost nothing over the years.'

'But how can that be?' asked Sausage. 'We were all together last night. We were never out of the sight of you or Joel.'

Agatha smiled affectionately at her ever-optimistic friend.

'Sausage, dear, Sidney and Joel are here in an unofficial capacity.'

'We are on the run,' clarified Goodman.'

'To this end,' continued Agatha, 'They will be unable to furnish us with the alibi that would, at least, ensure we are not blamed for this one.'

'Is there a reward?' asked Joel archly. He knew the answer.

The question detonated like a practical joke at a funeral. The little Egyptian had made little secret of his dissent at Goodman's faith in Agatha's ability to assist them with their project. His plan of enrichment began and ended with claiming the modest reward that the police had offered for information that would lead to the capture of the three ladies.

'Yes. Of course this may change in the light of the new circumstances. The price on your head may go up,' conceded Goodman.

'How about you Sidney? Will your view change also?' asked Agatha, folding her arms.

'I see no reason we should not continue with our arrangement. The idea that your nephew's valet was once a burglar intrigues me, I must confess. I see greater potential in being patient and calling upon his experience than gaining a few francs for giving you up to the police.'

'Very reassuring,' said Agatha. She turned to Joel and glared at him challengingly. Seeing this, Mimi rose from her position and did likewise. She accompanied this with a growl which sent Joel scurrying towards the door while simultaneously reaching in his pocket for the pistol which was still unloaded as far as anyone knew. With a shake of his head he exited the room in a foul mood.

'Try to be nice to Joel. He is my conscience,' said Goodman.

'You have no conscience, Sidney and even fewer scruples,' retorted Agatha. 'That said, I would rather like to put one over that fake Comte.'

'I thought that you might, Agatha, but please, at the very least, try and control that Satanic creature you call a pet.'

'Mimi wouldn't harm a fly,' said Sausage defensively, stroking the stomach of the Doberman who had, upon Joel's exit, rolled onto her back. A sort of canine victory roll.

'I'm sure she's a little lamb, Lady Jocelyn, but all the same; make an old man happy and keep her on a leash,' said Goodman through teeth so gritted it seemed like it would take a week to unlock them.

'Well, we can't hang around here all day; we'll never solve the case stuck like this,' said Agatha with that hint of decisiveness in her voice that always suggested argument

106

was useless. Goodman sighed quietly. The sooner Aston's valet arrived the better for his mood. Mimi growled at this point which helped drive the point home.

'Are you mad?' exclaimed Joel who peeped his head around the door. 'The police will be all over the hotel.' This brought a series of defensive barks from Mimi who was on her feet with ears pointed to full demonic effect. This sent Joel back outside the room with what might have been 'please yourselves' although Agatha was certain she heard him add a few other words besides, that demonstrated his knowledge of Anglo Saxon.

'Looks like it's just us, then,' said Agatha walking over towards her niqab. Goodman sighed once more. Betty and Sausage sensed Goodman's reluctance, so they immediately did the same, thereby sealing Goodman's fate. Any argument against the move was academic as the ladies were dressed, unusually in Goodman's view, rather more quickly than their sex normally managed in his experience. They stood looking at him expectantly.

'Very well,' he said without enthusiasm. 'I just need to pay a visit.' Goodman left the ladies to visit the bathroom. Once he'd left the room, Betty voiced the concern that had been on Goodman's mind.

'Is this wise Agatha? I'm sure the police will have worked out that we're in disguise. We can't take Mimi.'

'Good point,' said Agatha bending down to stroke the Doberman. From the bottom of the stairs they heard Goodman calling them. 'Time to go.'

The three ladies descended the stairs carefully trying to ignore the disappointed whine of Mimi. It was a heart-

107

rending sound and all the more surprising given the Satanic source.

The heat of mid-morning hit them like a blow torch. Of course none of the ladies complained. To do so would have been an admission of weakness. Goodman was English enough to limit his comments on the weather to a 'It's turned out nice again.'

They walked slowly in a line through the crowded streets like wounded soldiers trooping to a dressing station following a gas attack. Agatha and the ladies felt the eyes of the male market traders boring in on them. Perhaps, thought Agatha, this was too much of a risk. They were difficult to ignore. It occurred to Agatha that the problem was Goodman and not them. He needed to adopt a costume that helped him blend in more effectively. He would, like all men, obey her. That was the way of things in her mind. Women decided, men obeyed. Life would be so much simpler and less violent if such an arrangement were more widespread.

The square where the hotel was located was a hive of activity. Policemen had set up a perimeter outside the hotel to keep tourists and curious locals away from the crime scene. One policeman guarded the door while another stood by an alleyway that presumably led to another entrance for the hotel.

'I'll try and find out what's happened,' said Goodman. He stopped for a second to check his pockets. Then he looked at Agatha. 'It seems I am temporarily embarrassed. I don't suppose...'

'For goodness sake,' snapped Agatha. She reached inside a pocket in the niqab and extracted some coins. 'Will this be enough?'

'Best be certain,' said Goodman standing his ground.

Agatha rolled her eyes and fished out some more money. Goodman looked at it for a second longer than was probably advisable which almost caused an eruption from Agatha. Then he wandered off in search of a policeman to bribe for some information on what had happened. He returned around ten minutes later with a troubled look on his face.

'I'm not sure if this is good news or bad for us. But it seems that the sad demise of our friend Berrada is something of a conundrum.

'Why is that?' asked Agatha.

9

'So we have a locked room mystery,' said Kit, scanning around the hotel room. His view took in the arched window which was barred like a prison and then the lock on the door which was broken when the hotel manager and guest had forced it open.

'Yes, it appears that way,' said Briant, a trace of a smile hanging on his lips.

'Have you ever read, '*The Mystery of the Yellow Room*' by Gaston Leroux?' asked Kit

'I preferred '*The Adventure of the Empty House*,' by your Conan Doyle,' replied Briant.

'My Aunt Agatha knows him quite well,' said Kit. He smiled as he saw Briant's reaction to this piece of news.

'I would love to meet him,' said Briant.

'Well, if you can avoid sending my aunt to the guillotine then perhaps you may have your wish one day. Now, I am going to make a rather large assumption here that you want myself and Mary to provide some assistance in this matter.'

'The best piece of assistance would be to find a way of bringing your aunt and her friends to us so that we may question them.'

Mary sidled over to Kit and took his arm. There was an impish grin on her face.

'If we work on the assumption that this does not happen, what role do you see for us in the investigation?'

Well, it was certainly to the point, which Briant acknowledged in his smile. Sergeant Raif, meanwhile, was caught between anger at the sense of prerogative of the young English woman and infatuation. He remained silent and decided to let the older man deal with this; Briant was in his thirties, so this made him virtually a geriatric in Raif's eyes.

Kit recognised that it was probably unfair to put Briant on the spot, so he offered an escape route for the captain.

'It's certainly a curious affair. Can you share with us what happened?'

Briant's eyes narrowed slightly before he nodded an acceptance of the olive branch.

'According to the hotel manager, Monsieur Lucien Moreau, Berrada returned to the hotel around six thirty in the evening and went up to his room. Around half an hour later, the manager heard a gunshot. Moreau ran upstairs. He found some of the guests on the corridor demanding to know what had happened.'

'Did the sound definitely come from Berrada's room? Could it have been elsewhere?' asked Mary.

This stopped Briant for a moment. He turned to Raif.

'We should check this,' said Briant. He tried to ignore the smile of triumph on Mary's face and the look of pride on Kit's. In the end he chuckled before continuing with his story.

111

'A gunshot was heard resulting in guests running out onto the upstairs landing. The only guest who did not was Inspector Berrada. By this time Monsieur Moreau was running up the stairs and noticed that Berrada was not among the guests. He saw the door was closed and began to knock on the door. When there was no answer he decided to open the door. He went downstairs and took the spare set of keys and came back up. However, when he tried to open the door, he realised it must be locked from the inside with the key still in the lock. He knocked once more, but there was still no answer, so he felt that he had no choice but to break the door down. He and one of the guests did this and fell into the room where they found the dead body of the inspector.'

'Berrada had a gun in his hand?' asked Kit.

'Yes, this was confirmed by both the hotel owner and a number of guests who were unfortunate enough to see the dead body.'

'And the gunshot wound was to the chest and not the head?'

'Correct.'

'Unusual, if it really was a suicide,' responded Kit, his eyes fixed on the large blood stain on the carpet.

'This was my thought also,' agreed Briant.

'You don't believe it was suicide?' asked Kit fixing his gaze on the captain.

'That is what we are meant to think, but no, I do not believe it was suicide. The post-mortem results are imminent but there did not seem to me to be the obvious signs of a shot so close to the body. Also, the way he fell...'

112

'Yes, it does look a little staged,' agreed Kit. 'I'm not sure that whoever killed him, if we go with this assumption, has ever had to do something like this before.'

'I agree,' said Raif.

Kit looked around the room for any possible way that someone might have entered the room. The only possible point of entry, aside from the door, was the window, but there were iron bars preventing anyone coming in. Just for his own peace of mind, Kit wandered over to the window and tried to see if the bars would move.

The room was not quite square, around thirty feet by twenty five feet. Aside from the bed, there was a small sink, a wardrobe and a chest of drawers. Kit went over to the wardrobe. It was already open and completely empty. Kit pressed against the back and found that it did not contain any secret entrance although given that the other side would have been the space of the stairs this would have been academic.

'Raif and I have done all this. There are no doorways, hidden spaces behind the walls. Everything is solid. There was no way in or out for a killer. The only logical conclusion is that Berrada committed suicide.'

'Except that he didn't. Why would he? Was there a suicide note?'

'I doubt he could write,' pointed out Raif. This was not as ridiculous as it sounded.

'Berrada was a Berber,' said Briant. 'They do not have a tradition in the written word.'

'So, locked room, dead body, meant to look like suicide, but without a suicide note or any obvious reason he would

113

do himself in. You know as much as I respect my aunt's intelligence, I think that even this would have been beyond her,' said Kit with a shake of the head.

Briant half-smiled at this before replying, 'I'm not so sure. She is unusual.'

This brought a look of pride to the faces of Kit and Mary. There was little to disagree with there. The heat in the room was overpowering so Raif went over to the shutters and opened them. This did little to improve the situation if anything it made matters worse.

Kit wandered over to inspect the window once more. There were no obvious points from which an expert marksman might fire a shot as the hotel was the tallest building in the square. Even then, how to explain the fact that the shutters were bolted from the inside? He gazed out over the square for a few moments and then turned to face the others.

'Well, I think we've seen enough for the time being. I don't suppose we could go to our hotel. It's been a tiring few days travelling by train and by sea.'

'And by air,' added Mary drily.

Kit coughed, 'Well the less said about that little adventure the better.'

'Very well,' said Briant. 'I will have one of the men drive you to your hotel.'

'Perhaps you and Sergeant Raif will join us for dinner this evening?'

Raif glanced over to Briant hopefully.

'We would like this very much,' said Briant. 'Is eight o'clock too late for you?'

'No,' replied Kit. 'Plenty of time to freshen up and perhaps Walter can show us around.'

'I will give you one of my men to drive you around and accompany you. I'm sure you understand,' said Briant.

Kit nodded and grinned back to the policeman, 'Of course. I imagine it will ensure we are not accosted unnecessarily.'

'Correct,' said Briant. 'We wouldn't want you disappearing like your aunt and her friends.'

Kit, Mary and Water Harris descended the stairs with Raif who delegated a Moroccan policeman to act as their driver.'

Outside the hotel as they waited for Raif to convey the instruction, Kit scanned around the square. It was still very crowded despite the afternoon sun. On one side a small market was selling fruit and vegetables. There was music playing from one of the cafes which competed against the sound of human voices.

Kit made a gesture with his hands which made Raif turn and frown.

'Is everything all right?' asked Raif.

'Just a fly or something,' replied Kit. He glanced at Mary whose eyes had narrowed. This made him smile which, in turn, made her smile.

'The hotel then,' said Kit who had decided that the investigation could wait a few hours while he gazed at that smile a little longer.

Across the square from the hotel was a group who were interested in what was happening.

'I say,' said Sausage, 'isn't that Kit and Mary?'

'It is,' said Agatha.

'Shouldn't we go over?' asked Sausage with that wonderful innocence.

'Not if you want to be arrested, dear,' pointed out Betty. She turned to Agatha for confirmation when she was stunned by her friend who was gesticulating with her hands as if she were typing a letter. 'What on earth are you doing?' she snapped.

'Speaking to Kit,' said Agatha. She waited a moment, satisfied that her message had been understood. Then she added enigmatically, 'He's a good boy, really.'

'What?' exploded Betty only to be shushed by Sausage. 'All right, all right,' said Betty a little remorsefully.

'Where's Sidney?' asked Sausage, suddenly aware that Goodman had disappeared from view.

'I don't think he wanted Kit to see him,' said Agatha. 'Anyway, I think we've accomplished as much as we can here. Did anyone see where Sidney went?'

Sausage pointed to the alley from which they had first emerged, so the three ladies set off in this direction.

'What did you say to Kit and more to the point, how?' asked Betty.

'Oh I used deaf sign language. I taught Kit this when he was a boy.'

'Was this one of Eustace's bright ideas?' asked Betty with just a hint of disdain in her voice.

'No, one of mine actually,' admitted Agatha. 'Of course, Useless laughed at me when I suggested it, but he soon saw its advantages. He became quite proficient. It came in useful a few times, I remember.'

116

'What did you tell Kit?'

'Christopher? Oh, just that we were in a safe place and that we would take care of Harry; he is to stay away from Harry. He comes on the boat tomorrow apparently. We need to let Sidney know.'

Betty stopped and looked at her old friend in a sort of awe, at least it would have seemed so, had Agatha been able to see her face.

'You did all that by just doing this?' asked Betty, who began moving her hands about like she was catching a recalcitrant butterfly for her collection. This attempt at parodying her sign language was ignored by Agatha.

'Oh there's Sidney,' said Sausage pointing to their erstwhile captor standing outside a café.

'Ah, ladies. I trust you managed to avoid attracting the attention of our friends in law and order. Was that your nephew I spied, Agatha?'

'Yes it was, Sidney. I didn't see Harry. I told Christopher to send him to the Minzen Hotel to await our instructions.'

Goodman's normally rather ruddy complexion seemed to turn pale for just a few moments at this piece of news.

'You spoke with your nephew?' he said in a tone that mixed no little shock with just a hint of disappointment.

'Don't ask,' cut in Betty on Agatha's behalf. 'Perhaps we could have a cup of tea,' she added, pointing to the café that Goodman had positioned himself outside. It was not The Ritz by any means, but right at that moment the three ladies and gentlemen were positively gasping for a cup of tea. Betty gazed through the fly-speckled window.

117

'Yes, this'll do.'

Goodman, however, looked a little embarrassed, half turning to the café and then to the ladies, he attempted a smile, 'As I mentioned I am temporarily embarrassed.' He pointed to his pockets.

'I'll pay,' said Betty, bustling forward, adding with a shake of her head at a rather forlorn looking Sidney Goodman, 'Honestly, you have to be just about the most inept kidnapper I have ever met, and I've met quite a few, I can tell you.'

10

Mary Aston did a twirl in the dress she had acquired in Paris from Coco Chanel. It was long, white and made no attempt to hide the slender frame of the wearer. It was nearing eight o'clock and the couple were scheduled to meet Briant and Raif in the lobby otherwise Kit might have opted to continue what had otherwise been a pleasant afternoon in their hotel room.

'I can see I'd better bring a revolver along just in case,' noted Kit drily.

'I'm sure the locals are much more polite than you think.'

'I was thinking about Raif. The poor man is head over heels.'

Mary frowned at this and put on a pale blue shawl. She gazed appreciatively at Kit who was wearing a white dinner jacket. Then she took his arm before they left the room. the two detectives were downstairs with Walter Harris. The three men were also wearing white dinner jackets.

'Captain Briant is very good looking for an older man,' whispered Mary as they descended the stairs.

'I doubt he's that much older than me,' replied Kit. Briant's dark hair was greying at the sides, but his face remained youthful and tanned. The War might explain some of the signs of ageing. He and Briant had never discussed their experiences, but there was no question in his mind that Briant had served and probably near the front line too. It was there in the eyes: the sadness, the guilt, the desensitisation to death and the acceptance of life's fragility.

'Where are we going?' asked Kit, the question addressed to Walter Harris who, having lived in Tangier so long, certainly qualified as the local expert.

'Café Haha, it's new and quite spectacular. I think you'll be impressed by the views'

'What about the food?' asked the Frenchmen in unison.

Raif drove them to the newly opened restaurant. As Harris had suggested, it was by the sea front, but the description 'spectacular' barely did it justice. The restaurant looked as if it had been sculpted into terraces on the side of the cliff. Tangier fell away in ridges of dense dark green far down to the long blue shimmering Bay

They sat at a table facing out onto the point where the Mediterranean met the Atlantic. In the distance the lights of Tarifa in Spain twinkled invitingly. A gentle breeze blew in from the sea, cooling the gentlemen in their dinner suits and providing a rolling rhythm of booms as it crashed against the nearby cliffs.

After they had ordered, Briant felt the eyes of the three English guests boring into him. He grinned in submission.

'I suspect this is the part where I tell you everything I know. Of course, Mr Harris, this is not for wider circulation.'

Harris nodded. He'd made a long career out of exaggerating the truth and keeping secrets. His judgement on when to do either was finely honed. Meanwhile, Mary's raised eyebrow and half smile confirmed this was exactly what she wanted to hear.

'Where shall I start?' asked Briant in mock innocence.

'Perhaps we could start with this ridiculous charge against my aunt and then we can move on to the murder or suicide of Berrada,' suggested Kit. There was just enough edge in his voice to remind everyone about the stakes for which they were playing.

'It was murder,' replied Raif. 'Berrada was murdered.'

Briant glanced towards his subordinate. The folly of youth is its certainty; uncertainty marks the end of innocence when right and wrong, truth, lies and everything in between is determined by context. Briant missed this sense of utter conviction but knew that faith is a risky substitute for experience.

'Do I believe Agatha Frost murdered Gabrielle Fish? No I do not. This expedition would be an utter waste of time if I did. It is because I do not that I am here,' began Briant.

Briant looked at the slightly puzzled faces of Kit and Mary with amusement.

'There are a large number of witnesses who saw your aunt shoot Gabrielle Fish on that night in December 1905. Equally, there are, or there were, a large number of people who will swear that it was a set up to ensure her safe passage out of the German Legation. I have spoken with senior officials who have confirmed that they knew of Lord Frost's plan to evacuate Gabrielle Fish. However, they will never confirm this in public. On our records, we have kept to the story that your Aunt Agatha murdered Gabrielle Fish.'

Kit stared in astonishment at Briant. Then he turned and looked in the direction of the ocean. He was silent for a few moments, sensing that the eyes of the table were upon him.

'You had a spy in the German Legation. A German spy. You are protecting him or her.'

The merest hint of a smile emerged on Briant's face. He began to speak once more.

'Without wishing to bring back sad memories for you, it must be said that even though Gabrielle Fish was murdered many months later in London, you cannot be certain that the body you recovered was hers, no?'

'Of course we can,' said Kit, but there was a hint of doubt in his voice; sadness too. He'd still been at school when the murder occurred. Gabrielle had disappeared one night, and it was assumed she had been murdered by a man who was caught a few weeks later attempting another murder. He'd confessed to killing Gabrielle but could not remember where he had buried her. Several months later she had been found around fifty yards from where the killer had claimed he had left her. Identification had been difficult and traumatising for her husband. The case was closed.

'The point is, we never investigated the fake murder. Your aunt left Morocco soon after and did not return for five years. France and Britain had the information they needed to prove that Germany had been complicit in committing atrocities in South West Africa. It helped tip the balance at the Algeciras Conference in favour of the Entente and in the division of Morocco between France and Spain with allowances for German business interests. Case closed. Or so we thought, but now, as you know, Morocco is in a state of rebellion again and this matter has surfaced for reasons that I can only guess.'

'Do you think someone is trying to drive a wedge between Britain and France?' asked Mary, who had been listening intently to everything said by the Frenchman.

'And Spain,' added Raif.

Briant nodded.

'Someone is supplying weapons to the Rif leader Abd-el-Krim and Raisuli. Their objective is clear: they want to free the country from its protectorate status. What better way to distract investigation into this than to dredge up an old murder dating back to the last time the country was at the front and centre of international attention? While the police are chasing your aunt, these insurrectionists have a free hand in running guns to the Rif people.'

'So where does the murder of Berrada fit into this? Why kill a man, a confederate of Raisuli, who is clearly helping this insurrection?' asked Kit.

Briant shrugged in a manner that was all too Gallic.

'I agree. It makes no sense except as a way of throwing more suspicion in the way of your aunt. I can't think of anything else. Berrada was, we know, in league with Raisuli. We put up with it because, well,' said Briant pausing to choose his words, 'this is Morocco. Things are different here. I can't see either we or Spain lasting much longer.

The Moroccans hate us. If it isn't the Rif rebellion it will be something else.'

'Britain has similar problems in Ireland and India. I can't see either staying with us much longer,' admitted Kit. 'Perhaps we shouldn't be there.'

'Do you believe that?' asked Briant, his eyes fixed on Kit.

'Don't you? What good do all these alliances, protectorates, colonies do us or the people we are supposed to be helping? The only result is bloodshed. A shot is fired in Sarajevo and millions die. Why?' Kit shook his head in disbelief. 'My aunt is on the run because some men in senior positions, not even in government I might add, have decided that national interest dictates that France and, probably, Britain cannot admit to a conjuring trick pulled off by Uncle Eustace fifteen or so years ago because it may expose a spy they have in Germany or that the Treaty of Algeciras was built on deceit.'

'It wasn't deceit. Germany was supplying Moroccan rebels and they had done terrible things in other parts of Africa,' pointed out Briant. 'We know this. They did so during the War, they might still be doing it now for all we know.'

'Very well,' said Kit. 'We'll worry about that for another time. Perhaps you can tell us about the sad passing of our friend Berrada.'

'Murder,' interjected Mary raising a smile on the faces of the three men.

'Murder,' agreed Raif.

124

'The death of Berrada,' said Briant pointedly, but with a smile, 'occurred around 6:45pm. Monsieur Moreau was dealing with a customer named Heinrich Keller, who owns his own import – export business in Frankfurt. The two men heard the shot. They ran upstairs and met other guests who were running from their rooms in panic.'

'I would have stayed in my room,' said Mary.

'I agree,' said Kit. 'Some questions on this. Was it Moreau and this chap Keller who broke open the door?'

'No, it was Moreau and a French gentleman staying in the next room, Charles Durand. He was downstairs at the time as was another guest, a gentleman from Switzerland called Julien Lefevre. All of them heard the shot and immediately ran up the stairs.'

'Tell me about Durand,' asked Kit.

Briant paused for a moment. A smile crossed his face and then it grew more serious. It was as if he wanted to say something. Kit waited for the revelation, but none came.

'Durand is from Calais, he says. He arrived just that day. He is to start work at the French Legation next week as a translator. He speaks fluent Arabic,' said Briant. Then he added cryptically, 'he seems an interesting man.'

'Why do you say that?'

'You'll see,' replied Briant ignoring the look of irritation on Kit's face.

'He had just arrived that day,' repeated Kit. 'Where had he been previously?'

'Algeria and Egypt. He works for the government. It's difficult to establish a connection with Berrada prior to his arrival.'

'Could he have been involved with the Rif insurrection. From memory, the Rif mountains are in the east of the country. I can see a supply route from Algeria for weapons.'

'Meet him and decide for yourself,' said Briant effectively closing that line of inquiry.

'And Lefevre?'

'He is middle-aged, just retired from business and on holiday. He is a widower.'

'Did he go in the room?' asked Kit.

'No, he stayed on the landing.'

'Who else went into the room?'

'A French couple named Paul and Angelique Bouguereau. They are middle-aged, but if your aunt is anything to go by, age is not an obstacle to murder.'

'Very funny captain,' said Kit, smiling. 'Can you tell me more about them?'

'He is retired, and they are travelling in North Africa, They too have been in Algeria and Egypt. This is the last leg of their tour. They return home to Nice once we release them to travel. He was a civil servant.'

'And she?'

'An actress,' interjected Raif with a roll of his eyes. Kit did not take this at face value.

'They entered the room too?'

'Yes. Madame Bouguereau fainted when she saw the body.'

'How dramatic,' said Mary, drily.

'Exactly,' said Raif.

'She does not have your constitution. Perhaps if she had eaten more overcooked Roast Beef, her stomach might have been stronger,' added Briant with a shudder.

'I would have thought the copious amounts of blood that you serve with your meat would have prepared her adequately,' responded Mary.

Just then the starter dishes arrived. They consisted of beef kebab with a grilled pepper and tomato salad.

'Some of your delicate food,' said Mary, 'how nice.'

Conversation about murder ceased for the duration of the first course; it does nothing for the appetite in general and is most off putting when it comes to meat dishes. When the plates were cleared, Briant returned to the critical minutes around the shooting.

'Aside from the people in the room, there was another couple staying on the third floor. This couple are American, from Boston. Both are teachers, unlike the other guests, they are on their way to Egypt and then Jerusalem. A Mr and Mrs Friedman. They both came down the stairs but did not enter the room once it became apparent there was a dead body.'

'Anyone else?'

'Aside from Heinrich Keller who was in the room directly above Berrada there was no one else upstairs,' answered Briant. 'Madame Moreau was in the kitchen of the hotel along with one of the waiters. She is the cook, I might add. Neither she nor the waiter, Jabir, went near the room. Both heard the shot but did not realise it had come from within the hotel.'

'They thought it came from outside?' asked Mary, beating Kit to the punch.

'No, they were not sure. It was a shot, everything happened very quickly. Both were in the kitchen so quite some way away from the room. Aside from Madame Moreau and Jabir as well as the people I've mentioned, there was no one else in the hotel when the shot was fired.'

The next course arrived as Briant concluded his summary of the people who were known to have been in the hotel.

'Would it be possible to speak to the people who were in the hotel, captain? I mean, what harm can it do?'

Something in Briant's face alerted Kit once more that there was something else at play. Briant, from experience, often played a multi-layered game that his Uncle Eustace would have understood and appreciated.

'You are welcome to speak to them. I fear that unless some new information comes to us, we are almost certain to conclude it was suicide,' said Briant, holding his hand up to Raif, 'whatever our instincts tell us. Our esteemed Chief of Police is very keen that we close the case with such a verdict at the inquest. It would everyone politically.'

'And the post-mortem? Surely it should be the key determinant of any verdict,' pointed out Mary.

'You would think,' agreed Briant, sadly, but Toussaint is an immensely powerful man.'

' I want to clear my aunt's name on both counts,' said Kit. 'I'm curious, though, why do you care about Berrada? Suicide or murder, it sounds like he was a thug, almost

128

certainly a killer himself. Why do you care what the verdict is?'

Briant was silent for a moment. The night was getting darker and a little colder now. He gazed out at the sea and found no inspiration, only darkness and danger. Why did he care if Berrada saw justice or not? In truth he cared nothing for the man. The world was better off without him and his kind. Yet, another part of him instinctively rebelled at such a callous disregard for human life. Lord only knows, life was cheap in this country and men like Berrada and his leader, Raisuli, had been responsible for this. Finally, he spoke. His voice was almost a whisper.

'I have killed men; probably I have killed more men than Berrada ever did. I did so because I was ordered to. The responsibility was not mine or, so I have been told. I see some of their faces still. I see their faces every day. I'll see them every day until I die. I promised them, my enemies that is, that I would work for a more just world. This is my penance. Maybe they'll forgive me. Maybe I'll forgive myself. Yes, you can speak to the guests, Lord Kit Aston. Perhaps, in this way, in finding the real killer, we can save our souls.'

11

Tangier: 8ᵗʰ July 1921

Kit and Mary were driven to the Sultan Hotel the next morning by their unofficial bodyguard or watcher. Neither Kit nor Mary minded as both were finding the hot weather troublesome. Kit never wore shorts. He was too self-consciousness about his prosthetic lower leg and Mary would have preferred to wear less but felt it would be inappropriate even in an international zone such as Tangier.

Briant and Raif kindly left them free to question the guests at the hotel. They had already taken copies of the statements which they had given to Kit including a diagram of the hotel. Kit held the diagram up as they travelled in the back of the car.

Floor Plan Hotel – First Floor

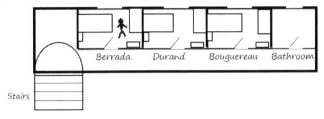

Berrada. Durand Bouguereau Bathroom

Stairs

Floor Plan Hotel – Second Floor

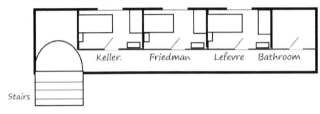

Keller. Friedman Lefevre Bathroom

Stairs

Kit and Mary looked at the floorplan together. There were two pages, one each for the first and second floors.

'So Berrada was in the first room, by the stairs with the bathroom at the end of the corridor. We must check each of the rooms to see if the windows are all barred.'

'They looked pretty solid to me,' said Mary glumly.

'Yes, I agree, and I suspect our friends from the Sûreté have already thought of all this: windows, walls, ceilings. There is no way in or out of that room except through the front door.'

The second page was identical to the first page, albeit with different occupants. Kit set it down and studied the floor plan again.

'I'm not sure what this tells us because if there is no access to the room except through the front door then...,' observed Mary.

'I agree,' said Kit. 'I can see some obvious ways that it could have been done, but we come up against a few stumbling blocks.'

'For instance?' asked Mary, her eyes narrowing.

'Well, no one can be certain that the gunshot came from the room. That means anyone could have fired any gun, not just the one found in Berrada's room.'

'But the police searched all the rooms and found no other weapon' pointed out Mary.

'Half an hour later or more. Plenty of time to rid oneself of any inconvenient gun.'

'Yes, find a gun and it would certainly blow the suicide theory out of the water. What else Sherlock?'

'Well, Watson, when I said "obvious ways" I probably meant just that one point. Singular not plural.' Mary's face was a mixture of derision and disappointment. She did this rather well and caused Kit to chuckle. 'The key is to establish means because the motive is probably obvious.'

'Revenge?'

'Correct, or assassination. That Berrada was disliked, I have no doubt. He must have had many, many enemies. I hope that the captain and Sergeant Raif can produce a connection between the guests and Berrada. Was he working on something besides Aunt Agatha's case that might mean his removal was expedient? I think we will have to leave motive to the Sûreté. Failing progress on this we are left with trying to work out how a murder that could not have happened based on the facts we have, was committed. I think Briant is happy to leave this one with us.'

'Or Aunt Agatha?'

Kit laughed at this, 'Indeed. I strongly suspect that she will want to investigate this herself. Incidentally, did you see how he reacted about this man Durand. I wonder why.'

'Me too. He was quite circumspect about him,' agreed Mary.

The police car pulled up outside the hotel. There were fewer people hanging around now as interest in the murder waned. Kit and Mary entered the hotel just as Lucien Moreau was barking out orders to a woman they took to be a cleaner.

Moreau's eyes lit up when he saw the couple as did his smile, new guests. Then he remembered seeing them with the police. The realisation of this killed his smile. He went over to greet them with a distinctly chilly, 'Bonjour.'

Kit explained why they were there in his faultless French.

'The police have asked us to assist them in this matter. Would it be possible to speak to you and then some of the guests?'

'Of course,' came the rather sullen reply. Moreau wasn't so much sweating as melting. A further cause for his prickly attitude was a degree of envy at the rather cool appearance of the two Anglaises. Truly they were a cold race, he thought.

He led them into his office which looked like it had not been cleaned since before the War. The window was open which allowed the noise from the street and the heat to enter freely making life uncomfortable for all.

'Can we go anywhere else less cauldron-like?' asked Mary.

Moreau shrugged in a "this-is-Morocco manner." Kit and Mary decided to make the best of things and not extend the interview unnecessarily.

Moreau told them about himself. He had arrived in Morocco just after the Treaty of Fez in 1912 when Morocco became a protectorate of France and Spain. Moreau had seen an opportunity in a country that would grow economically thanks to the benign and civilising influence of France. The locals did not see things the same way and riots were the result. This hurt business a little. Then the War hurt business even more. However, they had survived if not thrived. It was a struggle, but then wasn't life? Following the War, business began to improve and, finally, they could see the hotel's potential being realised. Then the Moroccan people began to do what they usually did periodically: rebel. First Raisuli and now Abd-el-Krim. It never ended.

Moreau was clearly at the end of his tether and the murder of Berrada was certainly not going to be a boon for business. Kit could see the Frenchman was close to tears as he described the potential impact.

'Perhaps it may attract business,' pointed out Mary hopefully. 'I mean, who wouldn't want to stay in the room that the infamous Berrada was killed. I imagine many would pay a pretty penny for this.'

Moreau's eyes suddenly lost their dull, defeated colour. All of a sudden he sat up, his eyes widened and something approaching a smile appeared on his face. There was some truth in this. With the right publicity in the right places he, Morceau, could make something of this.

'Can you tell me what you were doing on the day of Berrada's death?' asked Kit.

'All day?' asked Moreau, a trace of dismay on his face. His mind was already racing ahead with the how he would sell the room that Berrada was murdered in. Murder dinner parties. Tourist day trips. School trips; why not? There was so much he could do.

'Yes, all day,' replied Kit. 'Just summarise what you were doing, where, who you were with.'

Moreau took a deep breath while he tried to recall the events of the day.

'I was up around six in the morning. I went to the market to buy food for the day. We serve breakfast, lunch and dinner. I was back before seven. Our guests rarely rise before then. The inspector was the first to sit down for breakfast. This was around seven thirty. He never eats much, and he was on his way by eight. I did not see him again until his return at six thirty.'

'Did you speak to him?'

'I rarely speak to him monsieur. He is not one for conversation. I gave him his room key and he went upstairs. Ten minutes later or so I heard the gunshot.'

'After Berrada left for the day, who else came down?'

'Monsieur Lefevre came down but did not take breakfast. He went straight out, and we did not see him

135

until he returned around six fifteen. Next down to breakfast was the American couple, the Friedmans. They had breakfast and then spent the morning in the reception area reading the newspapers from the day before yesterday.'

'They speak French?' asked Mary.

'Yes, they are fairly fluent,' said the hotel owner, 'for Americans that is.'

This did not sound a ringing endorsement, so Kit pressed on to what they had done then.

'They left the hotel for a walk and only returned around two. They stayed in their room before leaving about five. An hour later they returned and went to their room. Neither are young, they both looked tired.'

'I understand Monsieur Durand was with you when you found the body. Can you tell me about him?'

'A young man who is here to work,' said Moreau, with no little approval. 'He took breakfast just before nine and then went out to the Legation. I did not see him again until after six, he took his room keys and then he sat where the Friedmans had sat earlier and read the paper.'

'Is that in the lobby?'

'Yes.'

'You can't actually see if anyone is sitting there, though, from the reception desk. There is a separating wall just where the seats are.'

'True, but he appeared within seconds of when I heard the shot. Where else could he have been? Certainly not upstairs. There was not enough time.'

Kit nodded at this and made a note on his small leather-bound notebook.

'Herr Keller?' asked Kit.

'He was already down before the inspector. He wanted to inform me that he'd had an accident and spilled something on his carpet. Then he went to take his breakfast. After chatting with the Friedmans in the dining room, he left the hotel returning mid-morning. He did not stay long. Later, in the early evening, he returned, just after Berrada. I was just going for his key when we heard the gunshot. Then he, Monsieur Durand, and Lefevre accompanied me up the stairs. That's when we found the inspector.'

'Who was with you in the corridor?'

'When we reached the top of the stairs we started to knock on the inspector's door. The Friedmans appeared on the stairs at this point but stayed there. Monsieur Bouguereau came out of his room followed by Madame Bouguereau. They are at the end of the inspector's corridor. He wanted to know what was happening and if the gunshot had been inside or outside the hotel. We ignored him. Durand suggested that we try and break the door down. I wasn't too happy about that. Who would pay for a new door? But then Keller agreed with him.'

'So it was Durand who suggested breaking in,' asked Kit.

'Yes,' said Moreau dolefully. 'I tried at first, but my heart wasn't in it so the second time we tried together, and the door gave way. That's when we saw the body of the inspector lying at the foot of the bed.'

'Was there a gun in his hand?' asked Kit. 'This is very important.'

'Yes, I saw the revolver.'

'You're sure?'

'Yes, because I saw and I said, "he' shot himself." You could see the blood on his white shirt.'

'Was he wearing his suit?'

'No monsieur. Just his shirt, trousers and shoes,' replied Moreau.

'Where was his jacket?' asked Mary.

'He had placed it on the back of the chair. Anyway, Keller joined us and then the Bouguereau couple. When she saw the dead body she screamed and fainted.'

'Where were you standing when this happened.'

'I was kneeling by the body. I wanted to check if he was dead or not. He's not the first person to die in the hotel. We had an old lady a few years ago. I know what signs to look for. I checked for a pulse. He was clearly dead.'

'Was he cold?'

'I cannot remember.'

Kit nodded, but he was a little frustrated that such a detail was not forthcoming. Perhaps the heat may have delayed the onset of rigor.

'So you were looking up at the doorway when Madame Bouguereau fainted?'

'Yes, we all were when she screamed. Then she collapsed in the doorway. Keller and her husband carried her back to the room at that point and I sent Monsieur Durand to find a policeman. I stayed with the body.'

'There was no one else in the room?'

'No. There is nowhere to hide. No one could have come in or out without me seeing them,' said Moreau. Kit believed him. Moreau had proved to be a good witness for the most part. His recollection was clear and there was no sense of doubt in his mind about the sequence of events.

'What did you do then?'

'I cleared the room of people and put a chair in front of the door to make sure the room was not disturbed any further,' said Moreau.

'Good thinking,' said Kit which made the Frenchman sit up a little straighter and smile. 'Are all of the guests in the hotel at the moment?'

'The Friedmans and the Bouguereaus are in their rooms. I do not believe Monsieur Durand is back from the Legation yet. Herr Keller and Monsieur Lefevre went out for a walk about half an hour ago, separately.'

'Very well, perhaps if you could ask the Bouguereau couple to join us in the lobby, we will question them on their memory of what happened.'

Moreau looked relieved that the interview was over. They all stood up and trooped out of the office. While the hotel manager went to find his fellow countrymen, Kit and Mary settled onto the sofas in the lobby. It gave them both a chance to observe the layout better. An open copy of the *Tangier Gazette* lay on the wicker table. Kit picked it up. The murder of Berrada was on the front page. At least, reflected Kit, Aunt Agatha was no longer the main news story.

From the sofa, it was possible to see the entrance to the hotel, but not the reception as it was covered by a lattice wood panel. While they waited, they saw a number of tradesmen enter the hotel. Madame Moreau appeared and sent two of them round to the back of the hotel where the

139

kitchen was located while a third was sent upstairs to fix the door of the room formerly occupied by Berrada. She pointed to him where to go and left him to his job.

The thick walls of the hotel meant that the temperature in the lobby was actually quite bearable. Four teas arrived, coinciding with the arrival of the French couple. Kit and Mary rose to greet them. Monsieur Paul Bouguereau was short, pleasantly plump with half-moon spectacles and a warm smile.

His wife, Madame Angelique Bouguereau looked like the mad aunt of American vamp actress, Theda Bara after a particularly convivial weekend drinking bottles of Absinthe. Her eyes were heavily made up with rather too much emphasis on black for any woman not employed in a Pigalle bordello. At any other time this would have raised a few eyebrows, but her Ostrich feather hat was more than a match for her eyes in the attention stakes. The black feather rose at a forty-five-degree angle from the black and silver hat adding at least a foot and half to her already Amazonian dimensions.

A swift glance at Kit told Mary to be on her guard. Her husband was unlikely to pass up such a gilt-edged opportunity to make her laugh.

'I hope, monsieur, that the fact you want to speak to us does not make us suspects,' said Monsieur Bouguereau after the initial introductions.

'I don't think we can put our head in the sand, Monsieur Bouguereau. Murder is a serious matter.'

There was loud, hollow noise, coming from Mary, moments after Kit said this.

'What was that?' asked Madame Bouguereau in a dramatically husky voice.

'It came from outside,' said Kit turning to the window. In fact, Mary had just kicked him under the table. This was not an uncommon occurrence. Experience had taught this particular husband to stay on the prosthetic limb side of his wife. Kit began to explain the purpose of the interview.

'The Sûreté have asked us to assist them in their enquiries on this matter. So far the investigation has been...flightless, we hope to change that.'

Kit noted that Mary was holding her hands together as if in prayer. Her knuckles were white. Another few puns and she might crack, thought Kit.

'The police will manage the lion's share of the investigation. Perhaps we can dust a few points out of the way.'

The French couple seemed confused by Kit's use of language but put it down to his not being a native speaker. Mary, on the other hand, was already cursing him and knew exactly what he was trying to do. She suspected the rest of the interview was going to be full of allusions to Africa, birds, feather dusters and silent movies.

Madame Bouguereau, at Kit's request, began to explain the events surrounding the discovery of the body. Mary bit her tongue in the hope that this would maintain some degree of decorum.

'You acted with great courage Madame,' observed Kit. 'No drama.'

Mary excused herself to go to the bathroom.

12

There was no little drama when Agatha and her friends returned to the house where they were staying or being held captive; the exact definition was becoming less clear by the hour. Joel greeted them with a face like a seditious seven-year-old denied his tea.

'That animal of yours,' said the Egyptian, stabbing his finger at Agatha, 'is destroying our house.' As if to emphasise the point, Mimi began barking frenziedly again as she sensed the arrival of her new owner.

Agatha made a point of staring at the paint peeling of the walls and the woodworm infested furniture before replying.

'Applying the coup de grace, I would have thought. No matter, let's go up and see how she is.'

'Insane as you,' muttered Joel under his breath. Agatha ignored this, but Betty glared angrily at Joel causing him to shrink behind a grinning Goodman.

'That's the spirit Joel,' said Goodman.

Mimi's evident delight at seeing Agatha was in marked contrast to Joel's dismay at the state of the room. Vases had been smashed, chairs chomped, and cushions chewed.

'She certainly missed you,' observed Goodman. He seemed remarkably unperturbed by the chaos of the room.

This was a pragmatic response to the fact that he was not the one staying in it nor was he, typically for a man, likely to lift so much as a finger to tidy it. 'Well, I shall leave you ladies to the task of clearing things up and discussing how we can advance our cause.'

'Don't forget, Harry is due in today. Have you thought about what I asked you to do?'

'All in hand dear lady, all in hand,' said Goodman who had put his own to good use by waving to them on the way out. The sooner he exited, the less chance he would be press-ganged into helping on a matter that was decidedly not his forte, never mind his responsibility.

Meanwhile, the ladies began to apply themselves to returning the room to its former state of inglory. This was never going to take long, but in the process Mimi earned a mild rebuke from Agatha which earned her, in turn, a more severe reprimand from Betty.

'You spoil that animal,' said Betty, holding what had once been a cushion up as evidence.

'Never mind that, we must apply ourselves to the task of helping Christopher,' replied Agatha, picking up bits of a vase from the floor. She looked at Mimi accusingly and said, '*Mauvaise fille*.' Mimi turned away and sloped over to the corner in shame.

'What do you suggest we do?'

'We need to despatch one of our friends to assemble as much information on the murder...'

'Suicide?' offered Sausage hopefully.

'Murder,' replied Agatha without missing a beat, 'as much information as possible.'

'Can't Kit use the sign language thing to tell you?' asked Betty in a tone that blended a hint of sarcasm with genuine curiosity. This combination is not easy to pull off, but Betty managed it so well that Agatha took the question at face value.

'It would take too long and, besides, it would be rather conspicuous. I could just imagine a crowd of Moroccans assembling to watch the performance.'

'So how will we obtain the information?' asked Betty.

'This is Morocco,' answered Agatha. 'We simply bribe one of the policemen.'

'Ah, silly me,' said Betty, shaking her head. She glanced over to Sausage who merely shrugged.

*

As Agatha was contemplating adding to their lengthening list of potential misdemeanours, Harry Miller was watching the boat from Marseilles dock into the port at Tangier. He was dressed in the standard uniform for any European traveller, light linen suit, Panama hat, white shirt with sky blue tie. At first he'd enjoyed the freedom of his travels. Visiting Paris and hearing the news about Ida had given him a greater lift than anything he could have imagined. However, boredom had set in on the passage to Tangier and he was ready, once more, for a little adventure.

His wish was certainly to be granted over the next few days.

There was large crowd at the bottom of the gang plank to greet the arrival of the boat. This was mixture of friends and family as well as locals hoping to persuade a passenger to take them on as an unofficial tour guide. Over the previous couple of days Miller had become if not used to the blast furnace heat, then a little less shocked by its intensity. With his coat slung over his back and suitcase in hand he descended the gangplank towards the waiting throng.

It seemed conversation in this part of the world could only be conducted at deafening levels. Everyone was shouting at someone else and soon Miller found himself in the middle of a swarm of people with his hand firmly on the wallet in his trouser pocket. He ignored the sound of locals begging him to come with them and marched with his eyes straight ahead. Then he saw a young man standing behind the throng. He was holding up a sign that read:

MR H. MILLER

Miller walked towards him. He was more boy than man. Not yet in his mid-twenties, small in stature, he had a moustache that emphasised his youth rather than disguising it. Miller had attempted something similar during the War but gave it up as a bad job following some well-deserved ribbing from his comrades in the trenches.

'*Bonjour, monsieur*,' said the small Moroccan. '*Parlez-vous Francais?*'

'*Un peut*,' replied Miller. He had brushed up on the language on the way over as he knew this would be the principal method of communication while he was here.

The young man introduced himself with a shy smile and spoke rapid French.

145

'I am Nassim. I am to take you to your friends. Please come with me.'

Much to Miller's dismay, it appeared as if they would be walking rather than driving in car or a horse drawn Caleche or bicycle taxi.

'Where are we going?' asked Miller.

'Hotel first then friends.'

This was a surprise because it implied that he would not be staying in the same accommodation as Kit and Mary. While it was unexpected, Miller correctly assumed that Kit would have good reason for doing this, as normally he would stay near them. It also suggested that his presence was not meant to be known. Miller wondered the reason for this.

'Why am I not staying with his lordship?' asked Miller. The response amazed Miller so much he stopped dead in the street almost causing a pile up behind him, such was the crowd on the narrow street on which they were walking.

'Who?'

'You mean it was not Lord Kit who sent you?'

'No monsieur. I was told to tell you that Agatha sent me.'

In order to take his mind off the heat, the pools of sweat under his arms and dripping from his forehead, Miller asked about the young man. This appeared to delight Nassim, and his back straightened slightly as he spoke.

Nassim was twenty-one years old. He worked in his family business making pottery and painting it. He was a painter who loved the work of Renaissance artists. Every Saturday he would sell his paintings at a market. Recently he had been given oil paints for the first time by a patron and he was learning how to paint in this medium. His progress had delighted his patron which was a source of great pride to Nassim and his family.

Around ten minutes later they arrived at a building with four stories. They walked through the arched doorway into a large, tiled courtyard with a fountain in the middle. It was quite delightful in Miller's view. There were tables and chairs arranged around the perimeter of the courtyard. It was empty except for a small man sitting alone drinking tea. He glanced up at Miller with a look that was bordering on unfriendly. Nassim brought him over to the man. He didn't stand up.

'You are Mr Miller?'

The man spoke accented English. He did not offer his hand, so Miller did not offer his.

'Yes,' replied Miller. 'And you are?'

'A friend. I am acquainted with the three ladies and that hateful animal.'

Miller smiled as he remembered that Agatha had adopted Mimi following the case involving the Bluebeard Club a few months previously. He sat down uninvited. Meanwhile, the man glanced towards Nassim.

'Take his bags up to the room.'

Miller looked a little unhappy at this.

'Just a precaution Mr Miller. We cannot book you into a hotel as it will alert the police. The name of the room occupant is our friend Nassim here. He is honest. You can trust him. He will stay with you and hold onto the key. No questions will be asked.'

147

'I see,' said Miller, who plainly didn't. The sight of such uncertainty bordering on distrust drew a smile from the man.

'I see you are unsure. This is understandable. You must understand that Lady Frost and the other ladies are still officially on the run. She is keen that your presence here remains secret.'

'Why?'

'She will tell you herself if you come with me, please.'

Miller groaned inwardly at the prospect of yet more walking in the hot midday sun. Thankfully, his mysterious friend was similarly disinclined towards strenuous activity and ordered a bicycle taxi which they both boarded. It took them through a series of winding streets that meant Miller was hopelessly lost within a matter of a seconds. A few minutes later they arrived at a square. Miller's companion jumped off the back and said, 'Can you pay the driver?'

Miller rolled his eyes and extracted his wallet to do the needful. A few sharp words from his companion to the driver ensured that he was not rinsed on the fare. They walked across the square towards a café where Miller saw a large man with a ruddy complexion that bespoke an Englishman, sitting with three women dressed in niqabs. This drew a smile from Miller. His admiration for the ladies was boundless, but this took things to a new level. What spirit! What ingenuity! What kind of trouble were they in?

Miller approached the café with a broad grin on his face but decided that a more solemn countenance might be the order of the day. It was, of course, too late by then.

'I don't know what's so funny, Harry. It's a sauna in this outfit,' said a familiar voice from behind the veil.

'Of course,' said a chastened Miller. He glanced towards the man who was with them at the table. He was large, in his sixties and appeared to possess an unusual combination of benign malevolence. Miller did not doubt this man was untrustworthy, but he appeared to want to make a good impression, so he made the effort too.

'Mr Miller, this is indeed a pleasure,' said the man holding out his hand. 'I hear great things about you.'

'This is Sidney,' said Agatha. She did not expand on her rather brusque introduction.

'Pleased to meet you. Call me Harry.'

'I shall indeed do so, Harry. As Lady Frost says, my name is Sidney. I am providing accommodation for the ladies in return for a small favour.'

This brought a snort from behind at least two of the veils. Miller guessed Agatha and Betty would be the most likely suspects.

'What can I do to help you Sidney?' asked Miller, but he already suspected what the answer would be. In his pre-War life, Miller had been a moderately successful burglar. The War and meeting Kit Aston, or to be more precise, rescuing him from No Man's Land had changed his direction in life.

'Why don't we order you a cup of tea and we'll discuss the details,' suggested Goodman with a broad smile. It felt, to him, as if he were nearing the end of a long race. The presence of the Londoner was surprisingly reassuring. This was a man that Goodman instantly recognised as being competent. He knew the sort and respected them enormously. He liked Harry Miller and suspected that most people who met him did so too.

Around an hour later the party had left the café and were standing outside the villa that Goodman had shown the ladies a few days previously. Miller was now fully briefed on the project. His first assessment of the villa was that it presented no obvious challenges, but that was without considering the presence of guard dogs and armed guards.

'There are no dogs, I am told,' assured Goodman. 'It is as you see. There are a number of local men who function as security.'

If Miller's ears pricked up at this, then it caused Agatha to turn sharply to Goodman.

'You never mentioned the guards Sidney,' said Agatha sharply. 'Who and how many?'

Goodman appeared to flinch at this. Never a good sign and particularly in this man.

'Just some local men I understand.'

But Agatha not only had the bit between her teeth, but she was also patently about to explode into righteous fury.

'Sidney, are these Raisuli's men?'

'Come now Agatha, how can I be expected to know all these things? I do not believe so, but who knows?'

'I thought you had that boy Nassim working there.'

'Only long enough, Agatha, to confirm the presence and location of the painting,' said Goodman hurriedly. He was sweating profusely now, and this was only partially due to the cauldron-like temperature.

'This changes things, Sidney. It's one thing to break into a poorly guarded villa. It's another for Harry to drop into a military stockade full of crack troops. Are you mad?'

Goodman's countenance lost its benign Pickwickian beam. In its place was a harder, more dangerous scowl.

'No I am not mad, Agatha. Nor am I on the run from the authorities. You would do well to remember this.' This comment stopped Agatha momentarily. Certainly long enough for Goodman to seize the opportunity to mollify once more. 'I'm sure that Mr Miller is more than capable of breaking and entering a house with no alarm, no dogs and no safe, where all he need do is remove a painting from its frame, roll it up and exit stage left.'

'Chased by a bear or, in this case, Berber,' snarled Agatha angrily.

'So we're agreed then. Harry will steal the painting and I shall arrange for your safe trip to Spain by boat.'

'You haven't shown us that part yet,' pointed out Betty.

'Insurance, my dear, insurance. I shall introduce you later this afternoon to the young man who will see you safely across the straits to Spain. He is American which, as you will know of this remarkable race, means he is very self-reliant, very self-confident and, I think, very capable. We have used him on a number of occasions and have had no cause for complaint.'

13

Julius Friedman had the knowing squint of a man who knew the answer to a question before you'd asked it, and it was a damn-fool question to begin with. He and his wife were both of a similar vintage to Agatha and her friends: mid-Victorian by birth, belligerent in behaviour, modern in mindset. Kit and Mary liked both at once, but recognised they had a job to do which involved clearing the good name of his aunt. The American couple, meanwhile, had not survived a civil war, a world war and Spanish flu just to lay down in submission at a couple of amateur detectives, English nobles no less, who seemed to have walked from the pages of a crime novel.

'You two are like something from a detective book. You know, Lord How-Do-You-Do investigates.'

Kit had not spent his early life verbally fencing with Agatha, Alastair, his father and now, Mary, not to know this game and enjoy it.

'We always get our man,' said Kit, modestly

'Or woman,' added Mary, in defence of the gentler sex who were just as capable of murder as their lord and masters.

'I'll bet,' replied Friedman, 'all in time for tea and cucumber sandwiches with the Essex Farquharsons.'

'Essex?' said Kit with a raised eyebrow.

'Other side of the tracks?' asked Mrs Friedman.

'Decidedly,' replied Kit with a grin. 'Now as afternoon tea is but a few hours away, would you mind if we ask you some questions, unless you want to confess right now.'

This brought a ghost of a smile from Friedman.

'Why are you doing the job of the police?'

The question, notwithstanding the sarcasm earlier, was a fair one. Kit felt an explanation was owed.

'I have helped the police before in a number of investigations and I have helped Captain Briant, specifically, on a couple. If this is not suicide then their main suspect is my aunt which, as you may surmise, makes me particularly interested in this case.'

'Conflict of interest if you ask me,' said Friedman.

'I didn't, but it's a fair point,' agreed Kit. 'Shall we work on the assumption, however, that you are witnesses and the beautiful couple you see before you are the fictional detectives you clearly so admire?'

'Fair enough,' said Friedman, satisfied that Kit wasn't such a fool.

'Can you tell us about the day, as you remember, from when you rose to the critical minutes around when the shot was heard?'

Mrs Friedman took over at this point. She liked the look of Mary who had seemed to enjoy Mr Friedman's comments. Anyone who liked her grumpy husband was a

153

good sort in her book. She rather liked him too and had done so for close to sixty years since they'd met as children.

'We were up around seven-thirty,' said Mrs Friedman.

'I was up earlier, you'll understand when you're older young man,' said her husband which brought a roll of the eyes from his supportive spouse.

'I like to take my time,' said Mrs Friedman, regaining the initiative. 'We went down to breakfast at eight. Before you ask, the inspector had already left, and we met Herr Keller there. We chatted with him about places to go for lunch and then he left us. We finished our breakfast and went into the lobby to read the European newspapers. They're a day or two old, but we like to keep up.'

'Then we went out for a walk around the port,' broke in Mr Friedman, keen to move things along. This brought a sideways look from Mrs Friedman who had enjoyed her moment in the interrogation spotlight.

'It's beautiful, but rather hot down there,' said Mary.

'Roasted my...' Friedman paused at this point to choose the least offensive word of which he could think. His wife tutted and shook her head.

'It is rather hot,' agreed Kit. 'And then?'

The couple took turns explaining their afternoon lunch at the port. They recommended a chicken tajine they'd had. From there they went back to their room to have an afternoon nap and to read a book.

'We left around five to take a coffee and came back after six.'

'Did you see Inspector Berrada at any point that day?'

'No,' answered Friedman. 'We saw him the day before when he arrived, but that was it. Neither of us entered his room; didn't see the body either before you ask.'

Kit nodded at this and then changed direction.

'You are on a tour, I gather.'

'Yes, We're off to Egypt next if we can ever escape Tangier and then Jerusalem. We've been planning this trip for years. You'll find out. When children come things change. It's not your life anymore. Takes a while for you to reclaim it.'

Friedman smiled as he said this, but his wife seemed sad. Her world revolved around her two sons and six grandchildren. This trip was for Julius. He'd been a good father, a good husband and a doting grandfather. She owed him that.

*

'I don't think they're hardened criminals,' commented Mary after the couple departed. Seeing the sadness on Mrs Friedman's face at the mention of their children had given her pause for thought. The idea of children was something she had not given as much consideration to as Esther. There was so much in life she wanted to do. Sometimes she wondered if she had any maternal instincts. Just then, at that moment when she looked into the eyes of the old woman who was clearly missing her children and grandchildren, feelings swept over her that were as unfamiliar as they were melancholic. She saw Kit looking at her with concern on his face.

'Is everything all right?' he asked, taking her hand.

Mary grinned back at him and said, 'I hope they're not involved. I liked them.'

'Yes,' agreed Kit. 'I'd love to chat more with him.'

Mary decided she would speak with Mrs Friedman again. Children was not a topic of conversation that had been raised with either Aunt Emily or Aunt Agatha. For too long with Aunt Emily there had been a war of sorts that, at least, appeared to have ended. The subject was too painful for Agatha. As a result, neither she nor Esther had ever been able to talk about something that was just taken for granted given their sex and their rank. She realised that she was confused about what she wanted, and, for the first time, Mary felt a little fear about what the future held for them.

The couple had to wait twenty minutes for their next interview. Heinrich Keller appeared at the reception. He was directed by Moreau over to Kit and Mary. Keller was a man of around fifty, with a light grey beard, round spectacles and standard light suit with Panama. When he took his hat off upon seeing Mary, it revealed close cropped grey hair receding severely. From his carriage it was clear he had been in the military. Kit used his stick to stand up which caused a raised eyebrow from the German.

'Cambrai,' said Kit, but there was a rueful smile on his face.

'I'm sorry,' said the German in English and seemed to mean it. 'It was a terrible war that I never wanted. I hope we never repeat these mistakes.'

'I hope so too but, for what it's worth, I fear we made a terrible peace at Versailles.'

Keller shrugged and sat down.

'You have not made life easy for us, certainly.'

Jabir appeared and the group ordered coffees. By tacit arrangement they spoke no more of the War. Kit looked at the German and guessed he would have been an officer. His English was faultless, and his manner suggested an intelligence he recognised from his time at Heidelberg. There were even some scars on his head that suggested he had indulged the sword fighting beloved of German students, Mensur.

Keller saw the direction of Kit's gaze and smiled sadly.

'The folly of youth,' said Keller.

Kit laughed and replied, 'I studied in Heidelberg before the War. A few friends asked me to take part. They were from Bavaria. I said "no" to them,' recalled Kit.

'You were very smart, sir. My friends invited me also. I did not want to seem a coward, so I joined them. They are not friends now.'

'Can you tell me about your memory of the day that Inspector Berrada was killed.'

'Was it not suicide?'

'Why do say that?' asked Kit.

'It looked, when we entered the room, that he had killed himself, but I must admit, it was a strange way to do it. I was in the army.'

'You mean he should have put the gun to his head?' asked Kit, but he already knew the answer. This part of the death had made no sense either.

'Precisely. The chest is not an efficient way of killing yourself.'

157

'Can you tell me about your day? We want to know what you saw at the hotel that day. Anything strange or anyone who should not have been there.'

'I was away most of the day and to be honest there are always tradesmen around the place. You know, with food, or selling their wares. After a while you do not see them.'

'Did you see Berrada at all?'

'No, he had probably left the hotel by the time I was at breakfast. The only time I saw him was in the room. We never spoke.'

'Were you in the hotel during the day?'

'Only briefly. I foolishly ruined the carpet in my room. I spilled some wine when I was having a drink with the Swiss, Lefevre. I offered to buy Monsieur Moreau a new one. He refused, but I felt honour bound. I can tell you the name of the trader I purchased the carpet from.'

'I think the police have that too?' asked Kit.

'They do,' said Keller shrugging.

'And the ruined carpet?' asked Mary.

'Monsieur Moreau has it now. He said he would try, and have it repaired, but I think that it is ruined.'

'So this was the only time you were back in the hotel?'

'Correct, this was around three in the afternoon. I left immediately and did not return until just after six thirty and then, of course, I heard the shot.'

'Where were you?'

'Just at the reception. Monsieur Moreau went to give me my key when we heard the shot. It seemed to come from upstairs.'

'Could it have come from downstairs?' asked Mary.

Keller thought for a few moments, trying to recollect the events that had led him to this seat and the two English people.

'It could have, but,' he paused for a moment, 'you mean outside the hotel?'

Mary and Kit both nodded.

'It's unlikely. It felt much closer and for sure it was not in the lobby of the hotel, so we assumed upstairs.'

'What happened then?'

'Monsieur Moreau and I ran upstairs, along with the Frenchman. Moreau knocked on the one door that remained shut. When there was no answer, I didn't know the inspector was in his room, but Moreau did. That was when he tried to force the door open.'

'Did he not have the key with him?' asked Kit, surprised.

'No, you are correct. He ran down to take the key then came back up, but the key did not work in the lock so there must have been a key on the other side of the door. Anyway, that's when they tried to force the door.'

'Did you help them?'

The German smiled ruefully and rubbed his shoulder before saying, 'No, I have you British to thank for that.' Mary smiled sympathetically. Kit, meanwhile, tapped his prosthetic lower leg with his walking stick. This caused a look of surprise on the German's face. 'A terrible war. Such waste,' added the German.

There was no disagreement from Kit on this point and they parted soon afterwards. Kit and Mary were now alone on the lobby.

'Well, I suppose we should return to the hotel,' said Kit. 'Durand won't be back until later. It's a little hot now.'

'Yes, I'll be glad to be out of these clothes,' replied Mary, using the newspaper as a fan.

'I'll help you,' replied Kit looking as innocent as a fat boy in a tuck shop.

They rose from the seats and went over to the reception desk past an open window on a corridor that led to the dining room. Kit went over to the window and looked out. It was an alleyway that ran the length of the hotel. To the right it led down to a door. On the other side it led up to the square. Kit could see one of the policeman standing guard at the top of the alley.

Moreau appeared from the office at the back.

'Would you like more tea or coffee?'

'No thank you,' said Kit. 'We shall return to our hotel and return later to speak to Durand. Can you let him know?'

'Of course,' smiled Moreau.

'By the way,' added Kit, 'Where does that door lead to at the bottom of the alley?'

Moreau replied, 'That is the kitchen. The tradesmen are meant to go there, but they never do. They always want to come through the main entrance,' said Moreau resignedly.

Kit and Mary thanked the hotel owner and left the hotel. They were met by the policeman who had driven them to the hotel. Just before they climbed into the car, a thought struck Kit.

'Can we just take a look at the alleyway.'

The policeman shrugged and led them back towards the hotel, past the policeman to the alley. It was around thirty yards long with high walls either side. There was only one window, the one which Kit had looked through and the door at the end. Kit looked around him and up to the thin opening which revealed the sky. Mary kept her eyes on Kit.

'Well?'

'I don't know what I'm looking for. I suppose I was wondering if a shot could have been fired here.'

14

Agatha's gradual assumption of control of the ill-assorted group was as much an economic imperative as it was a force of personality. Neither Goodman nor Joel had the strength of character to cope with the dynamism that Kit's aunt brought to the dual projects of relieving Bourbon of his Caravaggio and ensuring their own safe return to any country that was not interested in incarcerating them for murder. The former, from a purely moral point of view, decided Agatha, was not her affair. It was possible that Goodman had obtained the painting legally and it was possible the murder of the Turkish sailor was self-defence. While she had no doubt that Goodman remained untrustworthy, his native cunning and survival instincts, demonstrated by his getaway from prison, could be deployed most usefully in their second endeavour: escape.

At Agatha's suggestion and Goodman's ready acquiescence, they hired a caleche to take them to a cafe just off Rue de la Plage, a street leading towards the port of Tangier. It was here they were to meet the young man called Rick. By now, Agatha and Betty were funding their continued stay in the town. Their two captors had long since run out of money; their last act before leaving for the port was to borrow money, which Betty accepted she would never see again, to pay rent on the villa for the rest of the month.

'I'm pretty sure whatever the traditional approach to kidnapping and abduction is, this is probably not it,' said Betty as she handed money over to Joel to give to their landlord. The three ladies stayed out of sight at Goodman's suggestion. Their landlord, Faisal, was not a man to be trusted, warned Goodman. The snort that greeted this from Agatha was happily ignored by the big Englishman.

Two caleches were hired to take them down towards the port. Goodman travelled with Betty and Sausage while Joel drew the short straw and sat in an uncomfortable silence with Agatha. If Goodman was relaxed about the shift in power since the arrival of the three ladies, Joel most certainly wasn't. Only the prospect of obtaining the Caravaggio was holding him back from going to the police and claiming the reward. Although, if he paused long enough to think about it, his position as a man on the run might mean he was somewhat at risk himself.

The caleche arrived outside a large café. They climbed down from the carriage and walked inside. The café was filled with sailors so the sight of three niqab-wearing women led by a European was strange enough to raise a few eyebrows and ribald comments in French.

'Is that your harem?' asked one sailor.

Goodman smiled benignly and said, 'For a good price they could be yours.'

The sailor took one look at the three ladies and laughed uproariously. Their dress did nothing to hide the fact that they were no longer as slender as they once were. He was joined by a few of the other sailors who had heard the exchange. Goodman started chuckling as well. He knew that Agatha would probably disembowel him later, but for a few glorious moments he felt like a sultan.

'Get a move on,' hissed Agatha who, aside from feeling irritated at being the source of a joke from Goodman of all people, was concerned that this scene was attracting unwanted attention towards them. Out of the corner of her eye she saw a large man with an even larger black moustache behind the counter cleaning a glass with a dirty rag. It might have been a gun such was malevolence in his eyes. The man disappeared behind a beaded curtain. This was a mistake, thought Agatha once more.

They moved towards a young man who was sitting alone in the corner. He had been gazing at the exchange with undisguised exasperation. Agatha guessed this was their potential contact. He was in his early twenties with thick dark hair, tanned skin, a couple of days growth on his face. He wore a shirt rolled up to muscular arms. His dark eyes assessed them with a palpable shrewdness. He was no fool in Agatha's estimation and she would deal with him accordingly.

He didn't stand up when they arrived at the table and there was no shaking hands. Rick was obviously too angry.

'What the hell were you thinking bringing this three-ring circus here?' he snarled at Goodman and Joel. The two men looked a little shame-facedly at the young American.

This was their introduction to Rick. He had a point: half the people in the café were looking at them. The other half were sleeping or dead. Agatha was regretting this meeting,

164

yet she knew that it was not something she could leave to Goodman alone.

'Let's leave,' said Agatha in a tone sharp enough to cause Rick's head to jerk in her direction. She spun around forcing her friends to do likewise. They marched quickly out of the café and around a corner. Moments later they were joined by the three men.

Outside the café Agatha turned her fire on Goodman. If it was possible for a man so large to shrink like wet wool then Goodman did so at that moment.

'What on earth were you thinking, Sidney? We may as well have advertised our presence through the agency of a billboard and a town crier.'

'You were the one that wanted to come here in the first place,' hissed Goodman, finding something approximating to manhood in response to Agatha's ire.

'Of course, Sidney. That's because I don't trust you, but, at the very least, I thought you would have the wit to have us meet in a quiet place. Instead, every cutthroat in town, unless they are complete dolts, will know that you are harbouring us,' retorted Agatha who was moving quickly away from the café, the others trailing in her wake.

'Hey Goodman,' said Rick caustically, 'the price has just gone up.'

Goodman was appalled at this. He spun around to the American.

'Why? You knew the danger before we met.'

'I don't care about the danger, Goodman. It's the two days in a boat with that dame,' said Rick, pointing to Agatha.

'Ahh, indeed,' yes I can see your point,' replied Goodman, who was now, against his better judgement and physical qualifications, jogging to keep up with Agatha as she made her way through the town's twisting labyrinth of streets. Joel had been relegated to the role of helping Sausage who was struggling up some steps.

The reached an alleyway that seemed to be quiet, so the group reconvened. The air crackled with angry censure. Rather than have Agatha make things worse, Betty put a hand up, thereby silencing the group.

'Right, I think we have to move beyond what's happened. Mr Rick. We will need to leave earlier than planned. We will inform Harry. Can we move the night after tomorrow? This will give Harry time to accomplish his task.'

Agatha nodded in approval. Rick glanced at Goodman and Joel then nodded.

'It's your money. Night after tomorrow. Best to leave at midday. The port is crowded. No better time for moving unseen.'

'The early hours would be better,' said Agatha.

'Police will expect that,' said Rick. 'You'll be on the boat and away before anyone knows what's happened.'

There was not just a certainty in his voice, but a clarity too that suggested once more to Agatha that he was not a fool.

'Who are you Mr Rick?' asked Agatha.

The American shrugged.

'Someone who's on your side. What else do you need to know?'

'More,' responded Agatha sharply.

'Fine. I gave up college to fight in your war. When it was over I decided to stick around. I won this boat in a poker game and I've used it to,' he paused at this moment before adding, 'transport things that make me a good living.'

'I can imagine what you transport,' said Agatha.

'Well maybe you can lady,' said Rick, 'but I wouldn't get too snobbish about it. I'm helping you and you're not exactly flavour of the month with the authorities here.'

'I don't deal in death Mr Rick.'

'Nor do I. I'm not interested in politics. I'm a boatman. I go where I'm paid to go. I take what I'm paid to take: guns, stolen goods, people who need to disappear. I'm the only cause I'm interested in. You should be glad I don't ask too many questions.'

Agatha, Betty and Sausage listened in sceptical silence which was broken only when Rick had finished.

'Well I think it's jolly rotten what you do,' said Sausage folding her arms to signify the matter was closed. They all turned to Agatha who had listened in a silence that a novelist might describe as stony.

'I think under that cynicism there might be a sentimentalist trying to escape.'

This brought a humourless smile from Rick.

'The only people trying to escape are you ladies and whether you like it or not I'm the only one who appears willing to help you,' replied Ricky dripping in the cynicism that Agatha had accused him of.

The group parted company soon after confirming their arrangements. Much to Agatha's frustration, they had to do

167

what Rick wanted. He held all the cards, a fact that he was not slow in letting them know.

They started back towards the villa. The arid heat was having an enervating effect on all of them. The streets, meanwhile, teemed with people who seemed impervious to the stultifying air. As they trooped through the streets, men looked at them in mute astonishment. Normally women walked behind men, but Agatha was leading the way.

They passed a stout middle-aged man seated in a wicker chair, one hand resting on a stick, smoking a cigarette in between hacking coughs. He cleared his throat seemingly from somewhere near Australia. The he expelled what he'd dredged up just in front of Agatha's feet, the sound was like a bullet ricocheting off a wall. This seemed to amuse him as he began to cackle before his laughter merged into more coughing.

Had Agatha been carrying her umbrella she might have put it to a non-weather-related use. Betty, however, was outraged and when she reached the man, she kicked away his stick causing him to fall over. A few people stopped and laughed at him. He was on his feet immediately snarling angrily at the group. This explosion of anger was silenced in a moment as Joel pushed him back onto his seat and then fished out his gun and pointed it as him as they went past. It's amazing how brave one can feel with a gun in one's hand: even an empty one.

The group proceeded onwards to the sound of much swearing which required little by way of translation such was the volume and vehemence with which it was expressed. Their arrival was greeted with joy by the lonely Mimi who had chewed up yet another cushion. This brought a similar, albeit lower volume response from Joel. His rant concluded with an exhortation to Agatha.

'Can't you do something about that animal?'

Agatha fetched him a withering look.

'Don't tempt me.'

They had a visitor in the early evening. It was the young artist Nassim who appeared to function as a messenger for Goodman and Joel. He had news of the case.

'I spoke to the policeman as you advised,' he said, grinning broadly. By this he meant he had bribed him with Agatha's money.

Nassim proceeded to relate all that had been disclosed to Kit and Mary and the nature of the locked room mystery: the names, country and profession of the suspects as well as a very well-drawn diagram of the two floors of the hotel.

Agatha studied the drawing commenting, 'This is an excellent piece of work, Nassim.'

The compliment brought another grin from the likeable young artist and just a hint of pride in Goodman's eyes. For a while now he had been considering a project using the young man which would combine Goodman's deep knowledge of art with the young man's evident talent. How many artists had visited Morocco over the years? Who was to say they had not left some work behind them that could be uncovered by a man of rare taste and insight?

Everyone studied the floorplan of the hotel with Agatha. None knew what they were looking for except her. None spoke. Agatha muttered some things under her breath and

169

shook her head from time to time. Betty, a long-time observer of Agatha's reaction to clues took this to be a bad sign. Finally, after around five minutes of studying the floorplans, Agatha looked up.

'Well?' asked Betty in a more succinct version of the question circulating in everyone's mind.

Agatha scanned the eager eyes of the room. Even Mimi was looking up at her expectantly although this may have had more to do with a forlorn desire to be fed a snack than any insight into the possibility of learning how the crime was committed.

'Well,' began Agatha, 'I'm fairly certain it was not suicide. I mean why would you shoot yourself in the chest. Why bother doing a day's work, come home and then put a gun to your chest? May as well do it first thing in the morning and get it over with.'

'Is that what you would do?' asked Joel drily, earning a stern look from Sidney Goodman.

Agatha ignored him and pressed on, 'No, it doesn't make sense. Oddly, I think the murderer knew this too. I don't think he or, indeed, she, cared. What I'm grappling with is one key question.'

'What's that?' asked Sausage, edging closer to the floorplan.

15

'Was Berrada actually killed in the room?' pondered Kit as he and Mary returned to the hotel where Berrada had met his end. They climbed out of the police car and walked past the alleyway and saw a Moroccan woman appear from the doorway at the end. She ushered a tradesman inside and then the door closed.

'I was wondering that too,' said Mary, 'but the key was in the door at the other side, and no one could have escaped from the room when the others arrived.'

They walked into the hotel lobby to find there was no one on reception. Mary was about to reach over to ring the bell when Kit stopped her. Mary was surprised by this; a frown appeared on her face along with a smile. It was a combination that Kit rather liked. He walked around the counter to the bank of keys hanging up on hooks on the wall. He lifted down the two keys to Berrada's room to inspect them. The two Mortice keys, rather like the hotel, had seen better days. One of them had a tiny hole in the wardle. Kit stared at it to see if it had been made by rust. He showed it to Mary.

'What do you think?'

'It's a hole,' confirmed Mary drily.

'Holmes, you amaze me,' replied Kit before replacing the key on its hook.

'What are you thinking?' asked Mary. 'I have to say, it was rather easy for you to take those keys. I imagine if Monsieur Moreau is not around...' she left the rest of the statement unfinished.

'I was thinking that too. Anyone could have gained access to his room.'

They waited at the reception for another minute before Moreau appeared from the direction of the kitchen. He smiled automatically at the new arrivals before apologising for keeping them waiting. This was waved away by Kit.

'Monsieur Durand returned fifteen minutes ago. I let him know that you would like to speak with him.'

'You're truly kind. Could you let him know we are here?'

Moreau went upstairs to find Durand while Kit and Mary returned to the seats they'd occupied earlier. As they waited, another tradesman appeared carrying two Moroccan hanging lamps made out of tinted stained glass with wrought iron metalwork. He stood in the reception, but without hitting the tiny bell.

'I wonder why he does that,' said Mary.

'Yes,' said Kit staring at the man. He was dressed in a pale off white djeballah with a red fez. 'I suppose it's not done for a tradesman to do this.'

'Perhaps it would be considered a tad peremptory given that the nature of the relationship is different,' suggested Mary.

A couple of minutes later, a man appeared alongside Moreau. Kit and the man looked at one another in shocked silence which confused the hotel owner and Mary. When

Moreau had recovered he said, 'May I present Monsieur Charles Durand.'

Kit stood up and shook hands with the young Frenchman. He was as tall as Kit, slender of build with dark hair, a thin moustache and a monocle which, in any work of fiction, betokens the murderer, even in romance novels.

'Monsieur Durand,' said Kit slowly.

Durand nodded, a half-smile on his face. He turned to Moreau and thanked him. The hotelier departed leaving Durand alone with Kit and Mary.

'Mary, let me present to you Monsieur Durand. The last time I met him his name was Thierry Simon. Should we call you Durand or Simon?'

'Whichever you prefer,' replied Durand-Simon in a low, amused voice. His English was only slightly accented.

'Very well, Durand will have to suffice. I don't want to ruin your cover. You are part of the French Secret Service I assume?'

'I'm afraid that is a conversation for another time, Aston. First though, may I congratulate you on your recent marriage,' at this point Durand bowed to Mary and kissed her hand. Mary smiled and looked at Kit with narrowed eyes. An explanation was due and in short order too.

'I met...Durand at the Paris Peace Conference. I was investigating the murder of a French diplomat. A friend of Spunky's was the chief suspect. Anyway, to cut a long story short, we met in a nightclub where Durand told me to stop investigating. I don't suppose that message will be any different here?'

The Frenchman laughed at this. He seemed more relaxed this time around or, perhaps, his opinion of amateur detectives from the English nobility had altered since their first meeting. This was confirmed moments later.

'Well, I will concede you were a little less of a fool than I had bargained for on the last occasion of our meeting.'

If not quite fulsome praise, coming from a spy and a Frenchman to boot, it bordered on adulation.

'So,' said Kit, pausing for a few moments to find the correct words, 'was it you or the French Secret Service for that matter who killed Inspector Berrada?'

Durand looked thoughtfully at Kit; the smile did not leave his face. Finally, he spoke in a tone that belied the amusement on his face.

'Inspector Berrada was a thug with little to recommend him as an officer of the law. His principle use to us was as a conduit to Raisuli. Are you familiar...?'

Kit gave a curt nod which Durand took to mean that he should continue. Mary looked on in fascination. Each new revelation only increased her fascination with the man she had married. It would probably take a lifetime to find out all there was to know. She would use every second of their time together to do so.

'Raisuli has never made any secret of his desire to rid the country of Europeans. Sometimes he collaborates with us, more often he does not. Now that he and Krim, you know he is stirring up trouble in the Rif Mountains, have fallen out, the government felt that we should take more of an interest in getting Raisuli on our side. Killing Berrada, a man who might be considered his friend, would hardly help

174

us, don't you think? The Spanish are too weak and, frankly, too inept to prevent a rebellion. I am over here to understand the situation and report back. I can assure you, Aston, murder is the last thing on my mind or that of our government.'

'But his death suits you,' responded Kit. It was not a question.

'Why do you say that?'

'If Berrada was a known agent of Raisuli who you say is a potential ally, then finding his killer might facilitate his trust in you.'

'That is one way of looking at it. A poor way, I think. Technically, Raisuli and the Rif are fighting against Spain even if they are not allies.'

'You will be next.'

'They have to defeat Spain first. We'll happily wait for the result of that contest before stepping in. No point in wasting French blood on a Spanish affair.'

'How supportive of you. The Spanish must thank their lucky stars each and every day to have chummed up with you in Morocco,' said Kit sardonically.

Durand made a mock bow, his smile widening. Mary decided that she did not like this man. There was an arrogance that bordered on contempt for those who had not had the good fortune to be born French. Kit was not finished however, 'It still does not mean the secret service were not involved in his murder.'

'I am not a killer,' said Durand, rising from his seat.

'Nor is my aunt,' said Kit.

175

This seemed to surprise Durand. He sat down again removing his monocle at the same time.

'Sorry, did I understand you correctly? Lady Agatha Frost is your aunt?'

There was something in the question that worried Kit, but he was now committed. He nodded his head.

'Interesting,' replied Durand, rising once more. 'I think the best thing for you is to leave Morocco, Aston. You are meddling, once more, in matters that do not concern you.'

Durand did not wait for a reply. He strode off in the direction of the stairs, leaving Mary mystified as to what she had just been witness to and Kit vaguely uneasy that his disclosure about Agatha had somehow made matters worse rather than better.

'So, can you enlighten me on what all that was about?' said Mary.

Kit sat back in the chair to reflect for a few moments before speaking.

'I met Simon or Durand, as he is at the moment, when I was in Paris. I didn't like him then and I can't say time has improved my impression of him. Arrogant fat head. Well, perhaps not fat head. I thought he was a diplomat back then, but it's clear he's part of the French Secret Service. It's possible he participated in Berrada's death and I'm sure he would not bat an eyelid if an innocent person were imprisoned.'

Mary was appalled. She asked rhetorically, 'How can anyone justify such a vile act?'

'National interest, Mary. You can justify a lot of things using national interest as a moral shield for your actions:

176

war, murder, blackmail, extortion. I've never been quite so convinced.'

Mary shook her head, 'Dreadful. Doesn't decency exist anymore?' The answer to this was a qualified 'yes,' but Kit remained silent.

The last of the hotel guests arrived at this point, Julien Lefevre. Before he could introduce himself he broke into a fit of coughing. When it passed he apologised. By tacit consent they did not shake hands. The memory of Spanish flu was too vivid to allow for such close contact. Lefevre was in his forties with a sallow complexion not enhanced by a wispy grey beard.

'You were in the lobby when you heard the shot fired I believe,' said Kit.

'Yes, I was just going into the dining room when I heard a gun being fired.'

'Did it come from upstairs?'

'I can't say, monsieur,' said Lefevre apologetically.

'You were out all day?' asked Kit.

'Indeed, I must have walked the length and breadth of the town,' said Lefevre before another fit of coughing interrupted him. Kit called for a cup of water from the passing Jabir. While the young Moroccan went to see to this, Lefevre picked up where he had left off.

'I am thinking of moving to Tangier. The climate will be good for my health. As you can hear, I have a cough that I just can't shake. I was looking at different areas where I could live.' He paused for a moment and appeared to become emotional. "I am a widower. I have no children. It wouldn't be a problem for me to move.'

177

Kit and Mary nodded sympathetically. They chatted for a few more minutes. Lefevre, because he had not entered the room, could add little to what had been reported about the body of Berrada.

After Lefevre had departed, Mary said, 'So we've spoken with everyone then?'

'Not quite,' said Kit. 'There's one other person we should see.'

In the background they heard Moreau talking to a woman. Kit rose from his seat which made Mary do likewise. They rounded the corner to see Moreau talking to an attractive woman who appeared to be Moroccan but was dressed in European clothes. It was the same woman Kit had seen earlier in the alley by the kitchen door.

'Monsieur Aston, may I introduce my wife Lina.'

Kit and Mary both shook hands with Madame Moreau. Her dark eyes bristled with fear and, if Kit was not mistaken, anger. He was unsure if both these emotions were directed towards him. He gave her the benefit of the doubt and decided, as men usually do, that a smile and boyish charm will overcome any difficulty when dealing with the opposite sex. In truth, experience had taught him that this was far from a full proof approach, but one of the most underrated traits of men is their indefatigable optimism when dealing with women to whom they are not married. Of course, the opposite is the case when faced with the steely eye and temporarily hardened heart of one's lifetime partner.

'Madame Moreau, may I compliment you on the wonderful Krachel we had earlier,' said Kit.

Mary, picking up on the hint, added with a broad smile, 'They were delicious, you must give me the recipe. We must have a meal here sometime, darling.'

In the face of such sustained flattery from two attractive young people, Madame Moreau relaxed a little. Kit tested the water a little bit more.

'We've finished questioning the suspects Monsieur Moreau so we will trouble you no further. I understand you were in the kitchen when the shot was fired Madame Moreau.'

The face of the Moroccan woman hardened a little.

'Yes,' she snapped.

'It must have been quite a shock,' said Mary.

Madame Moreau snorted, 'It was no shock.'

Mary had been referring to the sound of the weapon being discharged, but Madame Moreau had taken an altogether different interpretation.

'Why do you say that?' asked Kit.

'He deserved to die. He was a murderer; a pig,' snarled Madame Moreau. This outburst made her husband's eyes widen in alarm.

'My dear, you should not say such things,' said Moreau.

She turned on her husband in a manner that would be immediately recognisable to men around the world.

'What do you know Lucien? That man has tortured and killed. He was evil.'

'You knew someone that he killed?'

'One? Many. Do you know, I spat in his food everyday he was here.'

So much for dining at this hotel, thought Kit. Then another thought struck him. The odds against it seemed astronomical as much because of the passage of time as the fact that Berrada would have had many enemies over the years.

'Did you know many victims of Berrada?'

'Many,' snarled Madame Moreau.

'When did you first encounter the inspector?' asked Kit.

'I've only just met him,' said Madame Moreau. This was a disappointment to Kit, but then she added more, 'but I knew him from a long time ago. From when he first came here to Tangier with that animal Raisuli.'

'What happened?' asked Kit.

She exhaled a loud sigh.

'What do you do when the men who are meant to represent justice are, themselves, the criminals? I knew one girl who worked at the German Legation who was tortured and killed by Berrada on Raisuli's instructions.'

'When was this?'

Madame Moreau shrugged and shook her head.

'A long time ago when he first came.'

'Would it have been around 1905?' asked Kit.

'Yes, that seems right.'

'Did you know the girl?'

'No, but I knew of her family,' answered Madame Moreau, tears welling in her eyes at the memory.

'I'm sorry to upset you,' said Kit gently, 'but can you remember why she was killed by Berrada. This is important. Anything you can tell me is important.'

Madame Moreau took a deep breath. The memory of what had happened was clearly distressing. Lucien Moreau appeared uncomfortable at seeing his wife so upset. He was on the point of intervening when she held her hand up sharply.

'I'm not sure how much of this is true. I heard that she had passed secret papers in the German Legation over to the English. I don't know anything else other than that pig Berrada arrested her. She was dead a week later.'

At this Madame Moreau burst into tears. Kit nodded to Lucien Moreau who comforted his wife. They left the couple and went out into the heat of the early evening sun. Neither felt like speaking. Instead, they trooped sadly over to the waiting police car. Kit's gaze returned once more to the alleyway by the hotel. The policeman was still there. Then they were off back to their own hotel.

'He clearly made many enemies,' said Kit.

'That poor girl.'

Kit turned towards her and took her hand. He waited for Madame Moreau to regain her composure. It seemed to him this revelation was such an extraordinary coincidence.

'The young woman you mentioned. How did you know that she had passed on the papers.'

'We all knew. Such things do not stay secret long,' said Madame Moreau. She shook her head and began to sob once more.

16

Late afternoon and the Chief of Police, Colonel Emile Toussaint was sweating in every part of his body and there was a lot of body to sweat. Tangier was both a blessing and a curse to him. It was hotter than a restaurant oven at Mardi Gras; he had never liked the climate yet there was something about the country that he loved. That thing was slavery.

Morocco ignored the practice and many families in the city and certainly out in the country, where he rarely ventured, had slaves a-plenty. He reasoned that the slaves led a comfortable life compared to the cruel fate that often awaited the unfortunate, the sick and the poor in a country that appeared to have little value for life.

Toussaint was unmarried. He'd dreamed of finding someone to spend his life with and then he was posted to Morocco. A whole new world of possibility opened up that quickly confined the idea of matrimony to the youthful fancies of a naïve youth.

He had spent eighteen years in the country, boy and man. He would probably spend the rest of his life in the country like that effete Englishman, Walter Harris. He had never liked the journalist, too flamboyant, too egotistical, too mendacious, yet despite all this it was difficult to deny that he was a man very much like himself. They were unforgiving men in an unforgiving country that had beguiled them with possibilities denied them in their homeland.

Toussaint was in an unforgiving mood that early evening. Just as he had been on his way out of the office a message had reached him that had sent his temperature gauge surging like lava from a crater. His mood was volcanic, and someone was about to get covered from a great height.

'Captain Briant and Sergeant Raif are here,' said the fearful young policeman at his office door.

'Show them in,' snarled Toussaint. He had not liked the two men from the start. Too sure of themselves, too arrogant. They treated him like a country cousin rather than the Chief of Police that he was: their senior officer. He particularly disliked the young sergeant. When did the Sûreté become so desperate that they started letting his sort in? Standards were falling. What had become of his country? As much as he would have liked to send them packing, he knew that this was not possible.

Yet.

Briant and Raif entered the office. They saw Toussaint, his face red, his mouth twisted like car metal after a crash. Briant took a deep breath. He would need all his self-control when dealing with the martinet before him.

'You wanted to see us, sir?'

'Yes,' said Toussaint. His voice was a low rumble. 'I noticed that you were in the office a lot today. May I ask how this was helping to progress the Berrada murder case?'

This did not seem so bad, thought Briant, but he remained on his guard.

183

'We have been looking into the background of the suspects.'

'And?'

'Nothing unusual has turned up. No one has been remotely connected with crime and Durand, we know, is obviously not connected.'

'Good. So what you are saying is that we are no further forward.'

This was probably true and Briant did not like one bit the tone of mocking malevolence. He remained silent. Raif shifted uncomfortably in his seat. He, too, sensed that something was imminent. He did not have long to wait.

'I gather, though, the questioning of the suspects has been progressing while you have been here. Is this true?' Toussaint's tone remained controlled, almost amiable. It was anything but.

Briant had expected this. How could he not? He had intended for this to come up. Insofar as he had a plan, this was it.

'Can you explain to me,' began Toussaint, 'why we have delegated the questioning of suspects to someone who is not only outside the police, but an English nobleman?'

The last couple of words were spat out with a level of vitriol that impressed the man from the Sûreté. Such indignation was as impressive as it was amusing to him. What did this man know of anger and frustration? Sitting behind his desk, he resembled nothing more than a fat pig melting in the heat. Briant knew all about this man and what he knew disgusted him. He fixed his eyes on the Chief of Police and smiled benignly. As much as he would have

184

liked to, Briant decided it would not be a good idea to mention the driver from the police force that he had assigned to act as a taxi service for the English couple.

'I have had cause to work with this Englishman before on two cases. He is extraordinarily perceptive. I would place my trust in him cracking this case,' said Briant with a friendly equanimity.

Toussaint wasn't sure that cracking the case was either required or, indeed, advisable. The appearance of an investigation was surely sufficient. Who knows what might turn up if someone actually tried to find the killer? His face began to turn scarlet and, for a moment, Raif wondered if it would pop like a balloon.

'I don't care if this man is the bastard son of Sherlock Holmes,' screamed Toussaint causing flecks of spittle to bathe the two policemen like a light rain. 'There is only one thing I want you to do, and you will do it immediately.'

*

Las Gilipollas was a Flamenco bar near the port of Tangier. Although the town was Moroccan it was *de facto* under international control, principally the French. There was, however, a strong Spanish look and feel to the town owing to the town's proximity to the Iberian peninsula. Kit and Mary arrived at the bar and glanced at one another. There was a radiant vitality to Mary's face that drew attention to the mischief in her eyes.

'Are you sure?' asked the policeman who was acting as their driver. He motioned with his head towards the dark street lit only by the moonlight. Dark shadows were cast by the houses from which one could see eyes peering out.

Kit was certainly not sure. The back streets of Tangier, albeit near the port, were not ideal for tourists during the day never mind the night. All around them they sensed danger in the air. Leaning in dark doorways were men who seemed to be awaiting instructions on who they should kill next. Unseen dogs were barking out a conversation probably about the weather if they were anything like English dogs

'Walter always did like to mix in strange places,' commented Kit.

'He's certainly,' replied Mary before pausing a moment to find the right word, 'flamboyant. He reminds me of Rufus.' Rufus Watts was a police artist who had helped them on a number of cases.

They watched as two local men walked in their direction staring at the couple as if Kit and Mary had insulted their fathers' right to be described as such. Kit felt his muscles tensing up and he gripped his walking stick in both hands. In a moment it would become a small sword.

The two men walked past the couple; their eyes fixed on Mary. She drew her shawl more tightly around her. Further ahead, a group of men sat huddled together laughing mirthlessly like they were planning a surprise party for an enemy.

'Friends of yours?' asked Kit.

'Didn't we meet them at the Fitzrobbins' last year?'

They nodded to the policeman and walked towards the entrance of the bar. A large man dressed in a black djeballah stared ahead without acknowledging their presence. Descending the steps they entered into a large open room with two dozen tables circling a small floor. The tables were mostly filled with Europeans, although there were a handful of Moroccans too. In the middle of the floor were two people. A Spanish guitarist dressed in black, and a beautiful Flamenco dancer dressed in a low-cut red dress which remained decent by a gnat's whiskers. The stamp of her feet echoed through the bar, punctuated by occasional and rapid bouts of clapping.

Mary found the performance altogether compelling. Initially, she had thought the dancer quite young, but now she realised she was older than she'd first thought, but no less beautiful. She struck dramatically stiff poses and moved her hands in a series of intricate yet sensual movements. The dance ended, the applause breaking Mary's reverie. She felt a touch of her arm as Kit led her towards their dinner companion for the evening.

Seated right at the front, on his own, was Walter Harris. He, too, was dressed in the manner of the locals, wearing a white djeballah with a red belt. Harris rose to meet the couple, his face was serious, however.

'Is everything all right?' asked Mary, immediately picking up on his mood.

'Not entirely,' said Harris, inviting them to sit down. Just at that moment the dance finished, and he paused while the audience began clapping. Once they'd finished he leaned over towards the couple. 'Emily sends her apologies by the way. She won't be joining us. Aside from that, two pieces of news have reached me which are concerning to say the least. Firstly, the post-mortem on Berrada has confirmed what we already knew. It was murder. Forgive me Mary for being explicit, but there were no signs of powder burns near the wound or on the clothes. I gather this had already been noted, hence why the police have been treating the matter as murder.'

'Has the post-mortem only just taken place?'

'No, it happened two days ago, but the results have only just been released. Anyway, this is rather academic when I tell you the second piece of news.'

Kit and Mary leaned forward expectantly.

'I hear that Raisuli is in Tangier. Berrada and he grew up in the same village. As far as it's possible to be a friend of the man and I think I almost qualify in that regard,' said Harris modestly, 'Berrada would almost certainly have been one. This can only mean one thing.'

'He'll want revenge,' said Kit finishing the sentence.

'He'll want revenge,' confirmed Harris. 'I don't want to worry you, but I've known men who cross him end up with their head hanging off railings. If you're lucky you might just end up with white hot coins placed on your eyelids or a few fingers cut off.'

'A friend of yours you say?' said Mary with a smile.

Harris grinned back at Mary and admitted in a voice tinged with fond reminiscence, 'He kidnapped me once. Held me for a few weeks and then, when my paper and the government refused to pay a ransom, can't say I blame them by the way. He let me go.'

'What's he like?' asked Kit, fascinated.

'Cruel, capricious and charming in equal measure. He's barbaric, but not a barbarian if that makes any sense? Lord knows it doesn't to me, yet I can't quite describe him in any other way. He's dangerous, utterly unfair in a fair sort of way and likes chess. Perhaps you could give him a game sometime, Kit.'

'What if I beat him?'

'He's not much good so unless you've lost your edge old boy you'll certainly do that. I'm not sure what he would do. You may end up returning home on a different boat from your manhood.'

'I'd let him win,' said Mary.

'Well, I suppose I'm not the player I once was,' acknowledged Kit.

'You wouldn't be the man you were either if you beat him,' chortled Harris.

They settled down to watch the next performance. Two Spanish dancers glided onto the floor in bright red and green dresses with black and white fringes. Each had castanets on their fingers. In the shadows the guitarist began to pick out a melody and soon the two ladies were swaying to the music while punctuating it with their percussive fingers. They gazed in silent appreciation of the dancers until the end of their performance. Warm applause greeted them as they disappeared from the floor.

'Have you heard from your man, Kit?'

'Yes,' replied Kit. 'He sent us a message earlier at the hotel this afternoon. I think, it best if we remain apart for the time being. He met with Aunt Agatha and the others. It sounds as if they are up to no good.'

Kit went on to explain the contents of the message including the part about robbing them of a painting.

189

'What painting?' asked Harris. 'I know that Tangier has often had visitors from the art world. I suppose it's possible one of them left behind a valuable painting.'

'Yes, he didn't say,' admitted Kit.

'Pity. Perhaps it's a Matisse or a Delacroix. I met Sir John Lavery a few times. Nice chap,' said Harris. 'He did a couple of paintings of me.'

'We don't have the artist's name, but we do have an address; no name for who lives there. I don't suppose you can find out?' asked Kit, scribbling an address down on a piece of paper from a notebook.

Harris glanced at the address.

'It's on the edge of town, but I've no idea who lives there. Leave it with me. So, tell me what you found out today,' asked Harris.

They ordered some food and then Kit took Harris through what they had learned from the interviews. When he'd finished he asked Harris if he'd met any of the suspects.

Harris said, 'No, police won't let me near the hotel. I can't say any of the names mean much to me. Interesting, though, about Monsieur Durand or Simon. That does put another complexion on the case. I wonder if Briant is aware of him.'

'Briant is certainly aware of him. He knew that I would recognise Durand and that he would know me.'

'So why not tell you in the first place?' asked Harris.

Kit looked thoughtful about this point.

'I shall have to ask him. Briant is no fool. He would not have kept it a secret without good reason. Perhaps, and I

190

am surmising here, he wanted to shake the tree a little and see what falls down. Maybe the French Secret Service did kill Berrada, but I can't see it myself. Nor, I think does Briant. If I were to hazard a guess, I think that he's using me to warn Durand.'

'About what?' asked Mary and Harris in unison.

'I don't know. There's something else at play here but I just can't put my finger on it. I suspect Briant can't either. Perhaps he's trying to extract more from Durand. As to what that is, we'll have to find out one way or another. I have a feeling that my telling him that my aunt was involved may backfire, but it's too late now to worry about that.'

Large copper plates arrived on the table each with steaming, saffron-infused paella. The meat was swimming in so much fat, Kit felt his arteries harden as he looked at it. He tried a piece. It was delicious. The conversation continued as they ate. Harris updated them on the ongoing conflict in the Rif mountains, which had heated up since the start of July.

'I've been hearing that the war is not going well for Silvestre and the Spanish. Can't say I'm surprised. Silvestre is an impetuous fool. Never liked him. Ridiculous moustache.'

'It sounds as if he'd have been at home in Flanders. We had a few of those too. Is Raisuli involved in this?'

'No, this is mainly Abd-el-Krim. Raisuli is somewhat jealous of him, I gather. He's younger and a more astute general. I wouldn't be surprised if Raisuli wants to throw his lot in with the Spanish or the French.'

'I thought he wanted them out.'

'He does, but don't forget, he's no longer a young man. He's ill, I understand. I think he'll settle for power under the foreigner if he can't expel them himself and, between you and me, he's admitted how difficult this would be anyway. That said, he's been known to play both sides. It would be right up his street to fall in with the Spaniards while facilitating arms supplies to the Rif. He certainly is complicated.'

Towards the end of their meal, a waiter came and handed Kit a message. They looked at one another in surprise then Kit opened the note. He spent a few seconds reading it and then he glanced up to the others.

'It's from Briant.'

He handed the note over to Mary who read it. Alarm spread over her face. She handed the note to Harris.

'Interesting,' was the only comment from Harris.

Mary took Kit's hand and without any obvious trace of fear asked in a matter-of-fact voice, 'What shall we do?'

Part 2: Add Spice

17

Tangier: 8ᵗʰ July 1921

The latest day of their 'captivity' saw the three ladies rise early as usual, don their niqabs, take their life in their hands on the stairs and head to a nearby café for breakfast. All this took place while their two captors slept in their respective rooms. This uncommon arrangement had long since ceased to be a subject of conversation. By now the only enemies they faced were boredom and the heat.

This was about to change.

On this morning, having returned from their breakfast, Agatha gazed idly at Betty who was practicing her golf swing. It was a persistent grumble of her great friend that Morocco was bereft of any decent courses which, in her book, was a mark against any claim it should make towards being a civilised country. Agatha's comment that the development of railroads was more important was invariably rebuffed by the twelve handicapper. She had added a few strokes over the years or perhaps was simply managing her handicap upwards to improve her chances in competitions.

Looking at Betty swing a broomstick Agatha suspected age was beginning to tell on the once mighty heaves that rendered holes a drive and a wedge. Her friend's swing had a certain jerkiness to it that had not been the case in her younger days when it was more free flowing. Time and additional pounds had gradually reduced its aesthetic qualities while increasing its brutal effectiveness.

Sausage, meanwhile, was lying on a makeshift bed reading a well-thumbed book by her favourite author. This was the third time she had read it. The novel in question was '*Bellmop Comes Over Queer*' by Ivor Longstaff. It had proved a popular read for the three ladies.

'I'm still not sure I understand the "why" at the end of the book even though I read it a couple of times,' commented Sausage. As much as she enjoyed detective books, the ending sometimes stumped her.

'Most detective books are a bit like that these days,' replied Betty mid-swing before following through. 'I'm not complaining. I suppose writing one can't be easy; always having to produce a new, ingenious crime and he writes two or three a year. Would you prefer one book per year that had been slaved over to within an inch of its life or would you rather get your hands on a Longstaff several times a year?'

'I suppose deep down, I'd like to have several Longstaffs every year,' agreed Sausage.

'My thoughts exactly,' agreed Betty.

Something about the conversation troubled Agatha, but she could not quite put her finger on it. Her mind was on the murder of Berrada. It was frustrating to have so little to go on. She needed to meet Kit and discuss the crime in more detail; little was being accomplished by their unenforced captivity.

'Aren't Sidney and Joel up yet?' asked Agatha. As prison guards went, they were an unfortunate combination of laxity and idleness. Neither quality recommended itself in a gaoler.

As she said this, she heard the sound of the front door being rapped loudly. Moments later, Joel shouted a few words in Arabic that the ladies took to be rather uncomplimentary about their visitor. Much to his credit and the evident admiration the ladies, Joel kept up the string of invective all the way down the stairs as he made his way to the door.

The ladies remained silent as the door being unbolted and opened. Frustratingly, they could hear little of what was being said. Footsteps up the stairs followed. Agatha felt her heart quicken. By the looks on the faces of Betty and Sausage they were equally concerned. Moments later they heard Sidney Goodman's voice.

'What on earth?' he exclaimed.

This was followed by silence.

The floorboard outside the door creaked. Agatha's mouth was now dry, and she knew that, for the first time, she was feeling fear.

The door opened. Goodman then Joel tripped into the room followed by the one of the most uncommon sights that either Agatha or the other ladies had ever seen. It was a woman wearing a black dress and a Hijab which covered her hair and neck but revealed her face. The woman was well over six feet tall and built like an Olympic shot putter.

She was square shouldered with large, powerful hands at the end of enormous arms that could wrestle a gorilla into submission, but this isn't what astonished the ladies.

One eye stared stonily ahead while the other scanned the room like a meerkat who has heard the coyotes are in town. Her mouth had an aggressive slant that suggested she would be particularly immune to Agatha's level of imperiousness. Agatha was caught between pride at meeting such a deadly incarnation of their species and quailing at the prospect of seeing first hand just how destructive she might be in deploying her formidable gifts.

'This is Fatima,' said a voice from somewhere behind the female mountain. The accent was French and dangerously familiar to Agatha.

A man stepped, quite literally, out of Fatima's shadow. He was tall, very good-looking in the French way and dressed in a linen suit with powder blue tie.

'Agatha, how lovely to see you again,' said the man.

'I wish I could say the same,' replied Agatha. Silence followed this riposte from Agatha and then Betty cleared her throat and raised her eyebrows in expectation of some enlightenment.

Realising that Betty and Sausage were owed an explanation and possibly an apology for getting them into this mess, Agatha said, 'May I introduce Comte Jean-Valois du Bourbon. I had the misfortune to meet him last year on the Aquitaine when we sailed to America and then once more in San Francisco. If you remember, I told you about the unfortunate conclusion to the episode concerning the Caravaggio. This is the man who dispossessed us.'

'Bounder,' said Sausage. This was the worst description in Sausage's, admittedly limited, lexicon of insults. Betty as a golfer of long-standing had at her command, access to a richer seam of abuse and proceeded to fire away with both barrels. This was greeted with a smile by the Frenchman, a scowl from Fatima who may not have understood the meaning, but suspected it was not complimentary and it also served to wake the sleeping Mimi.

The Doberman was on her feet in a moment, ears pricked to full Satanic mode, and she began barking.

Bourbon glanced in panic towards the dog. He raised his gun and pointed it at Mimi. If anything is designed to earn the censure of a freeborn Englishwoman then it is the mistreatment of animals, particularly dogs. Betty's tirade reached its apex in volume and intensity of invective.

Mimi hopped down from the seat and rushed towards the Frenchman. Fatima, one eye on the dog, the other on goodness-knows-what, stepped backwards. Despite her Amazonian proportions, she did not fancy fighting a Doberman with a foul temper. Help was at hand, or in the hand to be more precise. Bourbon stepped forward reluctantly.

'Arrêtez!' shouted the Frenchman in panic that he might actually have to discharge his revolver.

A word about Mimi. That word is 'French.' The Doberman's previous owner was a French officer of dubious moral character. Agatha had adopted the dog after the conclusion of her most recent case in Monte Carlo. When Mimi heard the instruction coming in French, her second language, she immediately skidded to a halt a foot away from the gun.

Bourbon looked in astonishment from the animal to Agatha and back again.

'*Assis-toi,*' said Bourbon. Mimi sat down and panted up at Bourbon. Without taking his eyes off the Doberman or, for that matter, his gun, Bourbon asked Agatha. 'Lady Frost, have you really trained your dog to understand French?' There was no mistaking the admiration in his voice, the pride. Most Frenchmen cannot understand why the world has not taken the one-time *lingua franca* of diplomacy and extended the idea so that it became the global language rather than English; God had put the English on an island and who were they to question the logic of such a move?

'I'm impressed Lady Frost, I really am. May I ask why?'

'It's a long story,' said Joel in a tired voice.

'We must go now,' said Bourbon, waving his revolver in the direction of the door.

'Do you mind if I pay a visit?' asked Goodman sheepishly. 'My bladder is the size of Andorra at the moment.' It was odd given a life spent involved with murder theft and now kidnapping that Goodman retained enough sense of Englishness to be faintly embarrassed at admitting he needed to visit the toilet. Bourbon looked confused while Agatha merely rolled her eyes. Goodman noticed this and said, 'No need to be like that. It's no fun aging.'

'Try going through menopause,' said Agatha.

'Try having a prostate,' retorted Goodman irritably. He lumbered towards the bathroom while Bourbon sat down on a nearby chair with something of a thump.

'Does anyone else need to go?' asked Bourbon.

'Actually, I need to go as well,' said Sausage.

'Glad you came?' asked Agatha, sardonically to the Frenchman.

'It wasn't my idea, believe me, Lady Frost,' replied Bourbon in a tired voice. It was barely nine in the morning, and he was already feeling the strain. This was going to be a long few days at this rate.

Agatha turned sharply towards the Frenchman. She fixed a steely eye on him and inquired, 'Whose was it?'

Bourbon did not answer, but the mirthless smile suggested that they would not find the answer a reassuring one. As soon as Sausage and then Betty had availed themselves of the facilities, a point had been reached when both Bourbon and Agatha would have happily given the venture up as a bad job.

'Now can we go?' asked Bourbon in a whining voice that Agatha unexpectedly had some sympathy for. No one spoke so Bourbon took this to mean they could leave. Everyone stood up, including Mimi.

'Not the animal,' said Bourbon.

'What do you mean?' retorted Agatha. 'You can't just leave her here on her own.'

'I can,' said Bourbon, pushing first Joel out the door and then Goodman. The ladies followed with only minimal prompting from Fatima. This was Mimi's cue to start barking. Bourbon picked up a small object and threw it to

201

the corner of the room. Taking this to mean the start of a new game, Mimi immediately went to retrieve it. It was only when she heard the door closing behind her that she realised she had been duped. She howled in protest, ran to the open window. There was no sign of her friends. She ran to the door and began to scratch underneath the doorknob. Desperate now, she ran to the window again.

And jumped out.

She landed on a terracotta roof feet below the window. The tiles gave way under feet, and she began to slip down. Aware that she was losing her balance, the Doberman began to panic. The more she tried to scramble back up the roof the worse was the grip for her paws. She was now sliding unhindered towards the edge of the roof.

Below was a forty-foot drop.

18

Harry Miller stared once more at the brief note from Agatha. It had been brought to him the previous evening by Nassim. The robbery had to take place that night. This was not much time to organise what he would need. Luckily, he had enough money to cover the expenses that he would almost certainly incur, and he knew where to find what he needed thanks to a combination of his own reconnaissance and the help of the enthusiastic Nassim.

Despite having "retired" from the profession of his youth before the War, Miller had, from time to time, been forced by circumstances and the rather unusual life he led with Kit Aston, to keep his hand in. As a result, he had lost little by way of knowledge, confidence or physical capability when it came to the commission of burglary. Furthermore, without having to confront a safe, one of the greatest risks to a burglar was immediately removed: the time required to spend at the scene. Added to this was a sense that the local police force was unlikely to pose many of the problems he would face if he were back in England.

Young Nassim was also proving a worthwhile addition to the project. The young man was full of enthusiasm and was proving no small help. In particular, he was able to furnish a getaway vehicle on the evening; a caleche belonging to his cousin.

Overall, as Miller stared out of his hotel window which gave him a panoramic view of the Mediterranean, he was feeling quietly confident that the task before him was achievable. Having bathed and shaved, he was ready to face the latest project in his on-off crime career.

Nassim was waiting for Miller in reception. He had become a *de facto* guide for Miller which was welcome. They had breakfast at a café near the hotel then Nassim led Miller towards the villa on the edge of town. At Miller's insistence, they walked. He did not want to leave anything to chance. Familiarising himself with the route to and from the villa was an added layer of reassurance. Acquiring this knowledge now meant he could focus everything on breaking in, securing the painting and exiting as quickly as possible.

'Collect me at two o'clock in the morning outside the cafe,' suggested Miller as they walked along a narrow street which was thronged with men and small stalls along either side. The noise was deafening, and Miller had to shout to make himself heard.

Nassim nodded enthusiastically. He was enjoying the experience of working with the Europeans. They treated him well and paid even better. Perhaps one day he would fulfil his dream and go to Paris. All of the great artists went there. It was the home of so many great new movements. He wanted to be a part of the extraordinary creative impulse that had characterised the last ten years in the city.

The walk up to the villa through the backstreets of Tangier took fifteen minutes. Miller was the only European on these streets which made him feel a little self-conscious although there was no sense of threat. Perhaps he would feel differently in the middle of the night if he were on foot.

They wound their way around past the Kasbah and further up to the edge of town. The square outside the villa was full of traffic; an odd Moroccan combination of horse-drawn caleches, bicycle taxis and motor cars with drivers that used the horn as a communication device and that communication was an uncomplimentary assessment of other peoples' driving.

When they arrived in the square, they parted company. Miller wanted to sit in a café situated on the square to think about what lay ahead. They would not see each other again until two in the morning.

The square was crowded with caleches, motor vehicles and people blissfully unaware of road safety. Miller looked on amused as some Rif women remonstrated with a European in an open-topped car. The argument escalated as a man who appeared to run a stall selling caged dogs and birds became involved for no obvious reason aside from boredom.

Miller took his seat at the café he'd been to the previous day. There were a number of Europeans there as well as wealthy locals. All were sitting outside at tables which had umbrellas to provide shade. It was mid-morning now; the air was hot, and Miller was finding it close to unendurable. He ordered lemonade and stared out at the villa. To his left on a nearby table, he sensed a man and a woman, both in their sixties, were taking an undue interest in him. Miller wondered if they were messengers from Kit or Agatha.

Unsure of what he should do, he waited for them to approach.

While he waited he focused his attention on the villa. He had already committed to memory the plan created by Nassim. Further questioning had given him a good picture of the interior of the villa. By two in the morning, the streets would be quiet in this part of the town. He would be free to scale the wall at the back of the villa and enter through the storeroom at the side of the house. Its inner door was never locked, and it was at the furthest point from the bedrooms. Critically, one of the iron bars of the storeroom covering the window was loose. It could be pried out from its hole allowing enough room for Miller to squeeze through.

As he was going through how the robbery could be achieved, he saw two large cars draw up outside the villa. He sat forward. This was not good. No burglary was without risk. If these cars contained reinforcements then it would make it almost impossible. He stared at the cars waiting to see who would emerge.

'Good Lord,' said a male voice from the other table.

Miller had to restrain himself from putting it more strongly than that. Across the square he saw, first, Agatha and then Betty and Sausage emerge from the cars without any attempt made to disguise who they were. Two men followed. One was large with grey hair, the other much smaller, younger and Moroccan in appearance. Following them were a couple of men and one extraordinary woman who looked big enough to give Jack Dempsey something to consider.

'What on earth?' said the woman nearby, but Miller no longer cared. He was on his feet now and walking out of the café. Agatha seemed under no duress and Miller doubted that anyone kidnapping her would really be in control. Still, the appearance of the Amazonian woman did not augur well in Miller's view.

Just then a man stepped in front of him. Although Miller did not know, he was dressed in a Berber costume consisting of a faded red cloth which was wrapped around his head like a turban and an ankle-length tunic. Miller was about to introduce the man to a very Anglo-Saxon slant on the English language when he felt something cold and sharp press into his stomach. Two other men appeared on either side of Miller; each man grabbed an arm.

There was little Miller could do. He saw in the distance Agatha and the others enter into the villa. Whatever plans they'd had were now up in smoke. As much as he wanted to shout, it was too great a risk. He relaxed his body and allowed the three men to lead him away from the square towards a caleche at the corner of the square. Miller was pushed onto the carriage; the three men followed him swiftly. No word was spoken. What was there to say?

Miller knew he was their prisoner and nothing in the expressions of the three men suggested that mercy was a word in their dictionary. Each man had a beard, dark eyes which flashed with the promise of violence. These were hard men. Warriors. They had fought battles, had known fear and in all probability had faced or inflicted death.

Then again, so had he.

Oddly, he felt the heat more than fear. Within a few minutes they were heading up the hill and out of the town. They were obviously taking him somewhere to meet someone, otherwise his death would have occurred before now.

The carriage picked its way up the mountain overlooking Tangier until the sea was no longer in view. They finally reached a plain surrounded by crags. Miller saw a small encampment with a dozen or so men, horses and a couple of campfires. He counted seven tents; one of the tents was at least three times the size of the others. Most of the men had rifles on their back as if they were expecting trouble any moment. They weren't going to get it from Miller.

A strange silence descended on the camp as the carriage rode through. Men stopped what they were doing, which wasn't very much, to come and gaze upon the prisoner.

When the carriage halted, the three men jumped down. One of them went into the large tent. It was around thirty feet long with no sides. It looked to Miller to be made from Camel hair. Another of the men motioned impatiently for Miller to come down. His mind was racing now. So was his heart. His head began to swim a little with this and the heat.

Uppermost in his mind was what they intended for him. They obviously wanted *something*. He'd read reports about how kidnapping Europeans had once been popular. To his knowledge most had been returned safely, following the payment of a ransom.

Miller jumped lightly onto the ground and waited for his next instruction. He wasn't long in waiting. The instruction took the form of shove in the back towards the large tent. Miller stumbled inside. The interior of the tent smelled of stale incense it reminded Harry of when he used to go to Saint Mary's church. It was surprisingly light. The floor was covered in carpets and cushions upon which sat three men, all dressed in dark robes with black headscarves. The sense of menace surrounding them was enhanced by their dark beards and angry eyes. Only one of the men was seated. He looked enormous. His face was bloated and seemed to be fighting a losing battle with gravity; his breathing was so laboured it sounded like it was coming from another room. Oddly, this made Miller relax a little. Moments later powerful hands threw him to the ground.

'Kneel before Raisuli,' said a voice in French.

Raisuli.

Miller had heard the name before. He remembered a long time ago hearing about the kidnapping of the American that had almost caused a war between the mighty United States and Morocco. At the hotel he had overheard a couple of men speaking about the fighting in the mountains.

Yet the man before Miller seemed anything but a lion of the desert. He looked ill, enervated by the heat or, perhaps, a life on the run, at war with the world just to survive. He stared down at Miller who had remained on the ground thanks to a heavy hand that kept him there. Finally, Raisuli spoke. His voice was rich and musical; it defied his blurred features. A man beside him translated into French.

'Who are you?'

'Harry Miller. I'm English.'

The response was translated, and then other questions followed.

'Why are you here?'

'Vacation.'

'You are lying. Why are you here?' snarled the translator who seemed to be caricaturing his master.

'I've always wanted to see Morocco.'

This caused an angry outburst from the large man. He rose to his feet with his fists clenched.

'Why were you standing outside the villa of Comte Bourbon?'

The translator's voice belied the anger of his master and was all the more dangerous for doing so. Miller knew now that his life was in danger. Hands seemed to claw at his chest and his breathing became even more laboured, but he was angry now also. He remained tight-lipped. Then Raisuli seemed to wave his hand in dismissal. He said something to the translator.

'Cut off his fingers,' said the translator. 'He'll talk then.

Miller felt two sets of hands pull him up from the floor and drag him outside. Each of the men was powerfully built and grabbed his arms. He struggled, but to no avail. Outside the heat was unbearable. The back of Miller's shirt was soaking with perspiration. A gag was placed around Miller's mouth. It was tied so tightly it seemed as if it would decapitate him.

A man clutching a scimitar approached Miller. He began to struggle more wildly but was once more thrown to the ground. His hand was placed on a rock.

Miller wanted to scream, but his throat was too dry. He kicked out, desperate, but the two men sat on his legs. He was trapped. His chin was scraping against the rocky ground and all he could see was a pair of sandals housing calloused feet. Red light filtered through his closed eyes as he waited for the sword to fall.

19

Kit lay on the bed and watched Mary change into her dress. It may have been his imagination, but she seemed to be spending an inordinate amount of time on this activity. There were worse ways to spend a morning he supposed. There was an air of expectancy in the room following the note they had received at the restaurant last night.

'So who killed Berrada?' asked Mary, fixing onto Kit's eyes which were directed elsewhere on her person. Aware that she was looking at him, he glanced up and smiled sheepishly.

'I believe it's allowed. We're married,' he pointed out.

'Answer the question.'

Kit was silent for a few moments before replying, 'Not a clue.' Mary made a face at this.

'Who do you think?'

Mary wandered over to the window which gave a wonderful view of the port. People were boarding the ferry for Marseilles. Alongside the ferry were two small tugboats being loaded with coal. The white sails of small boats looked like pearls cast out onto blue satin. She turned back to Kit and said, 'I suppose one should always go for the least likely suspect.'

'Who is?'

'They are,' corrected Mary, 'The Friedmans. Which is a pity because I rather like them. Monsieur Lefevre too, poor man.'

Kit nodded and said, 'Yes, I did too. What about our friend Durand?'

'Too obvious.'

'Why do you say that without lapsing into a rationale that would be laughed at on the pages of a detective novel.'

'The monocle is always suspicious, darling.'

'True. No evil doer is complete without one, but if, for a moment, we assume that it is not the arrogant, monocle-wielding Frenchman, what about Keller?'

'Motive?' asked Mary.

'Yes, I rather struggle there.'

'We're also struggling on how the murder was committed,' added Mary.

Kit remained silent on this point. He rose from the bed and joined Mary by the window. Outside the room they heard a clatter of feet ascending the stairs. By the sound of the voices they were the male of the species and decidedly French. They were also familiar. Kit and Mary exchanged glances.

There was a loud knock on the door. Rather too loud. It felt as if someone was putting on a show.

'Yes?' said Kit, walking towards the door.

'Police,' said the voice. 'Open up.'

Kit did not recognise the voice, but its tone did not suggest that a recommendation on local restaurants to visit was not imminent. Kit turned to Mary and smiled, then he opened the door.

Standing in the corridor were three men, one of whom was Briant and two uniformed policemen, one of whom was dressed in the manner of a senior officer. It was he who spoke first.

'Am I addressing Lord Kit Aston?'

'Yes,' smiled Kit and waved his arm to invite the men in. 'This is my wife, Mary,' added Kit in a tone of voice that suggested they had just met up for Cocktails at the Savoy.

'My name is Colonel Toussaint. I am the Chief of Police in Tangier. I have come to tell you that your stay in Tangier must end today. You do not have the correct visa.'

'Correct visa? Of course we do,' responded Kit.

'You do not; you must leave, this morning,' replied Toussaint sharply.

'I am sure if there is a problem with my visa then it can be easily sorted at the British Legation,' pointed out Kit, reasonably. This point was evident. What was the point of having a British Legation otherwise? Yet, Kit sensed that this point was unlikely to carry the day if the French colonel's red-faced fury was any guide. The colonel's posture was now stiffer than his moustache, no mean feat in Kit's book.

'Look here, captain, sorry I've forgotten your name,' said Kit. He saw Briant quickly hide a smile. In fact, the other policeman did so too. The colonel was not loved by his men, it seemed.

'It's colonel. Colonel Toussaint,' roared Toussaint.

'Well, look here Toussaint, you can't just break in here and tell us what we can and can't do. We're English, don't you know?' When called upon, Kit could play to the hilt the role of arrogant Englishman.

Toussaint's eyes widened, almost in pleasure. He was going to enjoy every second of this. The English were barbarians in his book. One only had to look at the food they ate. One certainly wouldn't choose to taste it.

'I am the Chief of Police, and I can assure you Aston, I do have the power to send you and your wife back to where you came from. Your Legation cannot sort this out. No, you must sort the problem out when you arrive in France. We will accompany you to the port. Pack your bags now and leave.'

All of this was said in a voice trying to control its anger or its pleasure. It was difficult to decide how much of it was acting, how much genuine. On balance, Kit decided the former. Throughout all of this, Briant had said nothing, merely smoking a cigarette. Mary turned to him and said, 'I didn't know you smoked.'

'I don't,' said Briant rolling his eyes.

'I see,' said Mary, smiling now.

Half an hour later having earlier gazed at the passengers boarding the ferry bound for Marseilles, Kit and Mary found themselves walking up the gangplank. The ferry had been held up to allow for the arrival of the English couple. As soon as they boarded, the gangplank was removed.

Standing at the side of the dock were the three policemen and two police cars that had transported the group to the port. The group remained there as the tugboat

215

pulled the ferry away from the quay. Kit and Mary stood on the deck and stared back at the policemen. Briant waved ironically to the couple much to Toussaint's evident irritation. This amused Mary so she waved back. So did Kit. With his white handkerchief. It seemed symbolic to Briant and was certainly taken as such by a gleeful Toussaint.

Soon the ferry was clear of the port, and it began to sail out into the Med under its own steam. Satisfied that the English couple were no longer in Tangier, Toussaint turned to Briant with a scowl.

'If I have my way, you will be on the next boat along with that pup of yours.'

Briant saluted him and walked off towards a café. He ignored the sound of Toussaint shouting at him. 'That's a promise, Briant. You'll be next.'

Part 3: Stew

20

Mimi's attempts at avoiding falling onto the street succeeded only in dislodging half a dozen tiles of the roof. The forty-foot drop beckoned to the terrified Doberman and duly she fell down, down yelping all the way. Onto a passing cart carrying cushions and carpets. This softened her landing somewhat and meant she would live to see another day. She clambered up onto her feet and leapt down from the cart, causing a couple of women to scream in fright at the sight of the black shape bounding towards them.

It took a few moments for her to gain her bearings and then it dawned on Mimi that she was alone in the world in a place that was thoroughly alien to her. This was only ever going to provoke one reaction and Mimi duly obliged. She stood in the middle of the street and began to howl for all she was worth. Men and women stopped to stare at the distraught Doberman. It was an uncommon sight.

A child, a young boy, taking pity on the poor beast, strolled over and began to stroke Mimi which quietened her briefly. Then the child was yanked away by a mother who proceeded to reprimand him in manner that would ensure the young boy would avoid showing any kindness towards animals in future.

Mimi stood in the street and watched as people took care to give her a wide berth. Any canine conjecture as to what to do next was suddenly interrupted and the decision taken out of her hands.

Bemused by her brush with death and abandonment, she did not hear the soft tread of a man behind her. One moment she was about to begin howling again, the next a bag had been placed over her head and she was manhandled into a cage. All was dark and nothing made sense. Terror gripped her and she fought fiercely to free herself, but the cage was small, and the door was well and truly locked. Soon she felt herself being hoisted up and set down on a cart.

Ten minutes later, the rocking of the cart stopped, and she felt the cage being lifted up again then set down. A moment later the bag over her head was removed. She began barking in a manner that suggested displeasure at her rather rough treatment. No one was listening. She stopped for a moment to look around her. There were other cages. Most seemed to contain other four-legged creatures like herself. They all began to bark a greeting to the new arrival.

Mimi joined them.

*

If Mimi's dander was up then it was no less than that of the three ladies who appeared to have exchanged gaolers and not for the better either, despite the superior nature of their new accommodation.

They walked through the gates of the villa into a courtyard with a small fountain and tall cypress trees that stabbed the blue sky. Jasmine and geranium fought one another for attention around the walls of the villa. It was quite beautiful, and the fragrance might have been a pleasant distraction from the arid heat had the ladies not been quite so dismayed by the turn of events.

Fatima led the group inside towards a set of stairs. The interior was sparsely furnished with wooden furniture. There were no pictures on the wall and no flowers. It was altogether a very male décor.

'You must have spent all of ten francs on the furniture,' observed Agatha drily. Bourbon smiled at this but did not rise to the bait. They went up a set of stairs that were distinctly safer than the ones in their previous accommodation. Agatha made a point of raising her eyebrows in approval to Goodman. He too understood that Agatha was making a point about the house from which they had been taken. He ignored her also.

The room they were taken to was around twenty-five feet square and without a window. There was no furniture, only a dozen cushions or so on which to rest weary bodies.

'Couldn't you afford some seats?' asked Betty archly.

'You won't be here very long,' replied Bourbon cryptically.

This did not augur well and succeeded in quietening any potential mutiny brewing amongst the captives.

'What will you do with us?' demanded Agatha, turning to Bourbon, hands on hips. She felt partially responsible for the trouble they were in. This guilt extended, she realised to her amazement, towards Goodman and Joel.

'That is not for me to decide.'

220

This brought a frown from Agatha. While she had no reason to trust Bourbon, she had never felt any real threat from him either. The memory of their time on the **RMS** Aquitaine had shown him to be a gentleman, albeit a crooked one. There was little sense of genuine malevolence in him. He made everything seem like a game. That he was deferring to someone else was not good. Agatha wondered who this might be.

Five minutes later she found out.

Bourbon left the room with Fatima on fixed point duty by the door. She sat down by the door and stared implacably ahead with one eye while the other looked around at her hostages. It was disconcertingly compelling.

'Who is this man?' asked Betty in a voice that was trying and failing to suppress its sense of anxiety.

Agatha explained the brief history she had shared with Bourbon from their meeting on the ocean liner through to the moment he had dispossessed them of the painting by Caravaggio.*

'I wonder who he means,' said Agatha out loud after she had concluded the story.

'Who?'

'Bourbon. There's someone else here.'

Betty knew her friend was not one to fret over things beyond her control, but she sensed an edge. Agatha became aware of her friend's eyes on her.

'I'm sorry dear. I've really put us in a bit of a stew this time.'

'Stop,' ordered Betty. 'We've faced worse than this before and come through it.'

Strictly speaking, this was true, but only because they did not know what they were facing in this situation. Moments later they knew. The door opened and in walked a man that Agatha had not seen in years.

'Aunt Agatha. Long-time no see.'

Agatha, Betty and Sausage gasped collectively. It was Agatha who found her voice first.

'Oliver,' said Agatha in a half whisper.

Lord Oliver 'Olly' Lake** walked into the room, a broad grin on his face. He walked up to Agatha first and regarded her with evident affection.

'Have you missed me?'

*see *The Frisco Falcon*
**see *The Chess Board Murders*

21

Captain Briant sat alone in a café a few streets back from the port. He stared at the packet of cigarettes that Raif had given him. They reminded him of the War. He'd started smoking in the first day he went to the front. He stopped the day the War ended. It felt to him as if he were in a new war against an enemy he could not see, whose reach extended all around the world yet could melt into the shadows or the boardrooms at the first hint of contact.

While he was waiting, he ordered another coffee. It was a little bitter for his taste, but it succeeded in helping fight against the enervation one felt in the stifling heat of Morocco. Soon he felt a hand on his shoulder. He looked up to see a man and a woman.

Kit Aston held out a chair for Mary and then sat down himself. Briant indicated to the man at the counter to bring two more coffees.

'So, Captain, do you want to tell us what all of this conjuring trick was in aid of?'

The conjuring trick in question involved Kit and Mary boarding the ferry bound for Marseilles, making a show of waving goodbye to Toussaint who Briant knew would stay to see them off and then, unseen by the Chief of Police, climbing from the ferry onto the tug that pulled it out to the sea and returning back to the port. By then Toussaint and Briant had departed.

'What else was I supposed to do?' asked Briant in a reasonable manner. 'It was the best I could produce in the time I had.'

This answer lacked the detail Kit was hoping for, but he suspected he knew what was coming. He raised his eyebrows to encourage more from the French policeman. Briant sighed and continued.

'I knew that you both would come over to help your aunt. Under any other circumstances this would have been no problem except there was one rather large problem. Berrada was murdered and...'

'Durand-Simon or whatever his name is,' said Kit.

'Correct. He would know you, resent your involvement and report you to Toussaint. Which he did. Hence the sudden expulsion from the country. I guessed that all of this would happen and prepared accordingly. I allowed you to interview the suspects and waited for this particular comedy to play itself out. And so we are here.'

'You don't suspect Durand, though, of Berrada's murder?' asked Mary.

'No, it's too unlikely. The French government is trying to drive a wedge between him and Abd el-Krim. Why would we kill his friend? The situation in the Rif mountains is deteriorating and I have no trust that the Spanish will be able to deal with it. If Raisuli can be bought off then it might make the Rif rebels think again.'

'Can he be bought off?'

Briant shrugged in an all too Gallic fashion.

'I don't know and, frankly, it's not my problem. Among other things, I just have to find out who killed Berrada. Toussaint is convinced it was Durand which is another reason why he was terrified of your involvement. I gather Durand gave a surprisingly complimentary assessment of your capability.'

'There is something I meant to mention to you.'

'The gun that was in the drainpipe outside in the alleyway?' said Briant with a smile.

Kit smiled at this, and Mary frowned. She had missed this and was not happy that the two men had seen it.

'I'm sure Durand was equally complimentary about your ability too.'

'Was it the gun that killed Berrada?'

'No,' confirmed Briant.'

'Fingerprints?' asked Mary hopefully.

'None,' said Briant.

'So you put it back?' said Kit, with a half-smile, sitting back in his chair.

'Correct. We had hoped the murderer would come and pick it up. He or she has not done so. There is no way of finding out who owns the gun. It is old and could have been obtained in Morocco illegally.'

'But it does narrow your list of suspects to Keller, Durand, Lefevre? Assuming one of them did fire the gun and throw it outside the window, we are still left with the same problem: if the murder took place outside the room, how did the body get into the room?'

'And how was the room locked,' finished Briant glumly.

'I think I have an idea on that,' said Kit.

'You do?' exclaimed Mary fixing a gaze on Kit that would be recognised by husbands the world over. Kit's response had all the hallmarks of a man who knew the doghouse awaited.

'Didn't I mention it?'

Nothing in Mary's unforgiving glare suggested this information had been forthcoming. Perhaps his charm and boyish good looks would overcome his egregious oversight. He wasn't sure if the idea would work, but he was committed now.

'Perhaps I can demonstrate when we go to the hotel. Presumably, Durand has left for the day. Where is the sergeant?'

'He's been trying over the last two days to recreate Berrada's movements on the day of the murder. Not as easy as you might think. Berrada was on his own so Raif has been visiting known informers to piece that together. We don't know anything of his movements after midday.'

When they finished their coffees they made their way to the hotel. Briant made an observation as they drove that had occurred to Kit also.

'We have until tomorrow night to solve this case. By then the ferry will have arrived and I suspect your absence will have been noted.'

They arrived at the hotel. Briant's first action was to dismiss the men guarding the front door and the alleyway. Lucien Moreau's face fell when he saw the three enter and Kit could not blame him. It looked as if he was building up to saying something.

'Captain, I must beg you...'

226

Briant held his hand up which silenced his fellow countryman.

'I have dismissed the men. Your guests will be free to go tomorrow.'

This appeared to brighten Moreau's day. His manner changed and he offered the new arrivals something to drink. This was declined by Briant for all of them.

'Monsieur Moreau, please can you give us the keys to the inspector's room.'

Moreau immediately disappeared to retrieve the keys. As he did this, Sergeant Raif appeared in the doorway. He seemed thoroughly unsurprised to see Kit and Mary. He nodded to Briant. This was greeted with a hopeful look from his captain. Raif quickly dispelled this hope with a shake of his head.

'Nothing Captain. From the pint at which he took lunch at Café Tangier his movements are a mystery. No one saw him.'

'What time did he leave the café?' asked Kit.

'Not sure, but it was no later than one in the afternoon.'

'What are you thinking?' asked Mary.

Kit shook his head. It was still a mystery to him. Just then Moreau held out the two room keys.

'You can show us what happened?' asked Briant.

'I hope so,' said Kit. 'Let's go upstairs. Mary, may I borrow a hair pin?''

Mary took a metal pin from her hair and gave it to her husband. Kit looked at it for a moment and said, 'Too thick.'

'Just like us apparently,' said Mary with a grin.

'Monsieur Moreau,' asked Kit, 'have you a needle and thread that can be used for sewing.'

Moreau put his hands up and his mouth formed into a 'search-me' shape. He left the group to go into his back office returning two minutes later with a spool of thread. Kit took the spool and cut a length. Intrigued, Moreau followed the policemen and Kit and Mary up the stairs. As they climbed, Kit carefully pulled the sewing thread through the hole in the wardle of the key using the needle.

'If I'm right, I think this is how the murderer was able make it seem as if the door had been locked from inside.'

They reached the room. Kit unlocked the door and stepped inside. He knelt down by the door and pulled the thread through the keyhole. Then he delicately placed the key on the inside lock in a position that he could pull it into place. Standing up he pulled the door shut very gently. With the other room key he locked the door from the outside and took the key out. Finally he pulled the key on the inside of the door into place.

It fell.

The sound of the key dropping onto the floor was greeted by a few choice words in Anglo Saxon followed by an apology to the amused Mary. She took the needle and thread from Kit and said, 'Let me try, Sherlock.'

'Be my guest,' said her rather disappointed husband.

Mary re-threaded the needle and put it through the hole in the wardle. Then she repeated the exercise undertaken by Kit. She shut the door very gently before slowly locking it from the outside. Drawing the key out she pulled the sewing needle back. It took a minute of fiddling, but she was able

228

to withdraw the needle from the hole in the wardle of the key. She held the pin up triumphantly to the group of men.

'Well done dear,' murmured Kit appreciatively. 'Very dextrous,'

The two French detectives looked at one another then Briant spoke. He said, 'Bravo, I think that explains at least one part of this crime.'

'Of course this means that almost anyone could have done it,' said Mary. 'Tradesmen, guests, the police even.'

'I know,' said Raif who admired what he had seen from the Englishman but had already anticipated its implications. 'The number of people coming into this hotel is ridiculous; it's like a thoroughfare.' This made Moreau blanche, but there was little he could say to deny this. Raif continued relentlessly, 'Anyone wishing to take revenge on Berrada would have had no trouble in doctoring the key and then returning it to its hook while he waited for an opportunity to gain his revenge.'

'Has Berrada stayed here before?' asked Mary.

Moreau and the two policemen all answered 'yes' at the same moment.

'Gosh,' said Mary. 'This could have been weeks in the planning; months, even.'

'Can we establish absolutely no connection between Berrada and any of the guests?' asked Kit

'None whatsoever,' confirmed Briant.

'Well, at least we know one other thing,' said Kit, with something approaching a grin on his face.

Everyone turned to face Kit with looks of high expectation following his coup de theatre.

'If it needed confirming, there is no way my aunt could have pulled this off, I am sure you will concede that.'

However, Briant was already walking off down the stairs accompanied by the sound of Kit laughing.

'So, what do we do now?' asked Mary as she, Kit and Raif started to follow Briant down the stairs.

'We find a place to stay or perhaps Sergeant Raif and Captain Briant have organised this.'

Kit turned to Raif who nodded in response.

'We had your bags moved to Hotel Minzen. I understand there is an English gentleman called Mr Miller staying at the hotel under an assumed name. Perhaps you know him.'

Kit declined to acknowledge the sly remark except through a smile. It was time to meet up with Harry and find out what was planned for him. Hotel Minzen was only a few minutes away by car. They arrived to find Walter Harris standing outside with an elderly woman.

'Who's that with Walter?' asked Mary.

'That,' said Kit, 'is Emily Keene who is also known as the Sharifa.'

'Ahhh,' said Mary. The lady in question looked as if she had been cut from the same quarry as Aunt Agatha. Although both could see Kit and Mary, neither seemed particularly happy. Minutes later after introductions had been made, the reason became clear as the elderly English ex-pats explained what they had witnessed earlier.

'Who are these people at the villa?' asked Kit.

Raif had the answer.

'The owner of the villa is a French national who goes by the name of Comte Alexander Dumas.'

The group turned to Raif in astonishment. The young sergeant shrugged and said, 'That's what I was told.'

It was Kit who spoke next. There was hard edge to his voice.

'I think I know what this is all about. Not the Berrada murder, that's still a mystery to me. Dumas is clearly not this man's name. I think he is really Comte Jean-Valois de Bourbon.' Briant whistled at this. 'You know him?' asked Kit

'ORCA*,' said Briant.

This was news to Kit. For the second time in the last twenty minutes, his eyes widened. When he finally found his voice he said, quietly, 'This is worse than I thought.' He turned to Walter Harris. 'Can you describe the men you saw?'

Harris described the six men who had emerged from the two cars as well as the extraordinary woman who was accompanying the group.

'An older man very stout and a small man who might be Moroccan,' said Kit looking at Mary.

Mary turned to Raif, her eyes narrowing. Kit smiled as he anticipated the question that she would ask.

'Sergeant Raif is there any way you can check if two men have escaped from a Turkish prison in the last year? Their names are Sidney Goodman and Joel Israel.'

'I will send a telegraph now,' replied Raif, indicating a telegraph office further down the street. He set off, leaving the group outside the hotel

231

'Are these men working with ORCA?' asked Briant, fixing his eyes on Kit.

'If they are,' replied Kit, shaking his head in disbelief, 'then ORCA's recruitment standards are slipping somewhat.'

At this point the Sharifa, Emily Keene spoke, and her words chilled the group.

'This may not be our biggest problem. There's one other thing we forgot to mention.'

The group turned to the venerable old lady who had caused so much controversy in her life.

'Agatha communicated to me that she wanted me to keep an eye on your young man Harry Miller. I asked some associates of mine to do so. This morning when Walter and I saw Agatha, Betty and Jocelyn taken away, we also saw Harry Miller there. He saw them being taken away too. The young man, to his credit was on his feet immediately and walking over to do something about it although I cannot imagine for the life of me, what. Three men came and abducted him on the street. Walter and I are convinced they are Raisuli's men.'

'What does this mean?' asked Mary taking Kit's hand.

It was Walter Harris who answered.

'Look, try not to be too anxious. It's the Spanish that Raisuli reserves his dislike for. Raisuli is a strange cove, trust me, I've seen all sides of him first hand, but he has an odd liking for the English.'

Kit wasn't sure if this was quite what he needed to hear at that moment.

*See *The Chess Board Murders* and *The French Diplomat Affair*

23

'Stop,' shouted an English voice.

Even in the middle of his terror, Miller couldn't help but wonder what use speaking English to the man clutching the scimitar would have. He hadn't struck Miller as being a linguist or perhaps he was simply prejudiced.

Much to Miller's amazement and overwhelming relief, the urgency of the voice worked in postponing the moment when the sword separated Miller permanently from his fingers.

'Stop this moment,' said the man, this time in Arabic. Miller could not understand what had been said, but something in the tone was similar to how he had spoken a moment earlier. The Berber put his sword down by his side and stepped back. Miller was still being held down, but he gave himself permission to relax a little.

'Are you English?' asked the man.

Miller squinted up into the sun and beheld a quite extraordinary sight. The man before him was a giant. At least six feet four or more. He had an eye patch over one of his eyes and dark, leathery skin.

Miller nodded. His throat was too dry to speak. The gag didn't help matters either.

'What in God's name are you doing here you damn fool? Do you know who this is?'

Miller had been pondering just such a question himself. He was also pondering how he was meant to answer the man's stream of questions with a gag in his mouth. At this point the penny seemed to drop for the giant. He knelt down and untied the gag while shooing away the men holding Miller down. He put a canteen of water to Miller's dried lips. The little Londoner drank greedily before wiping his mouth and sitting up.

'Who are you?' asked the man.

'Miller. Harry Miller.'

'What are you doing here?'

'I was kidnapped.'

This seemed to make complete sense to the giant. He offered Miller some more water and then sat down on the rocky ground beside him.

'The name's Sarll. Thomas Sarll.'

The two men shook hands like they were in a London Tea Room. For a moment there was silence then Sarll spoke again.

'Look, why would they kidnap you?'

Miller thought for a second about where they had picked him up and what he'd witnessed with Agatha and her friends.

'I don't know, but I have to get back. My friends have been kidnapped.'

'Has Raisuli taken them too?'

'No. Someone else,' replied Miller.

'You're all having a run of bad luck and no mistake. They're in Tangier?' said Sarll, taking a slug of water himself. Then he rose to his feet and helped Miller up too.

Miller gazed up at Sarll. He looked to be in his forties. His slender frame suggested great strength and there was just a hint of wildness in the eyes that suggested he was not a man to cross.

'What are you doing here?' asked Miller.

'Me? Oh, that's a long story. Suffice to say I went to interview the rebel Rif leader, Abd el-Krim and ended up here as a sort of emissary to find out what Raisuli's intentions were. They seem to trust me. More than they do one another. Raisuli and I have crossed paths before. He rather likes the English.'

'You could've fooled me,' said Miller.

'Oh don't be a baby. I think he was just playing around. Trust me, if he meant to cut off your fingers he wouldn't have sent me out to stop it, but really, Harry, you have to tell him what you're doing here. He's rather changeable.'

'Thanks for the advice. Can we see him, then? I need to get back.'

The two men walked towards the big tent. Sarll was fairly bouncing along, and Miller had to step lively to keep up with the enormous stride of his unlikely saviour. The arrival of Miller was greeted by a ripple of laughter among the half dozen men in the tent. This was perhaps not what he had been expecting and it certainly did little for his mood to know that he had been the subject of a rather elaborate and certainly malicious practical joke.

236

Soon Sarll and Miller were standing before the rather bloated brigand. A smile crossed Raisuli's face and he spoke once more to the same man by his side who had translated for him earlier.

'Are you ready to tell us who you are and why you were outside that house?'

From the corner of his mouth Sarll said, 'You better bloody well tell the truth this time son or we're both for it.'

24

'I must confess Aunt Agatha, I was hoping for a warmer welcome than this,' said Olly Lake in a faux sad voice. The smile on his face and in his eyes belied any obvious feeling of wretchedness.

'What became of you Oliver?' asked Agatha. There was genuine inquiry in her voice and no little sense of sadness. This was a boy she had seen grow up into a fine young man that any mother would have been proud, a war hero, someone who had risked his life for his country, first in Flanders and then in a Russia that was turning to communism. Then something had happened. There were rumours of his drinking when he returned from the War, abusive behaviour in his club, Sheldon's.

All of these stories had turned out to be a front for something more malevolent. He had joined an organisation whose intent was not yet clear, but whose actions seemed designed to create terror wherever they acted. Already they had been linked with assassination attempts on Lenin, on Georges Clemenceau and a host of other public figures. The organisation was known as ORCA, short for *Organisation des Révolutionnaires, des Communistes et des Anarchistes.*

'I woke up Aunt Agatha.'

'Don't call me that,' snapped Agatha.

'Very well. I shan't do so,' said Lake, pulling out a cigarette and lighting it. He enjoyed a smoke for a few moments. 'You deserve an answer I suppose, so I shall give you one. Now, the question was, what became of me, I believe?'

Agatha was not one to repeat herself; it was almost an article of faith for her that if you did not have the decency to listen in the first place then a second chance was out of the question. This brought a smile from Lake as if a point had been proved to his satisfaction.

'You never change Agatha.'

'You did.'

'I woke up, that's all. I woke up when I saw half my regiment slaughtered in sixteen, the other half maimed. And do you know what I thought?'

Lake didn't wait for answer.

'They deserved it. We all deserved it,' said Lake contemptuously. He stared at the group who regarded him in shocked silence. 'Do you know I met a young man, a poet, when I was there. He hadn't written many poems, they were sketches, ideas more than anything, but one of the lines he wrote I remember it so well. It was, "What passing bells for those that die as cattle?" Isn't that beautiful?'

Lake's eyes were wide. It was as if he was in the grip of madness.

'What passing bells for those that die as cattle? Extraordinary and true and there was I, Oliver Lake of

Hertwood, like a damn fool, in the middle of it all. If I'd caught one then it would only be what I deserved. I'd walked into it with my eyes open. Actually, no, that's not right. I was sleepwalking. We all were. By the way, I looked up the chap who'd written that wonderful line that was so true, so real. He died. Shot and killed just before the Armistice. Symbolic don't you think? A war that destroyed so much beauty, so much life caused by old men moving chess pieces around a board like they knew what they were doing. For what? Yet we all were complicit. We all went off to fight. We all took the cheers of our family, the kisses of our sweethearts. Our chests swelled in pride as the band played us onto the ships to take us on a one-way trip to hell. Oh yes, we deserved everything that came to us. Yes, I changed Agatha. Did I ever bloody change? I promised myself, if I came out of it alive, I would create some change myself in the world. That chap Marx, the one you met, he had a lot of things right. The ultimate solution was wrong, but my goodness the analysis was brilliant. If he'd only stopped at the overthrow of the existing order with control being exerted by an elite, all would have been well. He had it all there, but he had to take it a step further: the dictatorship of the proletariat. What rot! That way lies hell. Socialism robs men of their vigour, their ambition, their ability to think for themselves. Better to have an elite who ensure law and order and national security. After that let men live their lives to shape as they see fit without restriction and limited only by their capability.'

Agatha's eyes never left those of Olly Lake. When he had finished speaking she shook her head and replied, 'I

240

disagreed with Karl then, I do now, but at least what he wrote was borne from some desire, however misplaced, to help his fellow man, to help those of all abilities. What you propose is nothing less than a modern Sparta. The weak will be abandoned to their fate.'

'Yes and we will all become stronger as a result,' countered Lake. 'A gradual pruning so that what is left is strong, vital and able to build a better future for all. This is true equality, not what Marx proposed. I am a socialist, not some hand-wringing do-gooder. Leave that to the Salvation Army. I want the individual to thrive. He can only do that when he is free of any consideration for caring for others except himself.'

'Or herself?' interjected Agatha. 'What role do you see for women in this world that you have created? You talk of free men, yet most women are not free. You talk of equality, yet it is a man's equality not a woman's. What freedom do we have in your world? We will still be expected to bear children. We will still be expected to rear them. We will still be the homemaker while men go out into the world and shape it solely because their sex allows them to, free of the responsibility of ensuring there is a next generation. In your world what are we? Don't answer Oliver, I think I know, and it appals me. Your world venerates selfishness as destiny; it esteems strength when all I see is exploitation and it sees caring for others as weakness. Everything you say is refracted through the prism of being a man. I will fight you and people like you until the last breath in my body because there is one thing missing from your Utopia; it is the one thing that all women share because we have to: compassion. You can keep your world Oliver. It sickens me.'

Betty and Sausage never felt prouder of their friend or sadder for her than at that moment. Her denunciation of Olly Lake had been as passionate as it was bitter. It was as if seventy years of resentment at seeing women denied the opportunity to live a life without the legal restraints they had faced and were only now beginning to overcome: the ability to vote, to stand for Parliament, to go to university on the same terms as men. She turned her back on the former friend of her nephew.

Lake hadn't finished though, he added, 'I'm disappointed in you Agatha. Unlike Kit, I thought you might understand.'

This was greeted with a snort from Agatha.

'Understand? I understand that you are assassins and gunrunners.'

A sly grin crossed Lake's face and he replied quickly, 'Oh we're much more than that. Do you know how easy it is, when you put people in the right places, to substitute records. We did a trial run with you in Paris and London. I have to say, it's succeeded beyond our wildest expectations. You're public enemy number one now in Morocco.'

This was met, as Lake expected, with absolute shock by Agatha and the others. She stared at Lake then replied, 'I hadn't appreciated how far your tentacles stretch.'

'Well, it's always good to be re-acquainted with old friends,' said Bourbon with a chuckle as silence enveloped the room. 'Speaking of which, Olly.'

Lake nodded his head and turned to the unlikely group before him. He gestured dismissively towards Fatima.

'I have no intention of harming you if you all behave. Step out of line, however and I shall set Fatima on you. What she lacks in beauty and intelligence she more than makes up for in brute strength.'

At the mention of her name, Fatima looked around to Olly Lake. She smiled fearfully. Lake ignored her.

'There you go Agatha. There's something you can feel compassion towards; an illiterate monster,' said Lake, standing by the door.

'You're the monster,' said Agatha without looking up, but Lake had already slipped out of the room. Bourbon smiled and followed him out. As he went through the door, he snapped his fingers which saw Fatima immediately turn to join them.

This left the three ladies and their two former captors alone in the room. 'Was it really necessary to upset them?' asked Goodman.

Agatha glared at Goodman but did not deign to reply. Betty was on her feet immediately and over to the door. It was locked, of course. Worse it was made from a heavy oak. This meant any attempt at trying to break it down was impossible. The windows presented even less opportunity. They were barred from the outside. Betty walked over and gave each bar a jolly good shake, but they were immovable.

'Looks like we're stuck here, girls,' said Betty.

'Could be worse,' said Sausage which was greeted with astonishment by her four companions. Normally, Sausage would immediately be cowed into silence by such a

243

reaction. However, Agatha's words had lit something within her breast, and she stood up from where she had been sitting.

'I jolly well mean it. The room is a distinct improvement on our previous accommodation,' said Sausage. She saw a rather downcast look on Goodman's face and suddenly felt a wave of guilt. 'I mean you tried your best and all that Sidney, but this is a little bit cleaner and nicer. Furthermore, I don't believe Olly means us harm. He was always a rather wild boy, I'll admit, still is, as far as I can see, but he's not going to harm us.'

'I hope you're right,' said Joel who was sitting sullenly in the corner. 'So what do we do now?'

Everyone turned to Agatha because she was the most likely source for any plan, but she seemed far away in her thoughts. For a few moments nothing was said, then Agatha finally spoke.

'I think it's up to Christopher, Mary and Harry now.'

The mood was too low for this remark to provide the fillip everyone needed at that moment. Then Sausage wondered out loud about Mimi. The group sat in mute dejection for a while. Once more, Agatha felt the weight of a guilt that was for her alone to bear.

Fatima returned to the room and sat down by the door with her arms folded. Her good eye roamed the room like a spotlight searching for a trapeze artist. It was oddly compelling to watch it.

'How did you come to be here, Fatima?' asked Agatha in Arabic after ten minutes of silence had elapsed. Fatima glowered at Agatha and shook her head. Not a conversationalist apparently. In fact, Agatha wondered if her tongue was removed until soon after she knocked the door and called out to someone who was guarding outside.

A few minutes later, the guard arrived carrying a tray with cups and a jug of water. This was a welcome relief as the heat in the room was almost unbearable. To Agatha it showed also that there was a streak of humanity in the extraordinary woman who was their guard.

The water revived the spirits of the group, and they began to discuss how they might escape from this unusual prison. No one thought that overpowering their guard was likely to achieve success. They would have to wait until she left, but in some senses, she was the least of their worries. She was unarmed. The other guards, decidedly less impressive as physical specimens, more than compensated for this through having rifles. Rather old rifles in Agatha's view. They might have dated back to the Zulu wars.

None of this helped them advance far forward and soon a gloomy silence fell over the group. As they entered the second hour of their captivity, they heard noises outside their room. They turned to one another. There was another English voice. It sounded familiar and it was shouting.

Then the door flew open.

25

Mulai Ahmed al-Raisuli, the former Pasha of Tangier and a leader of the Berber tribe in Morocco, well, one of them, anyway, stared at the chess board with mounting frustration. Across the table from him sat Harry Miller who had just won his second straight game of chess against his potential gaoler.

'How did you do that?' snarled Raisuli, his words quickly translated by the ever-present man Miller now knew to be called Chafiq.

Miller had been the beneficiary of several chess lessons from Kit who was one of the foremost chess players in Britain. As tempting as it had been to throw the match against Raisuli, Sarll had warned him not to do so. Raisuli would hate to be beaten, but worse than defeat was any sense of pity from an opponent. This made sense to Miller, and he proceeded to defeat Raisuli fairly handily.

Miller glanced at Chafiq; he raised his eyebrows as he indicated the pieces. Raisuli saw the gesture and nodded. The two men across the table pointed to the board at the same time. So Miller began to lay the pieces out for another game. Once he had done this he said, 'The best opening move is this.'

He moved his King pawn two squares forward.

'Bloody hell,' said Sarll, shaking his head. He rose his enormous frame from where he had been sitting on the ground and stalked out of the tent.

'The best players in the world all do this,' said Miller, fixing his eyes on Raisuli. A smile crossed the lips of his erstwhile captor as he listened to the translation.

Twenty minutes later Thomas 'Tiger' Sarll's cigarette break was interrupted by a shout from within the tent. The shout was one word and it sounded distinctly like his own name.

'Coming,' shouted Sarll through clenched teeth, which is no mean feat. Try it...

Sarll trooped into the tent like a recalcitrant schoolboy who is no longer the coolest kid in the class. Even Sarll recognised that any feelings of jealousy towards Miller were somewhat misplaced when both their lives remained in the hands of a capricious madman notwithstanding his odd charm and affection towards Britain.

'Yes?' said Sarll in a tone that Miller immediately recognised as peeved. This was dangerous territory for an Englishman. The next level of anger up from this was "a bit put out;" at this point countries started to be invaded. Enough said.

Raisuli swept his hand over the chess board which was now laid out in the manner that suggested a game was imminent.

Chafiq barked, 'Sit,' to Sarll which confirmed the sickening realisation that he was to play Raisuli at chess. Again. He'd already defeated him on a couple of occasions in the past despite the fact that Sarll would never have considered himself much of a player.

'Move,' said Chafiq whose manner had become increasingly like an old schoolteacher of Sarll's. Sarll had parted company with English education when he was a teenager with little regret on either side. Even the big Englishman would acknowledge that he had a coltish indiscipline back then that made him rather a difficult child to teach. His teachers' assessment would have been considerably more forthright and single syllable if expressed verbally.

The game began with the Englishman sensing something was a bit odd. Then it hit him; he was playing white. Normally Raisuli played white. The Berber leader hoped this would give him an edge. Against the second division opposition in the camp, it usually did. However, when moving up a division to face Europeans it rarely proved any advantage.

Sarll lasted five minutes before Raisuli, with a roar of triumph, put him to the proverbial sword. The former brigand, kidnapper of Pedicaris and Kaid McClean leapt to his feet and danced a jig of delight joined by his equally delighted translator, Chafiq.

'What the bloody hell did you show him?' asked Sarll through the side of his mouth. 'He'll be even more unbearable now.'

Miller smiled and shrugged modestly. As far as he was concerned he had all but bought his freedom, but Miller wanted more. A plan was forming in his mind that was as daring as it was dangerous, but Miller had been through the

Great War. He'd rescued Kit Aston in the middle of No Man's Land with the Germans a few hundred yards away.

In for a penny.

*

'I'll say this for you Miller, you have a pair,' said Sarll. The two men were sitting side by side watching Raisuli's men ready a cart. Six Berber tribesmen would accompany Miller. They were, as anyone with two eyes to see, which Tiger Sarll did not, men not to be messed with.

It was late afternoon, and the heat of the sun was beginning to wane. As much as Miller would like to have left earlier in the afternoon, Raisuli had refused. His men were napping in their tents and even the great leader was loathe to disturb them while the midday sun was at its hottest.

Following the game in which Raisuli had so comprehensively defeated Sarll, an offer from the Englishman for a return leg had been met with a loud laugh. This seemed like a refusal in any language. It was then that Miller with an instinct for the human condition learned on the back streets of London, pressed his case.

'Can I ask a favour?' he'd said in French to Chafiq. To say this was met with a raised eyebrow would be somewhat understating the reaction it provoked in Sarll, never mind Chafiq. Raisuli's man more out of curiosity than any desire to help, had translated Miller's request to Raisuli.

'My mistress Lady Frost and her friends are in trouble.'

Sarll was about to clout Miller, an action in which he would have been fortunate to beat Chafiq to the proverbial punch, when to the astonishment of all, Raisuli uttered the

249

only English words that Sarll, or indeed, Chafiq, had ever heard him speak.

'Lady Agatha Frost?'

It was heavily accented, but there was no mistaking what he had said. Raisuli stood up and walked towards Miller. The sight was enough to make Miller quake inwardly. Had he misjudged the moment. The look on Raisuli's face certainly inspired no confidence in the length of his life expectancy.

'Who killed my friend Berrada?' asked Raisuli.

When Miller heard the translation his face must have betrayed his complete ignorance of what had happened. Then, to Miller's astonishment, Raisuli smiled. Miller had seen warmer smiles in his life than this and that included a King Cobra near Amritsar. However, there was enough in it to reassure him that his life was not in immediate danger.

While they waited for the midday sun to lose its intensity Miller and Sarll had stayed in one of the nearby tents. Miller got to hear more about the extraordinary life Sarll had led. Although Miller's own short time on the planet had been no less adventurous, he envied the freedom of his companion as much as he admired the blindly optimistic confidence in his own ability to cope in the face of whatever situation he faced. Sarll had faced death and ruin on countless occasions in his sojourns to some of the lonelier and wilder spots of the planet, but had bounced back, unwilling to accept defeat. Miller wondered if this would be yet another occasion in both their lives when they faced danger.

As they were parting, they shook hands. The pair had been the subject of much merriment from the Moroccans due to their contrasting sizes.

'Are you sure you won't come with me?' said Miller who had genuinely enjoyed the company of the unusual fellow Londoner.

'Sorry Harry. I go back to Abd el Krim today. Not sure what use I'd be to you.'

'Well, Tiger,' pointed out Miller, 'you'd be a much bigger target when the shooting starts.'

Sarll roared with laughter at this; much to his credit in Miller's eyes. He helped Miller up into a covered cart that would take Miller to the villa. The party consisted of half a dozen of Raisuli's men. All were armed with rifles. Miller, on the other hand, was unarmed. Sarll assured him, however, that the mere mention of Raisuli's name would be enough to gain the freedom of his friends. Miller wasn't so sure, but he felt reassured by the confidence Sarll had in the Berber leader.

The group set off for the half hour journey back to Tangier. Miller had, on two occasions, been shipped away from the front in France, during the War, in a makeshift ambulance. Those were, by quite some distance, the two most uncomfortable journeys of his relatively short life. This one came third. The driver of the cart appeared to be targeting every pothole in an already rocky road. The result was Miller spent most of the journey being thrown all over the back of the cart. His regular and often heart felt swearing was greeted with laughter by a driver who was as unsympathetic to his passenger's plight as he was clearly inept at managing a cart.

The sight of the sea and the white buildings of Tangier brought some hope to Miller as he felt a welcome sea breeze counteract the stifling heat which the cover to the cart did little to reduce.

However, for reasons passing all common sense, they began to descend the rocky road at a clip which had Miller lying on the floor gripping the sides. His confidence in the ability of the driver to handle the cart had long since eroded. This was not helped by the occasional cackle that erupted from the madman as they bounced over yet another rock. The most recent one was witnessed by one of the other riders who shouted a volley of abuse at the driver. Inevitably, an argument followed, but the result was a more sensible pace adopted.

Miller was almost in tears as they arrived back in the square, and not of joy either. His back hurt damnably and he didn't think he'd be able to sit comfortably for a week. At least the road was much better and, if not quite the smooth purr of Kit's Rolls Royce, the roll of the cart's wheels along the road was a distinct improvement on the previous thirty minutes.

Chafiq, Raisuli's translator and, Miller realised, second in command, came alongside the cart. 'We have arrived,' he said, indicating with his eyes the villa where Aunt Agatha, Betty and Sausage were being kept.

'Are you just going up to the gate?'

Chafiq laughed and replied, 'We are from Raisuli. Of course we are. They must let us in.'

Miller was unsure whether this was reassuring or concerning. He glanced around at the men on horseback. It was an impressive sight. If it came to a fight he would back this group against most.

Chafiq climbed down from his horse and banged on the gate. A minute later, face appeared at a small grill; a Moroccan peered out. He and Chafiq spoke rapidly in Arabic. The latter gesticulated a lot which was either in an aggressive manner or it was not, Miller hadn't a clue. Italians could be similarly expressive when discussing what they would eat that night.

After a couple of minutes, Chafiq and the man parted. Moments later the gates opened to allow the Berbers through. Chafiq climbed back onto his horse and waved the band of warriors to follow him.

'I will take you to your friends.'

Miller was rather hoping that it would be the other way around. He was about to say this when two European men appeared. Both were wearing light linen suits with ties which was bizarre. Miller had long since dispensed with his.

Chafiq jumped down nimbly from his horse and walked over to the two men. To Miller's eyes and great hope, there seemed little affection on either side. Then Chafiq pointed to the cart with Miller on board. The two men looked at it briefly and then chatted more with Chafiq. By now, Miller's pulse was racing like a greyhound at Wimbledon. One thing was for sure, he'd had enough of sitting on the cart. Moving his legs was a challenge as they had stiffened up, but he managed to persuade them to move. He jumped down from the back of the cart and walked around to join Chafiq and the two men.

'You are Mr Miller, I believe,' said the darker-haired man. He was tall, elegant and very French. 'It's a pleasure to meet you. I gather you wish to see Lady Frost and her companions.'

'I wish to take them away,' pointed out Miller.

'Why?' asked the Frenchman amiably. 'They are safe here from the police.'

'Are they?' asked Miller fixing his eyes on the Frenchman. This was greeted with a smile. During this time, Miller had not paid much attention to the other man, whose back had been half-turned away from him. The man turned towards Miller and spoke.

'So you're the man that carried Kit back from No Man's Land. Thank you Harry. My name is Olly. Olly Lake. I'm an old pal of Kit's.'

The man held his hand out and before Miller could stop himself, he instinctively shook it. Then he looked into the face of Lake. Miller could not believe his eyes. For a moment he had a flashback to the previous year when he had broken into the mansion of Lake's father and discovered that the man had an interesting collection of medieval torture devices that suggested an uncommon interest in the darker side of romance.

The man before Miller was tall with fair hair, blue eyes and, except for the moustache, he could have been Kit Aston's brother. No, that was not right, he *was* Kit Aston's brother.

How had no one seen this before?

Before Miller could speak, Chafiq said a few words in a low voice to the Frenchman who nodded. The two men walked away from Miller and Lake towards the cart.

'What's going on?' demanded Miller. There was an edge in his voice that was more anger than anxiety.

'You'll come with us to join your friends.'

Miller heard the sound of a bolt action on an Enfield Rifle behind him. He spun around and saw three Berbers with their rifles trained on him. Miller turned back to face Lake. There was no smile on Lake's face. Instead, he saw cold, hard eyes staring back at him.

'Don't do anything foolish, Harry Miller. You won't be harmed. Now, come with me. I'm sure Aunt Agatha will be delighted to see you.'

There was nothing he could do except follow Lake into the large villa. They trooped through the large entrance hall and up a set of wide wooden stairs to a second floor. Miller saw that there was a guard outside one door.

'Your friends are here Harry, none the worse, I might add, for their unscheduled stay.'

'What do you plan to do with us?' snarled Miller.

'We'll see. I would love to see Kit again and meet the lovely Mary. I gather she's rather a beauty.'

Anger flared up in Miller, he was about to rush Lake when he felt two sets of powerful arms grip his. Realising that escape, or simply sticking a fist on Lake's smug face was impossible, Miller gave himself up to a few remonstrations that were Anglo Saxon in character and decidedly uncomplimentary in nature. The door to the room opened and he was thrown inside. He fell to the ground with a thump.

'Good Lord,' said a familiar voice. 'It's Harry.'

Miller looked up and saw three familiar female faces looking down at him with concern. He sat up and rubbed the back of his head which had connected rather forcefully with the ground.

'I've come to rescue you,' said Miller, ruefully.

26

'I can call upon a few friends to keep watch at the villa. I'm not sure we can storm the place, however,' said the Sharifa, Emily Keene to the group. 'My son is the Sharif now. His men will do anything he says.'

Briant smiled and held his hands up in a manner that suggested this would not even be considered as a last resort. The one thing they were not going to do was launch a full-scale assault on a villa when they had no idea of its defences. Also, and he caught Kit Aston's eye as he thought this, the last thing they wanted was to attack the villa with Aunt Agatha and her friends inside. At worst it would put them at risk from being hurt by their captors, at best they would be in the hands of the police. Neither option was palatable. They needed a plan and Kit, at that moment, was fresh out of them.

'Thank you Emily. I don't think that a battle is on the cards,' said Kit speaking for Briant.

'We have to do something,' exclaimed Walter Harris in a defiant manner. 'We can't just let Agatha and the others be held captive by these rotters.'

Kit nodded in agreement. All of this was true, but just at that moment they were up against a number of challenges that were insurmountable. It was Briant who spoke next.

'We need to go to the Moreau Hotel first. Our esteemed Chief of Police still expects me to be running the investigation into the death of our friend Berrada. Perhaps if the Sharifa could organise some of the friends she mentioned to keep an eye on the villa while we are at the hotel. Send for us immediately if something happens.'

Emily Keene nodded and rose from the seat.

'Perhaps you could assist her, Walter,' said Kit. It was obvious the journalist was itching to do something. Aside from this, there was an interesting story in the middle of this stew that would not need to benefit from the usual penchant for exaggeration.

The group parted with Harris and the Sharifa headed for the villa while Kit, Mary and the two French policemen were bound for the hotel of the murdered inspector. The mood in the car muted any prospect of conversation. When they reached the hotel, Mary asked a question that Kit had been wondering about too.

'Won't Colonel Toussaint be alerted if we are seen here.'

It was Raif who answered.

'Only if Durand is there, but he left a couple of hours ago.'

'Let's hope he doesn't return,' said Kit. 'One question for you, sergeant: from the statements you have taken of our list of hotel guests, are there any of them who have time unaccounted for by any witness?'

'All of them,' said Raif sadly. 'I am excluding Durand of course. As it happens he does have witnesses to his

258

presence at the civil service so he would be discounted anyway.'

They left the police car and went inside. Lucien Moreau was not on reception, but his wife was. She seemed no more pleased to see the policemen than her husband had been.

'Are any of the guests here?' asked Briant to Madame Moreau.

The question was answered when they heard a man coughing nearby. The group turned to see cigarette smoke wafting from behind a partition.

'Monsieur Lefevre,' said Briant.

Madame Moreau pointed towards the kitchen and said, 'The Bougereaus and the Friedmans just went to lunch. Perhaps you could allow them to enjoy lunch first before they answer any more questions.'

'Lunch?' said Mary brightly before she remembered how the rather angry woman before them had added an unusual ingredient to Inspector Berrada's meal. She frowned for a moment as she met the eyes of the Moroccan lady. Just for a moment something unspoken passed between them, then Madame Moreau smiled.

'Do not worry. I only did it with that pig Berrada.'

'Did what?' asked Briant, confused.

'Trust me, you don't want to know,' said Kit. 'Shall we have lunch?'

'Is Monsieur Durand here today?' asked Briant.

Madame Moreau's brow furrowed at this, 'No, he left hours ago. He won't be back until six as usual.'

259

This decided the issue and they agreed to have lunch at the hotel.

'Will you tell us immediately if Monsieur Durand should come?' asked Kit just as they turned to go to the dining room. Madame Moreau glanced at Kit and nodded, but she was already dealing with the arrival of the laundry man, and she waved them away.

They arrived in the dining room to be greeted by Lucien Moreau's face falling faster than Madame Guillotine's blade at an execution. Then his professional manner kicked in and a hesitant smile crossed his face.

'Lunch?' he asked hopefully.

'Yes, lunch,' replied Raif.

This perked the hotel owner up a little. This was not going to be on the house and four covers was four covers. He led them to a table near the window and away from the other guests. Kit noted that a new couple had arrived at the hotel. They were Spanish and clearly in the middle of an argument if their faces were any guide. He looked frustrated; she seemed hurt. Silence reigned like an evil queen over a land turned to ice. Or something like that, thought Kit.

'The lunch is a buffet,' said the proprietor indicating a sideboard full of tajines containing an extraordinary and intoxicating aroma of different dishes. 'You are welcome to help yourselves.'

This required no second invitation and the group descended on the tajine dishes. There were four on the sideboard and each took one of the strangely conical lids and lifted them up. Moreau was now in his element. He

260

had a captive audience who were clearly beguiled by the magical potions created by his wife.

'The sergeant is beside the lamb tajine. This is made with lamb, chopped tomatoes, apricots, dates and sultanas. It is finished off with a hint of coriander and parsley. The young lady is with the beef tajine which has prunes with ginger, cinnamon and paprika. Captain Briant you are with the chicken tajine to which my wife has added onions, green olives, and lemon zest. The final one, sir, is a fish tajine for some of our guests do not eat meat. This has white fish with green peppers, garlic, cilantro, cumin, coriander, turmeric. I think this is as good as any Bouillabaisse.'

'Really?' said Briant doubtfully. He hailed originally from Nice, and this was tantamount to a calumny for the man from Provence.

Moreau paused for a minute then shrugged, 'Perhaps not, but it is quite wonderful, I assure you.'

Kit tried it and it was. Briant avoided it on principle, although Kit suspected there was enough patriotic fear that it might turn out to be a match for the great French fish dish that he decided not to risk any inner conflict.

Mary carried her dish over to the table by way of the Friedman table. She smiled and chatted with them for a minute then joined the others at the table.

'What have I missed?' asked Mary as she sat down.

'Raif was just saying he thinks the Friedmans are guilty,' said Kit taking a mouthful of the beef tajine.

Mary paused for a moment then her eyes narrowed slightly. She turned to Raif and said, 'If I were to kill my husband for persistent lying would any jury convict me?'

261

'None,' replied Raif.

'None,' confirmed Briant.

'Have you any thoughts on the method of execution?' asked Raif.

'I have,' said Kit, supressing a smile. 'It's certainly not been tried before to my knowledge, but I think if anyone can do it...'

There was a loud thud from underneath the table. However, once more Mary remembered that Kit had sat on the bad leg side of her. She coloured slightly and began to giggle. It was a welcome relief for soon the mood on the table became more solemn as they considered their options on how to liberate their friends.

As they considered this point, Madame Bouguereau made her way over towards their table. Kit noted that she and her husband had already consumed at least one bottle of wine. By the rather unsteady nature of her gait as she clattered into one chair after another like a blind slalom skier, Kit suspected they had downed a least two.

'Monsieur Briant,' said Madame Bouguereau, arriving at the table. She straightened up to enhance a dignity which had taken as many knocks as the chairs en route. 'When will we be able to leave? Surely you cannot believe that my husband is in any way connected in this vile affair.'

Clearly in Madame Bouguereau's view, it went without saying that she was innocent. Kit sat back in order to enjoy the show. Captain Briant did not disappoint.

'You are quite correct Madame. If I had known that your husband is a member of the French Secret Service I would not have pursued any investigation. I only hope that I

262

have not blown his cover. But you must not tell him we know. Or indeed that you do, Madame. This would be a national disaster.'

Madame Bouguereau's face changed colour and expression as Briant spoke. She was now considerably paler, but there was something else in her eyes that Mary certainly recognised now. A fire had been lit and she glanced over towards her husband who smiled nervously and weakly waved his napkin at her.

'Good day,' said Madame Bouguereau. No longer staggering, she marched proudly over to her husband with a passion burning in her heart. The man she had married was a national hero; probably highly decorated, a spy who had faced unknown danger every day before returning home to an ungrateful wife who did not see or appreciate him for the man he was. This would change. Angelique Bouguereau would be the wife that Paul Bouguereau deserved.

'I wouldn't be in his shoes for all the world this afternoon,' said Kit starting to chuckle.

'I doubt he'll need shoes by the look in her eyes,' grinned Raif.

Mary frowned at the three men before saying, 'A little cruel, don't you think? Do men ever grow up?"

'My wife would probably agree with you on this,' admitted Briant.

'You obviously don't think he is our killer then.' said Kit. As he said this they all turned to see the poor man being yanked from his seat by his more powerful wife. Bedroom bound, suspected all at the table.

'Probably not,' replied Raif. They watched Madame Bouguereau dragging her diminutive husband towards the dining room exit. Lucien Moreau smiled and nodded to the couple as they left.

'I hope the mattress is strong,' said Kit, as he watched Mary dip her fork into his stew. He scowled at her. She ignored him.

They returned to the subject of the murder of Berrada. Discussion centred around how it would have been possible to murder Berrada outside of the hotel.

'The problem is how to bring him back without being seen,' observed Kit. 'By the way, was there a laundry delivery on the day of the murder?'

'No,' confirmed Briant with a half-smile. It was clear he had been thinking along similar lines. 'But even if there had been, how do you explain the fact that Berrada was seen picking up the keys at reception. Moreau saw him. Not just Moreau, both Keller and Durand saw him too.'

'Disguise,' suggested Kit, but even he seemed a little unconvinced by this. 'Berrada was out of sight for a considerable portion of the day. There was certainly enough time to kill him, bring him back to the hotel, disguise oneself to be seen. I agree, though, there are quite a few parts to this. Too many areas could go wrong, and it would have required at least two people, men, to carry the body into the hotel and place him in the room.'

Kit shook his head and placed his napkin on the table. It did not feel as if they were any further forward. Lucien Moreau came over with Jabir to lift the plates away.

'Would you like anything else? Dessert, coffee?'

Coffee was requested. Just as Moreau turned to leave, Kit stopped him.

'Monsieur Moreau? When Inspector Berrada returned to the hotel did you see him properly?'

'Of course,' replied Moreau. 'He was as far away as you are now.'

'Was he wearing his hat?' pressed Kit.

Moreau took a moment and then replied, 'Yes, he was.' Then after a moment he added, 'And sunglasses too, I remember.'

Kit leaned forward. He asked Moreau, 'Did he normally wear his sunglasses inside the hotel?' Moreau looked a little nervously at the table. All eyes were trained on him. This felt like an important piece of information that he should have shared earlier. 'Don't worry Monsieur Moreau, it is just a small detail.'

Moreau seemed to relax at this and replied, 'No. No, I have never seen him wear sunglasses in the hotel before.'

'So the man you saw was dressed like Moreau; he was wearing his hat and sunglasses. Therefore, you saw the man you would have expected to see.'

Moreau nodded slowly at this. The events of the evening were beginning to come back to him.

Briant took over at this point.

'Please Monsieur Moreau, I want you to think very carefully about this. Did you spend long looking at Berrada. You saw him arrive. He asked for his keys. You went to retrieve the keys and he took them from you. Correct?'

Moreau nodded. This was what had happened.

'During this transaction, would you have looked at Berrada for very long.'

'No. Not very long. The brim of his hat was low. I saw the bottom of his sunglasses and his jaw. He was unshaven as usual.'

'Think very carefully, Monsieur Moreau. Is it possible that the man you think was Berrada might have been someone else?'

'But it is impossible,' said Moreau. 'It had to be Berrada. It looked like him. It sounded like him. I would not make such a mistake.'

Moreau seemed as if he were about to cry. Mary reached out and put her hand on his arm.

'Don't worry Monsieur Moreau,' said Mary. 'It may have been the inspector. We're just considering all options.'

Moreau went away to get the coffees while the group remained silent until he was out of earshot.

'It wasn't Berrada,' said Kit.

'I agree,' said Briant. 'This, at least, suggests that we are looking for a man who is not young. Berrada was unshaven. His beard was grey. This could only have been one of two men if the murderer came from the hotel.'

'Keller or Lefevre,' said Raif.

'Or both,' pointed out Mary.

'I still think Madame Bouguereau...' said Kit. He was unable to finish the sentence as he was assaulted by three flying napkins.

27

Walter Harris and Emily Keene returned to the café just before lunch having called in a couple of favours. Should a need arise to enter the villa without the permission of the owner then they had a large number of people that they could call upon for such an endeavour.

Walter Harris and the Sharifa had spent their adult lives in Tangier. It was a town they loved for very similar reasons: it had accepted them and the unusual choices they had made when it came to perilous terrain called love. They knew each other too well to ask questions and they liked one another too much to judge. Each had found freedom in Tangier, but this is its own prison. Neither could leave the gilded cage now; neither wanted to.

Despite the worry they felt for their friend, Agatha, they enjoyed not only being in one another's company, but also the chance to be of use. Of course, the Sharifa had her son, the Sharif, but what did that mean now? People like her, the European invader, had all but stripped the people of Morocco of any real power in the cities. In the countryside it was different. No one had control there, least of all the Spanish.

The passing years had not diminished either's sense of adventure. They remained moths hypnotised by the flame and who could not be beguiled by this country and Tangier? All around them they saw the reasons that they loved Tangier. The noise of the ululating women, the colours of their dresses, the stir of the market, the beautiful young men walking gracefully past the café.

Some men arrived at the café whom the Sharifa recognised. Her son had sent them. They were, to Walter Harris's eyes, men you would want beside you when there was trouble. Their headscarves hid most of the faces, but it was in the eyes. Tough men from Wazan, a town just south of Tangier. All carried rifles on their backs. It was strange, reflected Harris, such a sight in London would be greeted with hysteria if they were not army, here in Tangier no one batted so much as an eyelid. Tangier was endlessly intoxicating for this reason as much as any other.

Soon after the men from Wazan disappeared into the shadows cast by the mid-afternoon sun, Kit, Mary and Captain Briant showed up at the café.

'Where is Sergeant Raif?' asked Harris.

'He is looking into the Berrada case once more. It would not do for us to ignore it completely,' admitted Briant.

They joined Harris and the Sharifa at the table to gaze into the square. While the Sharifa updated them on the new arrivals, Kit pondered on how they could gain access to the villa without causing risk to life. He had no doubt that the villa was defended, but their knowledge of how many

268

men and how well armed they were, was scant. They needed inside information.

Around four in the afternoon, they received it.

It was Walter Harris who saw him first. The journalist had an eye for the local trade, young men in particular and this one seemed familiar. Where had he seen him? Had he been with him? No, he would have remembered that. Then it hit him.

'That's the young man we saw this morning with Miller. I'm sure of it.'

All eyes turned towards the square. There were a number of young men milling around the market.

'Which one?' asked Kit.

'You're right, Walter. That young man over there without the headscarf. I'm sure it was him.'

Harris was on his feet immediately and over to the young man. The young man turned to look at the café and then seemed to smile. He and Harris walked over to join the rest of them.

'May I present Nassim,' said Harris. 'He was with Miller earlier today as I thought. Tell them what you told me Nassim.'

The young man smiled and spoke rapidly in French. He told them of the plan to rob the villa of a painting and that he was to meet Miller at two in the morning to help him escape. It was clear that he had no idea that Miller had been captured.

Then they struck gold. As Briant bemoaned the fact that they had no idea of what they would encounter if they gained entry, Nassim spoke up.

269

'But I know the villa.'

This was greeted with astonishment.

'How?' asked Harris.

'I worked there for a week. Monsieur Goodman asked me to find out all I could about the layout of the villa and the number of guards.'

'Can you draw for us the layout of the villa?' asked Kit.

There was probably no better person in Tangier for such a task as Kit was to find out. Nassim nodded eagerly.

'What about the number of men?' asked Briant.

'When I was there it was not so many. There were three Europeans, two men and one woman, but I think the woman has gone now. Then there are three guards and one man, Faisal, who acts as a translator for the European men. Oh yes and there is another guard, Fatima. She is a slave. They use her to scare the staff.'

'How many staff?'

'Three. One cook and two servants. They are all slaves too. I was working with them in the kitchen until Monsieur Goodman had all the information he wanted. Then I left.'

'Three guards, possibly four,' said Briant. 'I like those odds.'

Kit nodded, but the risk remained too great to consider any kind of assault on the villa. Another thought had occurred to him. He turned to Nassim.

'You said there were two Europeans. Can you tell me what they looked like?'

'The one who owns the house is French. He has dark hair. I liked him. He smiled a lot.'

'And the other.'

Nassim fixed his eyes on Kit.

'He was English. He looks very like you.'

Kit wasn't sure if his mouth fell open at this point, but it was probably a close-run thing.

'Olly,' he whispered.

Briant frowned. 'What do you mean?' he asked.

'Olly Lake,' said Kit.

It was Briant's turn to look shocked. His eyes widened slightly, 'Do you mean Lord Oliver Lake?'

Kit nodded.

'He is one of the leaders of ORCA,' said Briant. There was a light in his eyes now. The chance to deal a significant body blow to an organisation that was spoken of in hushed tones of fear among senior policemen and politicians would be the greatest moment of his career.

Kit looked at the young Moroccan. He asked Nassim, 'You said that you are able to draw a plan of the villa?' This was greeted with a smile which Kit took to mean 'yes.' Kit took a notebook and pencil from his breast pocket and handed it to Nassim.

For the next few minutes they watched in fascination as Nassim drew a plan of the downstairs and upstairs parts of the villa. When he was finished he basked in everyone's acclaim.

'Where do you think our friends might be?' asked Kit. Nassim shrugged, but Kit had not held out great hope on this. He already had his eye on a large reception room upstairs. Knowing where they might be held was one thing. Finding a way to extricate them was something else.

Around five in the afternoon they saw a cart accompanied by half a dozen Berbers arrive at the villa.

'Good Lord, Kit. Isn't that your man in the cart?' exclaimed Harris.

'Bloody hell,' said Kit or something very like it which made Mary give him a sharp look. Kit smiled sheepishly for a moment. 'What on earth are they doing?'

One of the men appeared to be knocking at the gate.

'That's Chafiq,' said Harris. 'I'd know him anywhere. He's Raisuli's right hand man. What on earth would he be doing here?' Harris had risen to his feet and was on the point of calling out to Chafiq when Briant grabbed his arm.

They watched as the gate of the villa opened. A man appeared and he and Chafiq exchanged a few words. Moments later the gate opened fully, and the cart was ushered in. Then the gate was shut.

The extraordinary scene reduced the table to silence for a few moments then Kit turned to Briant.

'How many rifles do you think could be loaded onto that cart?'

Briant smiled. He had been thinking along similar lines. He paused for a moment to collect his thoughts on the size of the cart and then made a quick mental calculation.

'Including ammunition then I would say at least one hundred rifles.'

Harris was astounded by what he was hearing.

'Are you saying that these men are running guns to Raisuli?'

Kit nodded and then a smile slowly crossed his face.

'I have an idea.'

272

28

Harry Miller rose from his prone position and looked up at the concerned faces of the three ladies. He noted that the two gentlemen were somewhat less concerned and, if he had to put a finger on it, they looked a little peeved.

'So much for the Caravaggio,' said the larger of the two men who Miller learned was Sidney Goodman.

'How can you think of your painting at a moment like this?' snapped Betty angrily.

This was greeted with a shrug by Goodman. He was so close to the Caravaggio he could almost touch it. Why hadn't he asked Nassim to steal it? Then he realised this would have been too much of a risk due to the young man's inexperience. If he failed it would have tipped off Bourbon that someone was not only aware of its existence but wished to relocate it to a house that wasn't his.

Miller rubbed the back of his head and said reassuringly, 'Nothing hurt, only pride and any belief in my intelligence.'

'What happened?' asked Agatha,

'It's a long story,' said Miller. This was not enough to deter his new room mates who insisted on hearing everything.

'After all,' said Sausage. 'It's not as if we are going anywhere, is it?'

For the next few minutes, Miller related, in detail, his extraordinary encounter with Raisuli and Tiger Sarll. This drew gasps from Betty and Sausage who enjoyed the story and a look of regret from Agatha. When Miller had finished she patted him on the hand.

'I'm sorry Harry. I cannot tell you how much I feel responsible for the risks you faced today. I can barely bring myself to think about what might have happened. He's a very dangerous man.'

'I noticed,' said Miller with a grin. Then he took in their surroundings. The room was large and tastefully furnished. The windows had the inevitable bars. Then he went over to the door to study the lock. 'Shouldn't be too much of a problem.'

This perked up Joel. He joined Miller by the door.

'You can open this?' he asked in tones approaching awe.

'Yes, pretty straightforward.'

It was for Agatha to stick a pin in the rapidly inflating balloon of hope in the room.

'Then what would we do?'

'We still have to evade Fatima and the other guards.'

Miller frowned and said, 'Fatima? Is that..?' He put his hand up high and widened his shoulders. The ladies nodded. 'I wouldn't fancy tangling with her.'

Miller sat down glumly, as did the others. They were going nowhere anytime soon.

*

275

Bourbon led the Chafiq around to the side of the villa to a small, pastel pink, outbuilding. Taking a large key from his pocket, he opened the door and allowed Chafiq to peer inside. The interior was stacked with five feet long wooden crates. By the door was a crowbar. Bourbon handed it to the Moroccan.

Chafiq, oddly, wasn't sure if he fancied trying to open the boxes. It would be a poor show if he failed. He, in turn, handed it to another man and beat out a rapid series of orders. The man had no more idea of how to use the crowbar than Chafiq.

'*Mon Dieu,*' said Bourbon and took possession of the metal implement once more. He went over to a box and levered the crowbar under the lid. The lid splintering was like the crack of a rifle shot. Coincidentally, the crates contained British army issue Lee Enfield 303s. The eyes of Chafiq glinted at the sight of the weapons lying in the crate. There were another ten of these crates plus ammunition.

Then Bourbon motioned with his finger for Chafiq to follow him further into the store. He indicated another half dozen boxes. Just as he was about to hand Chafiq the crowbar, he thought better of it and decided to open it himself. If Chafiq had been happy before, the sight that greeted him caused him to dance a jig of delight.

'I thought you might like this,' said Bourbon. He started to chuckle at the childlike joy of the Berber. Then he watched as Chafiq shouted to the men in Arabic. It sounded like it was time to load up the cart.

*

276

Fatima reappeared in the room carrying another tray. This time it was coffee. By now her appearance was greeted less with mortal fear than a welcome relief from the morose monotony of the room. Agatha even attempted conversation with her.

'How long have you worked with the Comte?' asked Agatha. Her Arabic was remarkably intact given how infrequently she had been in the region since the passing of Eustace. Her facility had never quite matched that of her husband but, as she pointed out, he'd had a head start plus lecturers to help him. In response, he'd smiled that lopsided smile and agreed with her before toasting her with whatever drink he happened to be holding at that moment. How she missed him.

'They told me not to talk to you,' said Fatima, who left the room immediately she had performed her duty.

'Well Agatha, have you further thoughts on how we can extricate ourselves from this?' asked Goodman. His voice was drained of any energy or hope. It was almost enough to make one feel sorry for him. Almost.

'Further thoughts?'' said Agatha dismissively. 'I haven't managed the first one yet.'

This was enough to add another layer of gloom to the room which lasted for a quarter of an hour. Finally, Goodman rose from his chair and banged on the door. No response. He banged again. It opened and a rather irascible person demanded to know what he wanted.

'Can you tell our delightful young friend here that I need to pay a visit, ' said Goodman,

'Again? What on earth is wrong with you?' said Betty

277

This was greeted once more by a rather defensive Goodman,' my prostate. I've passed more water in the last few weeks than the Nile.'

Betty was beginning to regret bringing the topic up and tried to turn it to something less revolting, but, thanks to Agatha's Arabic, Goodman had already exited the room. About a minute after Goodman had left the room they heard shouts downstairs. Then two shots were fired.

'What on earth has Sidney done?' exclaimed Sausage.

More shouting. It was coming from downstairs. There were a lot of voices now and they didn't sound as if they were discussing cake recipes. A rush of footsteps up the stairs.

Then they heard something else which chilled all of them.

29

Olly Lake and Comte Jean-Valois de Bourbon stood and watched as the Berber horsemen assembled in the courtyard in front of the villa. To ensure things went smoothly they assigned an additional two men from their own guard to accompany the weapons back to Raisuli's camp.

Chafiq arrived on foot and climbed nimbly onto a horse that was being held for him by one of his men. He glanced up at the late afternoon sky. There were hints of red on the horizon and the sun was turning orange.

'Will you be back before night?' asked Bourbon in a voice that hinted at the frustration he felt. The group should have arrived earlier. Travelling at night, even well-armed was an unnecessary risk.

'Yes,' replied Chafiq. 'But we won't stop. We will move deeper into the country.'

'*Bon voyage*,' replied the Frenchman. Chafiq glanced towards the Englishman. He said nothing. If anything, he seemed a little bored. Chafiq didn't care. They had what they wanted; needed, even. These men were not his brothers. He disliked them, but that was not important.

They were useful. They were helping his master fulfil his destiny in ridding the country of foreigners. Recently, he'd wondered if Raisuli's heart was still in this great enterprise. The arrival of the weapons would surely reignite the fire that had once raged so wildly in the great man's eyes.

A nod from Bourbon and the gates opened. Chafiq said nothing more. He pulled his horse around and moved it towards the gate. His men and the cart followed. They went past the front wall of the villa into the square. A few people looked up at them, but there was not that much interest. Chafiq smiled as he gazed across at the carpet sellers, the caged animals, the men and women still bargaining for fruit and vegetables. Would they understand what he and Raisuli were doing? And Krim, in the Rif Mountains? Would they be seen as heroes? Also, what of him, Chafiq? This was the second time he had made this trip to bring weapons to Raisuli. There would be others. Was he not a hero too?

They formed a convoy with five horsemen ahead led by Chafiq, the cart in the middle, three more horsemen behind. The convoy turned right and headed back in the direction from which they'd come. This meant negotiating a few narrow streets which was not without its challenges and enjoyment. There was always a degree of satisfaction in seeing people diving into doorways to avoid being trampled.

The cart rattled along the road which had smoothed over the years. The next street signalled the start of their uphill ascent. Then the roads would become rockier. They would have to travel more slowly to protect the wheels of the cart.

They turned towards the hill and began to ascend. As they rounded a corner they saw a cart blocking their path. A wheel had come off. Chafiq exploded with anger and screamed at the man to get off the road. Perhaps, as Chafiq later reflected, rather than being angry he should have been thinking; been more alert to potential danger. You have a lot of time to think chained in a dungeon.

The man pointed to the cart and asked for help in putting the wheel back on. Chafiq was incensed, but there was no other choice. He had to help the man as there was no way he could replace the wheel on his own. He pointed to three of his men to dismount and help the idiot who was holding them up.

The front three riders did as they were ordered. They were on the ground in the blink of an eye and over to the cart. The wheel was not damaged, thankfully. Two of the men lifted up the cart while the third plus the cart owner started to put the wheel on.

Suddenly he heard a noise behind him. It sounded like a bolt action on a rifle. Perhaps it was just one of the men being careful. Too late it began to occur to Chafiq that they were horribly exposed just at that moment.

It's an interesting thought and perhaps one that may one day deservedly earn a Nobel Prize or some such award, that humans can often anticipate a disaster of unknown origin or consequence, a split second before it happens. Chafiq experienced that elevated moment of enlightenment and just as he was about to act on the insight he saw four men with rifles appear from the shadows dressed in tunics and headscarves. Two of the men trained their weapons on the two men holding the cart and the one on the wheel. The other two were pointing their guns directly at Chafiq and the other two riders at the front. There was no chance of responding as all had their rifles draped over their backs. Chafiq would also later rue this decision from the luxury of the dungeon in which Raisuli placed him.

Chafiq turned around and saw that the men at the back and the driver of the cart were similarly covered by the unknown assailants. The heart of Chafiq sank to the pit of his stomach. This was not good. How would Raisuli react? That was assuming he would survive this encounter, but the shocks were not quite over yet for the poor man whose only qualifying skill for leading these fighters was the fact that he could speak French.

One of the men at the front pulled back his headscarf. Chafiq stared at him in shock. He looked like the Englishman he'd just seen a few minutes ago, left at the villa. Was this a double cross?

'Lay down your weapons,' ordered the man in French. He waved his pistol to emphasise where the ground was which was a tad patronising by any reckoning. Within a couple of minutes the Berbers had been dispossessed of their weapons and led to a house. The next indignity for these warriors was only minutes away.

Kit strode over to the cart along with Briant. The Frenchman climbed aboard first and helped Kit up. They quickly opened the first crate, and it confirmed what they had suspected. It was full of rifles. Kit's attention was taken by the smaller boxes. They were in two sizes. He opened up the smaller sized box first. Ammunition. Thousands of rounds would be in these boxes, truly a deadly cargo. Briant, meanwhile, focused his attention on the second box. He gasped when he saw what was inside. The sound made by Briant persuaded Kit to peer over also.

'That's interesting,' was Kit's only comment. He turned to Chafiq. 'You will come with us.' Then Kit waved to his men who began to force the Berber tribesmen off their horses.

*

The guard at the gate of the villa peered through the grill and was somewhat surprised to see the face of Chafiq staring back at him. He glanced past Chafiq and saw the men on horseback and the cart all outside the villa. There was no question it was them. Chafiq seemed in his usual bad mood. Without paying too much attention, he opened the gate to permit access to the Berbers.

Bourbon witnessed what was happening from the front window of the villa. Something was wrong. Why had Chafiq returned? It made no sense. Had they encountered police or army en route? This could be the only explanation as delaying their departure meant risking making their journey just as night was falling. They were clearly well-armed, but it was a risk, nonetheless.

Olly Lake looked up at Bourbon from the table. He had a whisky in front of him and was mid sip when he saw the face on Bourbon.

'Something wrong?'

'Chafiq has just returned.'

'He's what?' exploded Lake, but Bourbon was already heading for the door. Half a minute later, Bourbon was striding into the courtyard. His senses were bristling with anger and something else. Worry.

'What's wrong?' he demanded; his eyes were fixed on Chafiq. What he saw made him stop in his tracks. Something was wrong. He turned to look at the other men. Then he saw two men in the cart. They were holding something in their hands.

Then he realised something was wrong. Absolutely and incontrovertibly wrong. Before he had time to think he was already running back up the steps to the door. Briant hopped down from the cart followed by Kit. He just had time to see Bourbon shut the door behind him and bolt it. Quite what the point of this was beyond Kit. Bourbon had seen what he and Briant were holding.

Dynamite.

Kit lit his fuse, as did Briant. Behind them Sharif of Wazan's men had opened fire on the reduced guard at the villa. Kit lobbed his dynamite towards the door, as did Briant then both men hunkered down.

An explosion reduced the door to matchwood. Kit and Briant made their way to the entrance but stayed either side. Both were clutching revolvers.

'I never liked this part,' said Kit.

'Me neither.'

'On the count of three?' asked Kit.

They started to count together.

*

'Good Lord, what was that?' asked Sausage, leaping to her feet. This was no small accomplishment for someone who had suffered a broken leg only four months previously

284

and a tribute to the shock that reverberated around the room.

Even in such moments of crisis, Agatha's best instincts always came to the fore, and she said acidly, 'I should have thought it was perfectly obvious what it was, Sausage dear.'

'Only asking,' said Sausage which made Agatha regret her intemperate response.

'Sorry dear,' replied Agatha. Then she turned to Harry Miller. 'Harry, I think now is the time to call upon your unique skills.'

Miller was on his feet in a flash, gripping a hairpin, which, as all devotees of thriller fiction will immediately appreciate, is sufficient to open all manner of doors, safes and treasure chests. Miller duly accomplished his task before returning the hairpin to its owner, in this case, Betty. They opened the door.

There, not so much standing in the doorway as filling it, was Fatima. Two arms flew out and grabbed Miller by his shirt, lifted him clean off the ground and threw him several feet across the room.

It seemed no one was leaving quite yet.

*

When the first explosion obliterated the front door it would be fair to say that it was not the only obstruction that fell away. Sidney Goodman had been having difficulty performing an activity that, although utterly natural and very common, has rarely featured in the great novels of our time. It would be difficult to imagine Mr Darcy, David Copperfield or Jean Valjean in quite the same way if Miss Austen, Dickens or Hugo had added extra such scenes.

285

Your humble chronicler has no such qualms about forging ahead into territory that is, quite literally, as dark as it is unpleasant.

But I digress.

Suffice to say that the explosion cleared more than one passageway in the house at that moment and Sidney Goodman, not the bravest of men at the best of times, was up and away in a matter of seconds from his rather vulnerable seated situation in the bathroom.

Although not courage incarnate, he was shrewder than a rich moneylender and just as kind-hearted. Not for one second did he consider rescuing his comrades in captivity. An opportunity had presented itself and he was just the man to grab it lovingly in both hands. The guard outside the bathroom had disappeared for the very good reason that there were explosions detonating around him. This left Goodman free to make his way along the upstairs corridor to a room that was of specific interest to him. The sound of gunfire saw Goodman quicken his step somewhat.

*

'Three,' said Kit and Briant in unison with their hearts thumping like Paavo Nurmi at the end of a race.

They crossed the threshold into the entrance hallway. It was covered with wood and brick. Smoke and the smell of cordite filled the air. Behind Kit and Briant followed a number of the Sharif's men. Rather impressively to the two former soldiers' eyes, they fanned out and began entering the downstairs rooms.

Kit and Briant made for the large drawing room which Nassim had indicated overlooked the front courtyard. Each took one side of the door and then Briant turned and kicked it open. The two men dived into the room.

It was empty.

They stood up, both feeling a little foolish. In the background they could hear shouts, but no gunfire. Kit scanned the room then his eyes fell on a cut glass tumbler on the table. There was some whisky in the glass. He looked at the bottle: a Macallan Single Malt Whisky.

'Olly was here,' said Kit, simply. He looked at Briant who was at the window.

'It looks like we have control. Let's find your aunt and her friends. You don't have much time. The commotion we've created will have attracted attention.'

Kit and Briant made their way up the stairs. At the top they were confronted by a rather uncommon sight. A woman, dressed in black, over six feet, wide, was point blank refusing to give way to one of the Sharif's men even though he was pointing a rifle directly at her. The arrival of Kit made her blanche slightly.

If she blanched then Kit certainly did. It took a few moments to decide which eye he should fix his on. One eye was staring directly ahead, the other appeared to have a roving commission. The sight of Kit made her stop. It was almost as if she was awaiting instructions. Briant glanced at Kit and said, 'I think she likes you. Ahhh, romance.'

Kit pointed to the door behind her. Much to everyone's amazement, she stood back.

*

Inside the room, Miller had dusted himself down and was preparing for round two. He didn't fancy his chances

287

much. Nor Agatha. She said, as he headed towards the door.

'I wouldn't if I were you Harry.'

Miller was about to comment on the vote of confidence he'd just not received when the door flew open. In walked a man dressed rather like one of the other captors. So did two other men, but they were more familiar.

'Christopher,' exclaimed Agatha.

Betty was a little less formal. She enveloped Kit in a bear hug that might have squeezed any remaining air out of him if Briant had not stepped in and said, 'You must leave immediately. The police will be on their way.'

This was probably not the time to quibble about definitions, but Agatha, true to form, did so anyway.

'I thought you were the police?'

'It's a long story,' said Briant. 'Now, move, please. There's no time to explain.'

Outside the room they ran into the large form of Fatima who had finally consented to putting her hands up. She was motioned to by the Sharif's man to go down the stairs and join the others who had been captured.

'Wait a moment,' said Agatha. 'Leave her.' Everyone turned around in amazement, none more so than Harry Miller who was still feeling the effects of his unscheduled flight across half the room. Agatha looked from Fatima to the Sharif's men and said in Arabic, 'She's with us.'

Agatha went up to Fatima and addressed her in Arabic.

'Are you a slave?'

Fatima nodded. There was shame on her face and for the first time Miller, without understanding the exchange

288

between Agatha and the extraordinary woman, sensed that there was more to her story.

'Come with us,' ordered Agatha in a manner that Fatima understood as authoritative.

She paused for a moment. Then a tear fell down from her one good eye.

30

As the two sticks of dynamite reduced the front door of the villa to smithereens, Chafiq made both the best and the worst of decision of his life. He took advantage of the evident mayhem to bolt for one of the horses. He was on it before you could say, 'Get me out of here,' which he did in Arabic. The horse, who was no more attached to the idea of hanging around the pandemonium than Chafiq, gladly obeyed and tore off through the gates before the Sharif's men had time to take in what was happening.

As he went through the gates he saw two caleches pull up. Seated by the driver was an old woman who looked familiar, but then his attention was diverted by the other caleche where a beautiful young European woman was staring inside at the carnage. Her face a mask of concern. It was only a brief moment and then Chafiq was riding for freedom at full tilt. On his way up the hill he passed the old man whose cart had caused the disastrous series of events that had seen him dispossessed of the weapons. Of his men, there was no sign and, frankly, he did not care. He did not have his sorrows to seek. He spat in the direction of the old man as he passed.

He missed.

*

Olly Lake was a little too tall for the tunnel that he and Bourbon were ambling along. Neither wanted to give the appearance of panic, but each knew that they could not hang around. The invaders would soon work out where they had gone.

'Were smugglers really so small?' mused Lake, whose back was beginning to stiffen by being crouched over. Bourbon was the perfect height for the tunnel and could walk along without fear of cracking his head against a low hanging rock.

The tunnel was not a long one. It was the perfect size for someone who needs to escape and quickly. It took them out into a house on the other side of the square. The house was occupied by the family of one of the guards at the villa. He had been instructed always to keep the door to his cellar open. Then Bourbon stopped and smacked the wall very hard. Lake frowned at the Frenchman.

'What on earth is up with you?'

'The Caravaggio. I must go back,' said Bourbon.

He felt a powerful hand grip his shoulder.

'Don't Jean. We must go. There's no time now.'

Reluctantly, Bourbon turned around and began to walk forward again. Lake was right, but he felt a stab of pain at having to leave the painting behind.

The two men emerged out into a small back yard. Outside, playing nearby was a small boy of about eight. He looked at the two men as they came out from the door that led to the cellar. Lake smiled at the young child, took off his Panama hat and put it on the child's head. The little boy's eyes widened in delight. He waved to the two men as

291

they walked towards the side of the house and then disappeared.

Out in the square they could see smoke rising from the villa. Parked in front of the villa were two caleches. The two men stood and watched some figures emerge from the front gate.

'Well, well,' said Lake. 'It could only be Kit. We will have to do something about you old boy. This can't continue.'

Bourbon looked at his friend and then back towards the caleches.

'I never said before, but you do look a little alike.'

'Oh, I know. We were known as the terrible twins at school. Actually, I was the terrible one. Kit was a bit of a goody two shoes. He has all the virtues of our sex and none of its vices. Hopefully, time and marriage will knock some of the virtue out of him. It can be rather tiresome.'

The two men turned and began to walk towards a caleche. They hopped on board, much to the surprise of its owner. Then Bourbon showed him some money. This hastened a change in attitude. Soon they were off and heading towards a road that led out of the town.

They journeyed for three quarters of an hour, well beyond the limits of the town. The road took them through a mountain pass to a flat strip of land around one hundred yards long. A flock of black goats lay in the shade of half a dozen cypresses that looked as if they would fall over with the next gust of wind from the sea.

There was a large shed made from corrugated metal. The two men paid off the driver of the caleche and sent him on his way. Then they walked over to the shed, both casually smoking their cigarettes. It would be the last ones they would have for a while. They lifted up the shutter.

'There she is,' said Bourbon proudly as if he was talking about an accomplished young child.

The two men looked at the source of their unlikely salvation. A two-seater B.E.2 biplane. Although they were probably safe from being caught, time was of the essence. Light was fading. They needed to make a start.

They pulled the plane out from the shed onto a flat piece of ground. This was the start of a makeshift strip from which they would take off. Bourbon climbed into the pilot's seat while Lake did the honours and started the propeller blades.

The sound of the engine kicking in brought a smile to their faces. Lake ran around the side and hopped on board. They pulled on their leather helmets and goggles. A thumbs up from Lake and Bourbon began to taxi down the strip. The plane began to speed up which was a relief for the mountain was rearing up on them a bloody sight too quickly for Lake's tastes. Then, just as disaster seemed like it would strike, Bourbon pulled the plane up and they soared over the top of the craggy rocks.

Lake's decidedly oath-laden opinion on what he was sure was a practical joke of Bourbon's was lost in the sound of the air and the engine. Soon they were hundreds of feet in the air and speeding across the Mediterranean. Below them the sails of fishing boats looked like white pearls cast casually across blue velvet.

The sun was setting now. Half of the orange orb had already been absorbed by the sea. Spain was only a few miles away. Ahead of them they could see the coastline rising up from the blue. It was a welcome sight. Spain and the chance to start again lay before them. This was a setback, but it was not the end. Their work was too important to fail.

Lake ignored the first cough from the engine. He had been in a plane before. These things happened. The coughing became more persistent, however and his concern grew rapidly.

Then the engine conked out completely. Lake watched as Bourbon started moving his controls frantically and swearing in French. Just a note on swearing in French. It lacks something of the majesty, the intensity and the sheer catharsis one can achieve using Anglo Saxon to vent ones feelings. Perhaps another reason why French never quite cracked it as a global language.

Lake's eyes flicked from the Spanish coast, a mile or two in front of them, to Bourbon, who was still trying and failing, to get some life from the B.E.2. Finally, Lake gave voice to the one question, rising like bile, within him.

'I say, Jean, is it supposed to do this?'

*

The sight of Mary sitting alongside the driver of one caleche and Emily Keene sitting in the other with Nassim, was a welcome one for the former captives of Olly Lake and Bourbon. Joel was now reunited with a rather cheerful looking Sidney Goodman. They exchanged satisfied smiles, noted Kit. He elected to join them on Mary's caleche along with Harry Miller.

The ladies, accompanied by Fatima and Walter Harris, went into the other. They had already said their 'goodbyes' to Briant, who was still inside the house, searching, fruitlessly, for Bourbon and Lake.

'Where to?' asked Mary.

Kit looked to Goodman and Joel. He was still shocked to have run into them again, but clearly they had helped keep Aunt Agatha and the others away from the police, so some form of ceasefire was in order.

'Where were you and my aunt hiding out over the last few days? Perhaps we can go there,' said Kit to Goodman.

'Let Joel direct our driver,' answered Goodman with great equanimity. The caleche set off around the square towards market stalls. Despite the extraordinary scenes across the square, life was continuing as normal.

'They seem remarkably unperturbed by the explosions,' said Mary.

'Well, I suppose there were only two,' said Kit.

'Yes, they were rather small too,' agreed Mary before giggling. She felt a little giddy with relief. Initially, she had felt angry that Kit had said he would go in with Briant, but she knew that there was no other choice. To have accompanied them would only have added to the risk they were taking. Walter Harris was like a schoolboy going on his first hunt. He'd been delighted by the plan and the chance to be part of the raid. He had already begun writing the copy in his head.

The mood was one of triumph as they passed the market stalls. A few of the men and women glanced up at them then returned to their own lives. The sight of the caged animals was a reminder to Mary that this was a country so very different from her own. The dogs were all howling in fear at what they'd heard.

One was barking.

Mimi, like the other canine captives had watched and listened in horror at what was happening across the square. Like the others she began to howl in protest at being kept in a cage, at being exposed to clear and identifiable danger. It was not fair, and someone was going to know about it.

As she was howling for all she was worth, something caught her attention. Her ears pricked up and she stopped. In a moment she was on her feet. She'd seen Agatha, Betty and Sausage. She began to bark, but the sound was drowned out by the howling from her fellow prisoners.

It was no use. Agatha's caleche went past.

Mimi's barking became more panicked.

*

'Be it ever so humble,' said Sidney Goodman as he introduced Kit and Mary to the accommodation that Agatha and her friends had enjoyed for several days. Kit smiled and stepped forward towards the staircase.

'I'd watch the third and fifth steps if I were you,' warned Goodman.

Agatha piped up, 'Eleven and thirteen, too.'

'Really?' asked Goodman, surprised. 'I must have a word with the landlord about the staircase. It's unacceptable.'

'Treacherous, you mean,' said Betty.

The staircase was negotiated without any fatalities, and they entered a familiar room once more.

'Where's Mimi?' asked Agatha. She was staring at the open window. She went over to it. The street below seemed empty. A sadness fell on her. Although she had only been in possession of the Doberman for a matter of months, she had fallen for the creature. Perhaps, intuitively she recognised their similarities. Mimi prompted fear in the people she met, yet she was also capable of deep affection despite her fearsome appearance and, it must be said, nature. Agatha collapsed onto a seat and could not stop the tears as they started to flow.

Betty, Sausage and Mary were over immediately to offer comfort as the four men and young Nassim stood looking on uncomfortably. Hundreds of thousands of years of evolution, hunting mammoth and the like had ill-prepared the species for dealing with emotion. Kit concluded that it was best to leave it to the experts. However, such a raw display of sadness could not, at least, help but spark a good idea and it came thirty seconds later. He turned to Goodman and Joel and asked them the only question a proud son of England's green and pleasant land could ask at that moment.

'Do you have any tea?'

Given that he was dealing with two bachelors, it must be said that Kit's hopes were not high.

'No,' admitted Goodman.

Nassim and Betty headed off to buy some tea while the group considered their options. Launching a search for the animal as night was falling was impractical. When Nassim and Betty returned with the tea the young man produced a startlingly sensible suggestion. He would dragoon his impressive array of relatives, to keep an eye out for the missing Doberman. This was an exceptionally good plan and soon Goodman led Nassim away downstairs to see its immediate implementation.

He returned just in time to hear Kit and Mary updating everyone on the investigation into the murder of Inspector Berrada. This served to take Agatha, Betty and Sausage's mind off their worry surrounding the missing Mimi. As they spoke, Agatha's brain inevitably clicked into gear, and she began to pepper the couple with questions. She had come across a couple of locked room mysteries in her time and was convinced, like Kit and Mary, that the murder was almost certainly perpetrated outside the room. The names of the suspects meant nothing to her but, then again, admitted Kit, they could be aliases.

A silence fell on the group and then Agatha looked shrewdly at Goodman.

'Where did you disappear to when all the commotion started, Sidney?'

'I think you know Agatha.'

'And did you, by chance, pick up the painting while all of this was going on?' pressed Agatha.

Under any normal circumstance, Sidney Goodman was second to none when a lie needed to be told and, more importantly, believed. Under the relentless scrutiny of the old lady before him, he realised dissembling was useless. He smiled and shrugged his shoulders.

'Joel, would you?'

Joel left the room and reappeared a few moments later with a metal tube. He unscrewed the top and shook it. A rolled-up canvas fell out. Looking around the room he saw several very curious sets of eyes staring at the canvas. He unrolled it.

'The Maltese Falcon,' said Goodman.

The group gazed in silent appreciation at the painting by one of the greatest artists of his or any other generation. The falcon of the Knights of St John lay half in shadow with light filtering down in a single shaft. It was beautiful prompting a few moments of awed silence. Then Kit spoke.

'We must take this Sidney. It has to go into a museum.'

Anger flared in Goodman's eyes. He leaned forward as if he would snatch it away.

'You can't,' he snarled. 'It's mine.'

'It belongs to the world,' said Mary. 'You can't keep it locked away in some squalid little room in a house where you are hiding.'

Harsh, but true, thought Kit.

'There'll be a reward,' said Kit. 'I'll make sure that it goes to you both.'

'How much?' said Joel, eyes narrowing.

'I imagine it would be tens of thousands of pounds,' replied Kit, who had no earthly idea, but thought that it would do no harm to fib a little. Sidney and Joel glanced at one another. There was an imperceptible nod. The decision had been made.

'May I?' asked Goodman. He picked up the canvas and stared lovingly at the beautifully rendered image of the falcon. Then he rolled it up and slipped it back inside the metal tube. There were almost tears in his eyes as he handed it over to Agatha.

All eyes fell on Kit's aunt. Some things remained unexplained. It was now her turn to enlighten everyone on what had caused the whole mess in Morocco in the first place. She went through in detail all that had occurred from the moment of her arrival at the German Legation to the point where Raisuli had appeared and then simply let them go. She ignored the eye rolling from Goodman when she reached this point, but Kit was confused by this point.

'Why would he simply let you go? It doesn't make sense.'

'Don't forget, Christopher,' replied Agatha. 'He had no idea of what had happened in the Legation. Perhaps if he had then it would have been a different story.'

At this point Harry Miller piped up, much to everyone's surprise. His story had not yet been told.

'I know why,' said Miller.

All eyes turned to Miller, and he quickly told them about what had happened to him with the extraordinary leader. Agatha and the others had already heard the story, but it was new to Kit and Mary. Both listened in fascination at his brush with death, his encounter with Tiger Sarll and the deception at the villa.

'Anyway, I forgot to tell you what he said when I mentioned your name, Lady Frost,' said Miller.

*

'Lady Agatha Frost?' said Raisuli standing up and striding over towards Miller. 'Who killed my friend Berrada?'

Raisuli's face was only inches away from Miller's. He could feel the hot breath on his skin. Once more, Miller felt himself in the grip of fear. Raisuli's eyes were boring into him.

'I don't know. I don't know. Who is Berrada?'

The next few seconds seemed to last an eternity. It felt as if these might be his last. Then Raisuli stepped back. A smile crossed his face. Then it faded. His face became more thoughtful.

'What are you to this woman?' whispered Raisuli. Miller melt his confidence ebbing away partly because he was surprised by the question but also by his inability to define what he was to her.

'A servant,' he replied.

'Where is Lord Frost?'

'He died ten years ago,' replied Miller. This seemed to take Raisuli aback. For reasons he could not explain, Miller felt the fear diminishing. There was something in Raisuli's eyes. For a moment, if pressed, Miller would have said it was sadness.

'Dead?' said Raisuli, stepping away from Miller. He turned and shook his head. 'That was a man.'

Miller glanced from Chafiq to Sarll. Neither had any more idea of what was going on in Raisuli's head than he did.

'That was a man,' repeated Raisuli, sitting down. 'Once, many years ago, he sent a message to me. He said he would

301

give me five hundred pounds in gold if he and Lady Frost could have free passage through Tangier one night. I thought he wants something, so I demanded double that. He bargained hard, but I won. I had my thousand pounds in gold. I was very happy. The next day I heard he'd tricked me. That night he stole something from my friends in the German Legation and carried it past me under my protection. I never told this to Berrada. He would not have been pleased. Yes, Lord Frost, that was a man.'

*

Well if anything was designed to perk up Agatha and make her sad at the same time it was a story about her beloved 'Useless.' She chuckled as tears moistened her eyes.

'He never told me,' she said finally. 'Oh Useless.'

'Really?' said Mary, surprised. She was of the modern school of young women. There were to be no surprises in her marriage. Everything was shared. She said as much. Agatha shot a glance towards her and shook her head.

'I've always believed any good marriage needs secrets. What would be the point of trust otherwise? You'll learn, my dear.' Then she added an afterthought, 'and you needn't worry either.'

Mary glanced towards Kit and smiled back at her adopted aunt. However, there was decidedly too much emotion in the room for the men and something needed to be done. Thankfully, the minds of men dwell less on feelings than they do on solving the next problem. Kit's mind had moved on. He still had some questions for his aunt.

302

'What exactly did Gabrielle pass on to you from the Legation that was so important?'

The expression on Agatha's face remained sad. Her voice was an angry whisper.

'We learned the extent of the massacre that had taken place in German South West Africa. We had heard stories that the Herero and the Nama people were being slaughtered in their thousands following an uprising. We had no proof until our contact in the Legation supplied us with the information we needed. It was true. A general by the name of von Trotha had herded the men of the Herero into the desert and kept them there until they died of starvation. Then he went after the Nama people too. They ended up in concentration camps. Now, I know Britain treated the Boers shamefully after the war ended, but this was of a different order of barbarity. Thousands died and these reports told us that some of the Nama had been used for medical experimentation. It was horrific and would have brought shame on the German nation if the true facts were known.'

Agatha stopped and shook her head at the memory of what she'd read. Then she added, 'Useless and I had many German friends, but he always felt there was a violence underneath the surface. He feared them, I think. Anyway, once the Germans knew we had this information the game was up for them at the Algeciras Conference. They could do nothing except watch as we made Morocco a protectorate of France and Spain.'

'Hardly in the best interests of the Moroccans,' said Sidney Goodman.

303

'Why not?' challenged Agatha. 'The French have built endless roads; they have opened hospitals and dispensaries, and everything has been done to avoid hurting the religious sensibilities of the people. I'm not going to defend colonialism, but you cannot tell me that the people would have better off under the cruel rule of tribal chiefs who not only permitted slavery but demanded it. Lyautey did what he could to abolish slavery in the cities and the concubinage.'

The discussion was threatening to veer off in a new direction, so Kit steered it back to the night of the faked murder. There was one remaining aspect that had piqued his curiosity.

'So, Gabrielle Fish's supposedly dead body was taken away by Dr Arnaud, in an ambulance.'

'Nothing so obvious,' said Agatha. 'This was Useless after all. No, even here he had one more deception.'

Agatha looked up and her smile became melancholic. She shook her head sadly and turned to look out of the window into the night sky. The murmur of women playing Taarija drums soothed her.

'Really?' asked Kit. 'What did he do?'

31

Tangier: 10th July 1922

Kit Aston and Mary joined Captain Briant and a rather sour looking Sergeant Raif outside the Moreau Hotel. Kit had noted the expression when he and Mary met them outside. Unusually for Tangier at this time of year, the morning was cloudy, making the day rather humid. Mary was wearing a light blue linen dress with a blue shawl that would be removed as soon as soon as they were away from the shocked eyes of the locals.

'You missed the show,' said Kit addressing Raif, further adding salt to the wound.

'Don't remind me,' murmured Raif.

'We threw dynamite at a door,' continued Kit with a boyish smile.

'Yes, yes, I heard,' said Raif stalking away to the sound of laughter. Not Mary's of course. As the only adult in the vicinity, she knew when humour overstepped its boundaries and became a weapon for overgrown schoolboys to wound.

'So what did we miss?' asked Kit as he and Briant entered the hotel.

'Our esteemed Chief of Police for a start and then, soon after, Monsieur Durand.'

Kit laughed, 'I suppose a few explosions would be enough to shift Toussaint out from his chair.'

'Indeed,' agreed Briant. 'He arrived about five minutes after you departed. Strangely he wasn't pleased to see me, but when we told him what we'd uncovered then his manner changed magically.'

'I suspect Durand was less pleased.'

Briant stopped and regarded Kit for a moment with a half-smile. Then he replied, 'You are correct. He was terribly angry. In fact, he accused us of disrupting an operation that had been months in planning.'

'He'd been keeping a watch on Bourbon?'

'So he says. I asked him why he had not arrested him and Lake when they had the chance.'

'What did he say?'

'He complained to Toussaint about my insolence and insubordination.'

'How did Toussaint react?'

'Let's just say that, for once, Toussaint was on our side. He sent Durand off with a few well-chosen words. No doubt someone from Paris will give him a dressing down, but Toussaint won't care. He can dine off this find for months. Harris promised to give him all the credit as the two men most responsible for the find will both step back into the shadows.'

Kit smiled and shrugged.

'Your modesty does you credit.'

They had passed through the entrance and were walking to the dining room. Inside there were some raised voices. Well, voice. It was Madame Bouguereau demanding to know what was going on while a rather irritable Raif was snapping back at her.

'Sounds like fun,' murmured Kit. In truth he was not looking forward to the next few minutes. He did not have a killer, just means, opportunity and motive. Unfortunately, several of the people attending could qualify on this score.

'Where is your aunt by the way? I thought she might want to be here for this,' said Briant.

'It's a long story,' replied Kit, 'involving a dog.'

'A Doberman by any chance?'

*

Agatha, Betty and Sausage just at that moment had returned to the scene of their flight to freedom. The reason for the return was that Agatha had recalled seeing a market trader selling animals. She'd heard the plaintive cries but, for once, had been too preoccupied by her own problems to act. By the time she reached Sidney Goodman and Joel's low rent accommodation, her decision came back to haunt her. The realisation that she might have passed Mimi broke her heart and sleep did not come easy that night.

As soon as the market opened, she wanted to be there just in case Mimi had somehow been captured and caged. They hired a caleche and went, undisguised, to the marketplace. The caleche had barely stopped moving when Agatha jumped down to speak to the owner of the animals.

307

'I am looking for a large black dog,' said Agatha in Arabic. Panic was rising within her. It was clear to her that Mimi was not there. This was confirmed a moment later.

'I am sorry, but we sold just such an animal ten minutes ago.'

Agatha extracted a description of the dog that had been sold. It matched Mimi's.

'What was the name of the man who bought her?' asked Agatha hopefully. This was greeted with a shrug. Agatha bit back an angry rebuke. This wasn't the time to discuss poor sales administration.

'Did the owner put the dog in a cage or on a lead?' asked Agatha. This was a strange question which made the stallholder frown.

'No cage,' he replied. 'The dog was on a lead.'

Agatha thanked him and joined her companions back in the caleche.

'We've just missed her,' said Agatha to her friends before adding to the driver of the caleche. 'Back to the villa, quickly.'

Just a few minutes earlier, a man had indeed purchased Mimi for a rather inflated price in his view, but the animal was magnificent, no question. Abu al-Wahad saw himself as a businessman, a trader who bought and sold goods; import and exports. The goods in question were human and demand for them was high amongst houses seeking to benefit from the prestige of owning slaves.

The recent passing of one of his dogs had left a gap that needed to be filled. The specification was simple: the dog must be big and fearsome. Abu was about to hit the mother lode on this morning as his caleche rattled into the square where, he had heard, a battle had taken place just the day before and a gun-running ring broken up. Such matters did not concern him. He was a businessman, nothing more, nothing less.

The purchase of Mimi would have been a protracted affair had Abu more time. Alas, he was time's slave. A deal was struck, and the dog loaded onto his cart. He tied the animal to a pole. Throughout the process the animal had stared at him in an unsettling silence. This had obviated the need to beat the dog with the stick that he always carried with him for protection, and occasionally disciplining animals belonging to him.

They set off into the town on the short journey to his business headquarters near the Kasbah. Arriving at the house, Abu made his big mistake, he reflected later. He forgot to take his stick. A false sense of confidence and a little bit of concern made him believe the animal was more passive than he would have liked.

He looked at the large Doberman as it lay inert on the cart. Then he climbed up and untied the rope from the side of the cart. This was the moment that Mimi had been waiting for. All at once the passivity evaporated. She was on her feet in an instant, sinking her teeth into the hand of the unfortunate slave trader. Abu screamed in agony, releasing his hold on the rope.

Mimi felt the rope slacken and was off in an instant. Abu looked from his bleeding hand towards the rapidly diminishing shape of the black beast. He howled in agony before unleashing a volley of abuse in the direction of the Doberman who had now, officially, disappeared.

Mimi's flight through the town was watched in awe by the inhabitants of Tangier. One or two brave souls tried to catch her but ended up with a few grazes as they hit the ground clutching air.

Ten minutes later, Mimi reached the villa and saw a familiar face outside. The familiar face in question was Joel. The little Egyptian was in a good mood as he fly-tipped rubbish from the villa onto the street. With the prospect of a large reward coming is way, his life was looking up finally.

He heard the familiar bark first. He turned around to see the diabolic black creature bounding towards him. Fear gripped Joel. The Doberman was barking like mad and heading directly for him. Mimi, meanwhile, was ecstatic. At last, a face she knew. Soon she would be reunited with the people she loved. She barked for all she was worth to show her joy.

Joel stared in terror at the shape coming for him. Instinctively, he reached into his pocket and pulled out his gun. Mimi was less than a few metres away now. He pointed the weapon at her and shut his eyes.

Then he pulled the trigger.

*

The caleche of Agatha, Betty and Sausage sallied through the streets causing men and women to throw themselves into doorways. Sausage, meanwhile, dispensed apologies like confetti at a wedding. Even if they had been understood, most were met with an angry wave of the fist. They reached the villa in just a matter of minutes.

'Good Lord,' exclaimed Agatha, who had been sitting in the front.

'Is it her?' shouted Betty from the back.

Two faces peered out from the side of the caleche. They saw Joel lying on the ground, Mimi on top of him, licking his face.

'Will you stop this animal?' shouted Joel irritably before being bathed once more in Mimi's saliva. At the same time he thought it expedient to hide the gun in his hand. The experience had been a traumatic one, but there was one important lesson he would draw from it.

Next time he would load the damn gun.

32

In an odd way, Kit Aston would have had a lot of sympathy for this feeling as he stood before the guests he'd previously interviewed in connection with the death of Berrada. Just as a gun is strikingly more effective when it is loaded with ammunition, solving a case is similarly enhanced when you have actual evidence and a specific suspect with whom you can associate it.

For the first time ever, Kit was beginning his summary of the crime with neither certainty that he had the correct means, never mind motive and no earthly idea who, as the writers of the most elevated form of literature would say, 'dunnit.'

'Thank you for agreeing to take part today,' said Kit to the guests who were seated at various tables in the dining room. Joining them were the hotel owners, Monsieur and Madame Moreau. Jabir was asked to man reception and to show Agatha and the others through when they arrived. Captain Briant and Raif flanked Kit, while Mary elected to sit near the Friedmans.

Silence followed this opening statement from Kit. Then it was broken by a cough from Durand. All eyes turned to him. They could see the anger on his face. Everyone immediately assumed he was guilty. Then Lefevre began to cough. He held up his hand by way of apology.

'Get on with it Aston,' snapped Durand. 'You're like something from a cheap novel.'

Kit was glad that Agatha was not around to hear such calumny. However, and rather frustratingly, the Frenchman had a point. This is something that no Englishman ever likes to admit. Kit was, indeed, prevaricating.

'Very well. I want to take you back to an incident that happened many years ago; 1905 to be precise. A party took place at the German Legation in which my aunt, Lady Agatha Frost, was seen to murder a young woman by dozens of guests. As you will no doubt have heard, the police have been looking for her for the past week. You will have a chance to meet her very soon. She is on her way here.'

This brought a gasp from Madame Bouguereau who was on her feet immediately.

'You are bringing a murderer here?' she shrilled. 'This is an outrage.'

Kit ignored her. His eyes were on Durand who was sitting impassively. Monsieur Bouguereau urged his wife to sit down. She obeyed immediately. There was a glint in the eye of the Frenchman and a certain colour to his cheeks that had previously been absent. Kit could not help but notice this. He glanced towards Mary who immediately covered the smile on her face.

'My aunt is guilty of nothing more than a certain sleight of hand and, what else? Oh yes, the theft of a top-secret documents from the Germans.'

313

Kit fixed his eyes on Keller. The German simply looked bemused.

'I won't go into what the documents said, but the contents were sufficient to embarrass the German government, weakening their position at a conference some months later at Algeciras. The theft took place under the nose of Inspector Berrada. The embarrassment must have been acute, and his response was brutal. The existence of the documents and their theft were assisted by a young Moroccan woman who worked at the Legation. She was among many suspects rounded up by Berrada and, under interrogation, or should I say, torture, she died.'

Kit went silent for a moment as he wanted this news to sink in for all those present. He wanted all of them to think about the young life sacrificed. Keller shifted uncomfortably in his seat. There was just a hint of anger on his face. The never-ending witch hunt of his nation was becoming unbearable.

'Of course, Yasmine, let us at least give her a name, was just one of many who died at the hands of this man. We will not mourn his passing and ordinarily I would have had nothing to do with this case were it not for the fact that my aunt is under suspicion for his murder. I think someone here knows otherwise.'

Kit let that hang over the room for a few moments before he continued.

'So we come to how Inspector Berrada was murdered. The killer locked the door and placed the gun in Berrada's hand to make it seem as if it was suicide. It was rather crude, and the post-mortem was always going to show that

314

there were no burn marks near the wound. So how was Berrada killed?'

'How indeed,' murmured Durand just loud enough for everyone to hear. The smile on his face was just smug enough to make Kit dislike him even more. It was if he knew Kit was playing for time.

'At some point after midday, Berrada was taken to a place and executed.'

Madame Bouguereau gasped and seemed on the point of fainting. These last few minutes had been very trying. To remain silent so long with everyone's attention elsewhere was something no woman, she surmised, should be forced to put up with.

Kit ignored her and continued, 'He was executed for the crimes he had committed against the innocent and then brought back to his hotel room and placed in a manner that made it seem as if he had committed suicide.'

'How?' exclaimed Lucien Moreau. It was unfathomable to him how this could have happened.

'Monsieur Moreau, you say that you saw Berrada arrive back at the hotel around six thirty on the day he was killed. What if I were to tell you that he, in fact, arrived some hours earlier, carried in a carpet that was ultimately destined to be put into Herr Keller's room to replace the one that he had ruined.'

Keller was on his feet at this.

'Enough. I have had enough of these vile insinuations. First you insult my country and then you all but accuse me of murder. How dare you. What did I do? Disguise myself as this policeman and walk around town pretending to be him. We look nothing alike.'

'In point of fact, Herr Keller, you are of a similar age, you both have a grey beard and with a few cushions in your shirt, sunglasses covering your eyes and a hat, I think we could easily take you for Berrada.'

This had its desired effect and caused the German to sit down. He was still enraged by what he was hearing.

'That is approximately what happened. I have my aunt to thank for helping me to solve this particular mystery. The killer bought a carpet from one of the many tradesmen in the town. He took the carpet to the location he had hidden Berrada, perhaps he'd hired a room, rolled the body up in it and then hired two men to transport the carpet to the hotel. He had already taken the key for Berrada's room when Monsieur Moreau was not at reception and was thus able to gain access without any trouble for the tradesmen. There are tradesmen in the hotel all the time. It would have passed without any comment. When they left, he unrolled the carpet in Berrada's room, he arranged the dead body as he wanted. Then, he took the carpet to your room, Herr Keller, room and placed it over the ruined carpet. I think you will find, if you go to Herr Keller's room that there are now two carpets there.'

All eyes turned to Keller. He was angry, but curious also. Beside him, Lefevre began to cough again while the Friedmans whispered to one another. They had their suspicions. Madame Bouguereau certainly did. She stood up and said, 'I demand you arrest the German, or I shall have my husband restrain him for you,'

This news was greeted with no little alarm on the part of Monsieur Bouguereau and some amusement from Durand and Lefevre. Kit turned to Briant who looked on a little sheepishly. Kit decided against looking at Mary. He suspected he would find little sympathy there.

'The body was now in place, but the killer's job was not complete. He had to convince people that the inspector was still alive. He left the hotel and returned to the rented room. There he changed into a white suit, hat and sunglasses that made him resemble Berrada before arriving at the hotel at six thirty, a time he knew would probably ensure there were a number of witnesses. He made a show of going up to his room. In fact he went to his own room, changed clothes and then returned downstairs. This was going to be the decisive moment. He went to reception and handed back his key to Monsieur Moreau. While Moreau replaced the key, the killer went to the window by reception and fired his revolver. He dropped the weapon into the drain, no doubt hoping to pick it up later.'

The guests of the hotel stared at Kit in mute shock.

'Of course we know what happened then. Uproar. The breaking into the room he'd locked from the inside using an old trick with a needle and thread. He stood with the others as the dead body of Berrada was discovered; an innocent bystander with the perfect alibi.'

'Who?' asked Durand in a bored voice dripping with scepticism. 'Keller? Me? Mr Friedman? Not Mr Bouguereau surely? Or Monsieur Lefevre?'

'That's Krapp,' said a voice from the entrance to the dining room.

317

Kit turned around and saw his aunt with Betty, Sausage, Sidney Goodman, Joel and Mimi.

'I say Aunt Agatha, that's bit strong,' said Kit, completely mystified.

33

It was Agatha's turn to look confused, but, true to form, she ignored the source of any misperception and forged ahead. She walked into the centre of the room and peered at one of the guests.

'Is that you, Wilhelm?'

'Kit's bewilderment rose a notch or two until three things occurred to him. Firstly, Krapp was a German name not just an opinion or, indeed, a by-product. Secondly, this meant that one of the guests had successfully managed to pull off a deception around identity which led to the third conclusion. Briant was already there on this score.

'Which one of you is Wilhelm Krapp?'

For a moment there was silence and then Lefevre started coughing again. When this fit had subsided he looked around to everyone and then said, 'I am Wilhelm Krapp. Or, at least, I was.'

'Did you kill Inspector Berrada?' asked Kit. Normally these situations require a certain amount of imperiousness of manner and a tone of righteous accusation. This was absent from Kit who now suspected he had all the pieces of the jigsaw in place.

There were tears in the eyes of Lefevre, but there was no sense of guilt in what he said next.

'Yes, I killed him. No, that's not right. As you said many times Monsieur, I executed him. He was an animal, guilty of many crimes. What I did was just. After what he did to those people, after what he did to that poor girl.'

At this point, Lefevre broke down completely. The Friedmans who were sitting nearby went immediately to comfort him. Durand looked on in disgust at the Swiss. Finally, he rose from his seat declaring, 'Well, I suppose that is that. If you don't mind and certainly I could care less, I will leave you to extracting your confession.'

The guests watched as Durand left the dining room. His footsteps echoed over the parquet floor with only Lefevre's coughing acting as a farewell. After a few minutes, the Swiss was able to speak once more.

'She was a sweet girl. An innocent child who carried a message. For this he killed her. By then I had left the Legation and fled to Switzerland. I am Swiss by birth. My mother was from Geneva, my father was from Germany. We went to live in Munich when I was ten and I joined the army when I was eighteen. My mother hated me doing this. She did not trust the Germans. But I knew best. My father knew best. How wrong I was.'

When I was posted to Tangier I began to see that my mother had been right. It was the arrival of Kaiser Wilhelm in 1905 striding off the ship like a nervous sheep that it became clear to me that Germany wanted war. Then I saw the reports coming from the South West of Africa. Horrible stories. I felt shame. Utter shame for what was happening. The massacre of the Herero and the Nama people was a stain on Germany and the army, and I wanted to let the outside world know.'

'So I contacted the British Legation through Yasmine. I asked that they send someone as I could not take the reports out myself. I knew nothing of the world of spying. Thanks to Lord Frost we had someone to give the report to, the rest you know. The contact was spirited out of the Legation in a carpet which gave me the idea for how to move Berrada back into the hotel after I killed him. I knew there would be an investigation about who had leaked the documents. I did not want Yasmine to be implicated, so that very same night, I escaped on a boat to Gibraltar and made my way back to Switzerland. I have lived there ever since as Julien Lefevre.'

Lefevre broke off once more as his cough returned. Mrs Friedman gave him a glass of water from which he drank greedily. He nodded his thanks to Mrs Friedman and continued from where he had left off.

'You may have guessed by now why I chose to return. This cough will only become worse. I was told perhaps I would live until the end of the year, but I don't care now. I have done what I needed to do. I have done what I wanted to do for fifteen years since I heard of what the vile beast did to that young girl. Believe me, I feel no guilt, only relief. If you want to arrest me, do so; my life is forfeit now.'

Lefevre broke down once more. This time there was to be no more from him. Kit turned to Briant. The two men said nothing. Only the slight shake of the head from Briant

321

gave any indication to Kit that Lefevre's last days and weeks would not be spent in a prison cell.

Agatha stepped forward and sat alongside the distraught man. She, too, seemed emotional. Kit joined her.

'You knew?'

'Yes, we knew it was Wilhelm or, at least, suspected. He seemed different from the others, and we wondered if he was the source. Then when we heard he'd left the Legation that night, we knew. Until today, I thought that he was a lover of the young girl, but perhaps this was the thinking of an old romantic fool. Poor Yasmine. She just carried some messages. Berrada was truly the vilest of men.'

Kit nodded without adding anything else to this assessment. He disliked the idea of capital punishment yet sometimes, sometimes...

At this point of high emotion when souls had been bared and deepest feelings shared, the last person one would have expected to say something sensible, something that would capture the moment, distil its essence and provide a way forward for all concerned, was Joel.

'We need to go,' said Joel.

Everyone turned to the little Egyptian. Caught in the glare of attention, Joel's speechmaking capabilities were found wanting. Thankfully, Agatha stepped in at this point to shed light on what Joel meant.

'He's right. We should go.'

"I don't understand,' said Kit.

'We have arranged a boat to carry us to Spain. It will leave with us on it, but we must go now. I am sure that Captain Briant will have no issue with this.'

Briant smiled an acceptance then added, 'I think that Lady Frost is right. If I am not mistaken, I think that our friend Durand will already be on his way to the Chief of Police to claim credit for catching Berrada's killer as well as the Morocco's most wanted old lady.'

'Less of the old,' snapped Agatha, but it lacked its usual bite.

The mention of Durand crystallised the issue immediately for Kit and he was on his feet. He looked at Lefevre and said, 'Come with us.' Then he glanced at Briant who once more smiled his acceptance, but Lefevre shook his head sadly.

'No, monsieur. I must stay and face what I have done.'

At this point a large shadow loomed over the Swiss. The owner of the shadow was a young woman named Fatima.

'Sorry, Wilhelm,' said Agatha. 'After a few weeks in Morocco I seem to have become infected by its penchant for kidnapping. You're coming with us.'

Then she said a few words in Arabic that Lefevre-Krapp understood to mean, 'Take him.' Lefevre looked up at Fatima and tried to catch one of her eyes. One was fixed on him with steely intent, the other appeared to be watching a tennis match.

Perhaps the idea of spending the rest of his life in a stinking hellhole of a prison did need some more consideration. In fact, further, and rapid, consideration began to suggest that a sanitorium in the mountains might be a better proposition.

'Go,' said Briant. There was urgency in his voice.

No further directive was needed.

323

'So who is this Rick?' asked Kit as they rode in the caleche down to the harbour.

'Someone that Sidney found,' explained Agatha. 'I suspect he runs guns along the coast.'

'Who for?' asked Mary.

'Whoever is paying him,' said Agatha in a voice heavy with disapproval.

They had two caleches to carry everyone. One of them was driven by the ever-smiling Nassim and his uncle. They road through the streets of Tangier at a pace that was breakneck for anyone foolish enough to get in their path, although, if timed on a stopwatch, probably was no faster than ten miles per hour.

'Who has the Caravaggio?' asked Kit.

'I do,' said Agatha. 'Sidney and I argued a bit about it again this morning. In the end he saw the wisdom of giving this historic painting back to the world.'

Mary had been listening intently to the conversation. She threw Agatha a look. 'You threatened him.'

'I might have pointed out some drawbacks to holding onto it,' replied Agatha, cryptically. She glanced towards Fatima in the other caleche then back to the road ahead. 'Ah, I can see our transport and Mr Rick.'

They had reached the harbour. About fifty yards away they saw a small fishing boat with a man wearing a white sailor's hat that suggested he was a skipper even if his vessel was old, needed a lick of paint and a prayer to navigate the high seas. A cigarette hung like a challenge from his lip. He smiled as he saw the approaching caleches. This was enough to make him rise from his seat. He wore a dirty blue shirt and cotton trousers.

'So you made it. Another few minutes and I'd have been off.'

'Distinctly poorer,' pointed out Agatha, stepping down from the caleche.

'I still have half,' pointed out Rick with a smile that revealed straight white teeth. He reached down and helped Agatha on board. This was the first time that Kit noticed a metal tube in his aunt's pocket. Mimi, who had no great love for caleches gladly hopped down and followed Agatha on board, much to Rick's dismay.

'Nobody said anything about a mutt,' he growled.

Mary was next on board. Rick took a little longer holding her hand as he appreciated the slender figure and delicately white skin.

'Are you with one of these jokers?' asked Rick hopefully.

'The blond one looking daggers is my current husband,' said Mary with a grin wicked enough to give the American serious thought about how to commit murder at sea.

Rick cast his eyes over Kit who declined any help on boarding the vessel. That would teach the American. The second caleche pulled up just as Lefevre boarded the boat. Betty, Sausage climbed down followed by Goodman who gingerly levered himself to the ground and Joel. The sight of Fatima gave Rick pause for thought on sailing away with the young English woman.

Betty, Sausage and Fatima joined the others on board as Rick began to take the rope holding them to the harbour away, the cigarette never left his mouth. Kit and Agatha stood at the edge of the boat.

'Well, I suppose this is it Sidney, Joel,' said Agatha. 'I should thank you for keeping us out of the way of the authorities.'

'It was nothing my dear Agatha. Look after our investment,' said Goodman pointing to the metal tube.

Agatha tapped the tube and said, 'All safe. Send me an address that I can reach you.'

Goodman smiled benignly as the small boat began to pull away. The smile suddenly transformed into something else as a police siren suddenly erupted. Goodman and the others on the boat saw a police car racing towards them.

'Stop,' shouted Agatha to Rick. The response to this instruction suggested this was around the last thing on the American's mind.

Joel acted immediately. He leapt onto the vessel and urged Goodman to do likewise. The police car was now almost upon Goodman. He turned from the group to the police car and then back to the group. He held his arms out and shook his head a little sadly. His bulk would have made any attempt at leaping onto the boat that was almost five metres from the jetty a folly.

'It's no use,' said Kit. The police car drew to a halt and two uniformed men from the Sûreté stepped out. They went towards Goodman, and each took an arm.

'No,' shouted Joel as he saw his partner about to be arrested. He turned to the others, his eyes wild with fear and anger. 'Do something.'

'There's nothing we can do,' said Kit feeling oddly desolate. He had no reason to like Goodman, but he had helped his aunt. This counted as a debt in Kit's book, one that he would make good. 'We can organise some sort of defence when we reach Spain.'

'Do something,' urged Joel. He was beyond reason now. Then, without any explanation, he jumped from the side of the boat and began to swim the twenty metres to the shore.

'Joel,' shouted Sausage, who had been the only one to develop a real liking for the Egyptian. 'What are you doing?' she said sadly. Joel was thrashing towards the shore. They watched as he reached the steps that led up to the jetty.

The boat was gathering speed now and they were now a hundred yards from the shore. They saw Joel being taken by the two policemen. Then both he and Goodman were out of sight and the vessel was in clear water.

'Aunt Agatha,' said Kit. 'Do you mind if I look at the painting a moment?'

Agatha turned to Kit and extracted the metal tube from her pocket. She handed it over to Kit. The group gathered around to look on as Kit unscrewed the top and pulled out a rolled-up canvas. He unfurled it and they gazed up at it. There, before them, cast in shadow was the painting of the Maltese Falcon. The chiaroscuro of Caravaggio was never more purely rendered. There was a glint in the eye of the Falcon which made it seem like it could come to life and swoop down on its prey.

The awed silence was suddenly broken by the sound of Kit's laughter.

327

Everyone turned to Kit who held up his thumb which had a dark, oily mark on it.

'The paint is still wet, I see,' said Kit. He began laughing again. So, too, did the others. When the laughter had subsided they settled down for the relatively short journey across the Strait. Up ahead the coast of Spain rose into view, but Agatha only had eyes for Morocco.

She sat and stared back at the land they were leaving, flanked by Mary and Betty. There were tears in her eyes.

'*Married in July, with flowers ablaze, Bitter-sweet mem'ries in after days. Married in July, with flowers ablaze, Bitter-sweet mem'ries in after days*, isn't that how it goes?' said Agatha.

She felt Betty grip her hand. Both had married their husbands in July. Agatha had lost Eustace ten years earlier also in July.

'Yes, something like that,' agreed Betty.

'I don't suppose I shall ever return now.'

'Don't say that Agatha,' replied Betty. Her voice was determined, but her face could not hide its sadness. 'You will, just you see.'

Tears trickled down Agatha's cheeks and she nodded.

'I will, but it will be to join him. You'll make sure, won't you?' Agatha turned to both Betty and Mary. The two ladies couldn't speak so they merely nodded. Mimi, with that extraordinary sense that dogs have, hopped to her feet and walked over to Agatha. This brought a smile to the ladies, and they stroked the Doberman's head.

'I miss him,' said Agatha.

*

Sidney Goodman and Joel watched the boat disappear from view. Nassim joined the two men and the policemen. Then Goodman turned to one of the policemen and shook his hand.

'Thank you,' he said with a pleasant grin. 'I think we better be off now before Joel catches a cold.'

He handed the policeman a number of banknotes then he, Joel and Nassim walked away from the jetty towards the waiting caleche.

'You do have the real Falcon, I hope?' said Joel, shaking water from his ear. Goodman tapped his inside pocket and said nothing. Instead, he took a couple of cigars out from his pocket. He offered one to Nassim who declined and the other to Joel.

'I think a little celebration is in order then perhaps we should move from this place. I fear things may get a little hot for us here Joel.'

'Where to?' asked Joel.

'I hear good things about Casablanca. What do you think?'

'Show me the painting,' replied Joel. There was tightness to his voice that belied the celebratory air around the three men.

Goodman lit their cigars and then took a metal tube from his pocket. He unscrewed the top and took out the rolled-up canvas. The group stopped just before they had reached the caleche. All three looked at the painting appreciatively.

'You did a remarkable job Nassim. I congratulate you. It certainly fooled our friends on the boat. What do you think Joel?'

'Sidney, I think this is the beginning of a beautiful friendship.'

The End

Acknowledgements

It is not possible to author a book on your own. There are contributions from so many people either directly or indirectly over many years. Listing them all would be an impossible task.

Special mention therefore should be made to my wife and family who have been patient and put up with my occasional grumpiness when working on this project.

My brother, Edward, has helped in proofing and made supportive comments that helped me tremendously. Thank you, too, to Debra Cox who has been a wonderful help on reducing the number of irritating errors that have affected my earlier novels. A word of thanks to Charles Gray and Brian Rice who have provided legal and accounting support.

My late father and mother both loved books. They encouraged a love of reading in me. In particular, they liked detective books, so I must tip my hat to the two greatest writers of this genre, Sir Arthur and Dame Agatha.

Following writing, comes the business of marketing. My thanks to Mark Hodgson and Sophia Kyriacou for their advice on this key area. Additionally, a shout out to the wonderful folk on 20Booksto50k.

Finally, my thanks to the teachers, particularly Mrs Kearney and Mr McNally, who taught and nurtured a love of writing.

This is a work of fiction. However, it references real-life individuals. Gore Vidal, in his introduction to Lincoln, writes that placing history in fiction or fiction in history has been unfashionable since Tolstoy and that the result can be accused of being neither. He defends the practice, pointing out that writers from Aeschylus to Shakespeare to Tolstoy have done so with not inconsiderable success and merit.

I have mentioned a number of key real-life individuals and events in this novel. My intention, in the following section, is to explain a little more about their connection to this period and this story.

Walter B Harris (1826 – 1897)

Walter Harris was a journalist, a traveller and socialite. He spent most of his adult life living in Morocco where he worked for many years as a correspondent for The Times. He settled in Tangier where his linguistic skills and appearance often meant that he passed for a native of Morocco. In the early part of the twentieth century, rural Morocco was regarded as off-limits to foreigners. Harris travelled freely, often at significant risk to his safety. On one occasion he was kidnapped by the famed brigand and leader Raisuli, but released after several weeks unharmed, but with a remarkable story to tell. How much of what Harris wrote is true or exaggerated is hard to say but he remains one of the most interesting characters to be associated with Tangier. His book *Morocco That Was* provides great insight into the period up to 1920 in Morocco.

Mulai Ahmed al-Raisuli (1871 – 1925)

Raisuli was a Sharif (noble, highborn person and a descendant of Muhammed the Prophet). He was born in the village of Zinat,16 miles outside Tangier. Raisuli is viewed as someone who falls between an English Robin Hood, a feudal baron and a tyrannical bandit. In his time he tried his hand at kidnapping, brigandry and being a Barbary Pirate. Among his most famous kidnapping victims were Walter Harris and the American Ion Pedicaris which caused Teddy Roosevelt to say, 'Pedicaris alive or Raisuli dead.' Or pay a ransom and give him a job as the head of police in the Tangier area, as they did. The Pedicaris affair was turned into a film starring Sean Connery as Raisuli – *The Wind and the Lion* (1975).

During the First World war he acted in concert with the Germans against the French and the Spanish. When the war finished he began, once more, to fight against the Spanish, but older, suffering from Dropsy, his impact was limited, and he had to be rescued by the leader of the Rif rebels Abd el-Krim. This was a humiliation for Raisuli who was jealous of the Rif leader. He died around the same time that a combination of France and Spain finally put the rebellion down. The latter used poison gas in their efforts to quell the uprising.

Raisuli was described as chivalrous, respectful toward his captives, friendly, generous to those who demonstrated respect and loyalty and a well-educated man. However, his many acts of cruelty are well known. He was very much a product of Morocco at this time. Walter Harris and Rosita Forbes both wrote about this remarkable leader.

Emily Keene, the Sharifa (1849 – 1944)

Emily Keene was an adventurer who went to work in Morocco as a governess for the Pedicaris family (see above), met and fell in love with a Muslim, the Sharif of Wazan or Ouzzane and married him. The marriage did not last, but they remained good friends and she nursed her former husband in his last days.

Keene stayed on and lived in Tangier. Emily devoted much time to improving health care provision for the women in Northern Morocco and to a hospital for the poor. Her charitable and social endeavours earned her titles such as the Officer of the Order of the Ouissam Alaouite and she was also promoted to Officer of the French Legion d'honneur. She also features in an episode of the series '*The Adventures of the Young Indiana Jones.*'

Her son Moulay Ali ben Abdeslam became Sharif of the region. He served as an officer in the French Army.

Captain Thomas 'Tiger' Sarll (1882 – 1977)

Tiger Sarll was an adventurer whose life reads like something from a 'Boy's Own' comic of the early twentieth century. He even appeared on '*This is Your Life*' on British Television.

Born in London, he went off to fight in the Boer War while still a young man. During the Boer War, he was wounded, decorated and promoted. He left the army soon after the end of the war. Over the next few years he hunted big game in Africa, worked in Canada on a ship, went gold prospecting in the Klondike, before returning to Tangier as a journalist. He met Raisuli for the first time around 1909 and played chess with him. A year later he was in Mexico and fought in the revolution, before returning to be part of the War effort.

334

After the War he returned to Tangier to trade goods. He also returned to journalism and followed the Rif War for The Daily News. One of his scoops was to have personal contact with the Rif leader, Abd el-Krim.

There is a biography of this extraordinary man by Godfrey Lias – good luck finding it.

Charlie Chaplin (1889 -1977)

It is, of course, impossible to convey in a paragraph or two the extraordinary life of the man from the back streets of Lambeth in London. At the time this book is set, 1921, Chaplin was, by quite some distance, the most famous man on the planet. He had just released *The Kid* and was at the peak of his fame. The suggestion he makes in the book was eventually to find its way onto the big screen in one of the very greatest films ever made, *City Lights* (1931). The conversation between Mary and Chaplin about the Bluebeard case suggests that this was the source for his post war film, *Monsieur Verdoux* (1947). In fact, credit for this idea must go to Orson Welles who suggested it to Chaplin.

Albert Bartels

Morocco was something of a magnet for strange, piratical characters at the turn of the twentieth century. Albert Bartels was one such character. He went out to Morocco just before the arrival of Kaiser Wilhelm in 1905 to work. As a German businessman living in Morocco he was imprisoned in 1914 by the French at the start of WW1. He escaped in 1915 to lead the local tribes as a Berber captain in the fight against the French until the armistice in 1918. He was eventually caught and spent a year protected as a prisoner in Spain before returning to Germany through Italy in 1920.

His book, '*Fighting the French in Morocco*' reads like a 'Boy's Own adventure. He was married to the daughter of an English Consul, but they separated in 1915.

The Rif War (1921 – 26)

The Rif War was rebellion of the mountain-based Berber tribes of Morocco against the occupying colonialists of Spain (assisted by France from 1924 onwards). The war raged between 1921 and 1926. The Riffians were led by Abd el-Krim. They initially inflicted several defeats on the Spanish forces using guerrilla warfare tactics and using stolen European weapons. Defeat became inevitable once France joined Spain to fight against Abd el-Krim's forces. The major landing of Spanish troops at Al Hoceima is considered the first amphibious landing in history which involved tanks and aircraft. Abd el-Krim eventually surrendered to the French and was taken into exile. For further reading I recommend, *A Country with a Government and a Flag*, CR Pennell.

Herero Genocide (1904-6)

The Herero Genocide took place in German South West Africa which today is known as Namibia. The Herero people, and later the Nama people, rose up against the German occupiers and killed 100 settlers although women, children, missionaries and non-German Europeans were spared. In response, Germany sent General Lothar von Trotha to put down the rebellion. By the summer of 1904 he had pushed the Herero rebels into the desert of Omaheke where between 24,000 and 100,000 died of starvation and dehydration. This was due to the German forces preventing the Herero from leaving the desert. News of Trotha's atrocities began to filter back to Germany in late 1904, early 1905. Chancellor von Bulow lobbied for a change of approach which resulted in thousands of Herero and Nama people being imprisoned in concentration camps where most died of disease, abuse through medical experiments and exhaustion. The actions taken by Trotha are now viewed by German historians as tantamount to genocide. I learned much about this appalling episode from Lawrence James's book, *Empires of the Sun: The Struggle for the Mastery of Africa.*

Slavery in Morocco
This is a sensitive subject and if you are interested I would *recommend Black Morocco: A History of Slavery, Race and Islam* by Chouki el Hamel. It covers the experience of enslaved black people in Morocco from the sixteenth century to the beginning of the twentieth century.

Tajine
A tajine is a conical earthenware pot and the dish prepared in the tajine pot shares the same name as its cooking vessel. Tajines are a form of Moroccan stew which can be made with meat, fish or just vegetables.

Printed in Great Britain
by Amazon

10600319R00198